Suddenly, the sound of alarms echoed through the building.

"INTRUDERS! BRUCE! RYAN! MAN YOUR POSTS! NOW!" Rob roared as he pulled out his .45 and started running towards the front of the building. Bruce picked up his sword and Ryan retrieved his shotgun and the two young men dashed to their posts in record speed, where they found close to fifty SWOT team members breaking in through the wall. Ryan and Rob began shooting as fast as they could while Bruce came up from behind and mercilessly started running the enemy soldiers through and beheading them with his sword. The SWOT members fired off many rounds, but missed their targets every time due to their fear of the sudden onslaught. A few seconds later, the other four militia members appeared with shotguns as the killing continued. Disturbingly enough, Bruce seemed to be truly enjoying himself as he slashed open body after body with his sword, spilling the enemy's blood and watching it run down the long, sharp blade and all over his hands. Then, to his dismay, he accidentally dropped the weapon…

Anthony G. Roof's *Left for Dead and Other Morbid Tales* is a collection of disturbing short stories that will haunt the dark recesses of your mind, weave your dreams into terrifying nightmares and leave you feeling sickened and uneasy as you helplessly crave for more. Find out what it's like to be "Left for Dead" as you follow George through a dismal struggle to be taken seriously enough to make a livable wage. Discover what it's like to commit "The Cardinal Sin," to be in a constant state of "Rigor Mortis," to encounter "The Centipede," and to witness the "Fall of the Feline King." These dark tales of doom take readers to the underworld where "Hell Unfolds," and leaves them with confusion and fear only to wander aimlessly "Into the Night." This book will frighten and repulse you and make you think twice about leaving the safety of your home unarmed.

THE
BOCKINGTON

BOOK COMPANY

LEFT FOR DEAD

AND

OTHER MORBID TALES

ANTHONY G. ROOF

THE
BOCKINGTON

BOOK COMPANY

THE BOCKINGTON

BOOK COMPANY

Lebanon, Pennsylvania

LEFT FOR DEAD

AND

OTHER MORBID TALES

ANTHONY G. ROOF

THE
BOCKINGTON

BOOK COMPANY

LEFT FOR DEAD AND OTHER MORBID TALES.
Copyright © 2008 by Anthony G. Roof. All rights reserved. Printed in the United States of America.

This book is a work of fiction intended for entertainment purposes only. Names, characters, organizations, places, incidents, and dialogues are either the product of the author's imagination or are used fictitiously and are not to be construed as real. Any resemblance to actual events or locales or persons acting in real-life situations, living or dead, is entirely coincidental.

Warning: This book contains coarse language and descriptions of explicit violence and gore and therefore may not be suitable for children or for readers who are easily offended or disturbed. For mature audiences only. Readers should not attempt to act out any of the stunts described within the pages of this book, as it is not intended as a guide to pursuing "morbid" behavior. Due to the graphic nature of this publication, reader discretion is strongly advised.

RATED: GENERAL ACCESS – MATURE

Written, edited, compiled, formatted, and illustrated by Anthony G. Roof.
Author photo credit: Jennifer E. Detweiler. Copyright © 2006 by Anthony G. Roof.
Cover concept and art by and provided courtesy of Lulu, Inc.
The Lulu logo is a registered trademark of Lulu, Inc.

The main text type for this book was set in 12 point Times New Roman font.
Published by Anthony G. Roof and The Bockington Book Company of Lebanon, Pennsylvania through Lulu of Morrisville, North Carolina.
Printed by Lulu and/or Lightning Source of La Vergne, Tennessee.

First Edition: Completed, published and released on July 3, 2008.
First printing: July 2008.
Printed in the United States of America.

Marketed by Lulu, Inc. and by The Bockington Book Company.
Mr. Bockington "Bocker" Crowley III and associated logos are trademarks and/or registered trademarks of The Bockington Book Company.

Lebanon, Pennsylvania, United States of America.

ISBN: 978-0-6152-3549-3

This book is dedicated to all of the people who have severely pissed me off over the years for being the scum-sucking weasels that they are and for making my life the living hell that it is. Although there are far too many names to list here, I owe a great deal of gratitude to these people because this book probably never would have been written if it were not for their constant commitment to piss me off – the source of my inspiration.

Of all those who have not pissed me off, I would also like acknowledge and thank the Lulu Company for helping to bring my idea into existence and for their online marketing services, Lightning Source for assisting Lulu with the printing and distribution of the finished product, Jennifer E. Detweiler for helping with much of the photography, formatting and manuscript printing, the ISBN Agency of New Jersey, Marybeth Peters of the United States Copyright Office, my mom for putting up with my ideas when I first told the stories verbally, and also, my friends who encouraged me to write this particular book: Michael Kirby, Mark Eberly and Myles Mione.

ISBN: 978-0-6152-3549-3
PUBLISHED BY THE BOCKINGTON BOOK COMPANY
http://stores.lulu.com/BockingtonBooks
Lebanon, Pennsylvania

Printed in the United States of America

Left for Dead and Other Morbid Tales is a book by Anthony G. Roof containing seven (7) short horror stories that were written between Spring of 2007 and Summer of 2008. Of them, The Cardinal Sin was the first to be written and Left for Dead was the last. Having turned out to be the longest in length at 28,538 words, as well as having required the greatest effort, Left for Dead was selected to serve as the focus and as the cover story for this book.

LEFT FOR DEAD (page 13)

George works at a grocery store. He hates his job because his managers take advantage of him. He spends six years doing everything that is asked of him and in many cases, he goes above and beyond the call of duty. But when he realizes that he was being lied to on a daily basis since the day he was hired, he becomes violently angry. The young man does everything in his power to try to cope with his anger, but when the day comes that the store closes forever without giving him any prior notice to find another job, George and a few other disgruntled employees feel left behind and declare war on the company that betrayed them.

THE CARDINAL SIN (page 75)

One day during a slow shift at his job as an auto mechanic, Mike looks out the window and sees a male cardinal with beautiful red feathers. When Mike innocently makes eye contact with the bird, he falls under its evil spell and eventually ends up in a mental institution. Traumatized, Mike has no idea that the demon-bird plans to haunt the rest of his tortured, miserable life.

RIGOR MORTIS (page 87)

Charlie is the happiest man in town. He shares a loving home with his wife, son, and their cherished pet dog, Fluffy. Charlie loves the dog more than anything else in the whole world and tries to do anything he can to make her happy. But one day, when the jolly old man moves the dog house too close to a fence, Fluffy climbs up on top of her house and tries to jump over the fence, hanging herself to death on the end of her chain. Charlie slips into a deep state of depression and falls in with the wrong crowd. It isn't long before he begins a life of crime and develops a morbid obsession with death.

THE CENTIPEDE (page 113)

When Elizabeth notices a common house centipede scampering across the floor in her living room, she becomes frightened and wants to kill it. Her mother, however, advises against this desire claiming that centipedes help to control the home's insect population. Elizabeth disobeys her mother and targets the creatures in a rampage of extermination during the late-night hours. When the insect problem gets out of control as a result, the girl's mother has the house fumigated. The only problem is that one centipede remains, and now mutated by the fumes, prowls around in the night with revenge on its mind.

FALL OF THE FELINE KING (page 125)

Sean always takes care of his grandparents' pet cat when they leave town. He feeds it, waters it, plays with it, and does anything else he can do to protect and please it. But one day when the cat turns on Sean and attacks him for no apparent reason and the grandparents choose to side with the animal claiming that the young man must have done something to deserve the attack, Sean decides the cat must die.

HELL UNFOLDS (page 135)

The small rural town of Oak Springs, West Virginia is a quiet and peaceful place to live and work until the town experiences a crime wave. As the crime rate increases, the local police department enlists the help of the most feared man in town: Frank. Living in an abandoned mansion in the middle of a cemetery, Frank uses an old hearse as his patrol car. When he catches violent criminals, he secretly locks them in caskets and deports them to the town of Hell, Michigan. Eventually, when the corrupt mayor of the town begins to suspect foul play, Frank makes him disappear as well.

INTO THE NIGHT (page 163)

Bill hates his life. Everybody takes advantage of him, lies to him, cheats him, and blames him for things that he did not do. Bill gets treated like crap at home, picked on at school, and taken for granted at work by bosses and fellow coworkers who do not appreciate his service. Eventually, Bill gets sick and tired of constantly being screwed over and as he takes an inward journey to his soul in a pathetic attempt to understand his place in the world, he goes insane and starts killing people.

ABOUT THE AUTHOR
(Pages 180-181)

THE
BOCKINGTON

BOOK COMPANY

THE
BOCKINGTON

BOOK COMPANY

Lebanon, Pennsylvania

LEFT FOR DEAD

AND

OTHER MORBID TALES

ANTHONY G. ROOF

"To penetrate and dissipate these clouds of darkness, the general mind
must be strengthened by education."

-Thomas Jefferson
Letter to Francis Adrian Van der Kemp, 1820

READER DISCRETION IS ADVISED

1

LEFT FOR DEAD

George works at a grocery store. He hates his job because his managers take advantage of him. He spends six years doing everything that is asked of him and in many cases, he goes above and beyond the call of duty. But when he realizes that he was being lied to on a daily basis since the day he was hired, he becomes violently angry. The young man does everything in his power to try to cope with his anger, but when the day comes that the store closes forever without giving him any prior notice to find another job, George and a few other disgruntled employees feel left behind and declare war on the company that betrayed them.

Left for Dead

"Beep, beep, beep, beep," sounded the cash register in a boring, but constant monotony as George relentlessly scanned groceries, caring about nothing but the ending of his long, after-school shift. George was a sixteen year old high school boy who worked at one of the town's local supermarkets, Turkowitz's Grocery Kingdom, five days every week except for Mondays and Tuesdays. He had been working at the store since October of the previous year and had been employed for about eight months. Despite the ease of learning the proper executions of his simple tasks, however, there was still a lot the boy did not yet know, therefore making him extremely submissive to instruction. While the other part-timers made fun of the poor, unmotivated, under-achieving adults who were employed by the pathetic, almost entirely kid-run business, George, instead strived to learn as much as he possibly could about the job, as sad as it was because all he wanted to do was succeed in the real world – and succeeding meant starting out at the very bottom and climbing up the ladder of the business hierarchy.

But as time went by and George remained employed by the grocery store, he saw many other employees come and go. They would get hired and work for a few weeks until eventually something pissed them off and then they would quit. This went on and on and on in what seemed to be an endless cycle, all the time while George maintained his position with the company in hopes of one day advancing into slightly better pay and more promising opportunities. In fact, George had been taught to always do his best, no matter how much he hated a job or an employer, so when many of his coworkers slacked off or made mistakes, George was always there to correct the problem; at that time, there was nothing he wouldn't do to show his dedication to the business. When the other kids called off or did "no-call-no-shows" or walked out in the middle of their shifts or simply didn't come back from their lunches and breaks, George was always there to save the day. He would willingly stay to cover the other cashiers' shifts, switch shifts with other people when necessary and would even come in on his days off. In this sense, George was always on call and could not make plans on his days off because he knew it was only a matter of time until the telephone would ring to call him to work.

George also did the work of other departments as well. It was not uncommon for him to have to stock milk and eggs, produce, sales displays, whole isles and even to have to round up the carts in the parking lot to bring back to the store, which they so passionately referred to as "pick-up." In fact, George often found himself doing pick-up, even in the hottest, sweatiest days of the summer, the most frigid of days in the winter, as well as in the rain and snow, simply because none of the other kids would comply when they were instructed to do the job, which was meant to be a rotating task. Rotate, it did not and needless to say, George was stuck with the task at least five times in a single shift every day that he worked. "Why should I have to do carts," the other kids would whine, "it's not in my job description! I'm not doing it! Why should I? Make George do it!" And to this, the employer complied.

George never, ever called off from a single shift of work, even when he was sick or injured, and was always good enough to come to work on his days off when other kids failed to show up. It didn't matter that the other kids were simply skipping work to do things like playing sports or to go shopping, because it was automatically assumed that George would be there to save the day. But then on the rare occasions that George needed to switch shifts with somebody, nobody wanted to help him out. It didn't seem to matter to anybody that whenever they wanted to switch shifts, George would gladly do it for them, but when he needed to switch, tough shit. And also, it was by this time that the boy began to notice how easily management would let these kids off the hook for not coming to work, all because they assumed that George would be there; it wasn't their problem, it was George's problem.

Needless to say, George was becoming very fed up with how everybody simply assumed that he had no life outside of work and thought nothing of taking advantage of him. By the time he had turned eighteen years old, he had done work in every department of the store except for the bakery and the meat departments, he had always done the pick-up job when it needed to be done and one top of it all, he still managed to do his job better than any of the other cashiers. In fact, he scanned groceries like a demon and received more compliments from customers about his superior customer service skills than any other employee in the entire store. Yet, George watched as all of the other cashiers who never did a damn thing they were asked to do on the rare occasions that they actually did show up to work, being rewarded with raises and promotions while George remained at his minimum wage –

16

and yet they still dropped like flies, quitting in greater numbers than they were hired in.

When George spoke with the management team about this injustice and made his points as to how he does everything that needs to be done and yet all of the raises go the lazy, unappreciative, snot-nosed brats who spend more than half their shifts reading magazines instead of working, he was told that when he works harder, he'll become eligible for raises as well. It seemed like every time George was inquisitive about the situation and why it was allowed to happen, the answers he was given always had something to do with him working harder or making a greater effort to be normal like everybody else. But then when the young man took the time and energy to observe and study the lazy, unmotivated work styles of his fellow associates so that he could assimilate to those standards of "normality," he would be reprimanded for not doing his work. And when George finally did manage to assimilate to be like everybody else he worked with, he was written up an uncountable number of times and harshly scolded by disturbed managers and supervisors who claimed that his actions and changes had "blown their minds," because they did not expect that kind of behavior from him of all people. "Whatever," George thought to himself, "I did what was asked of me and sure, they seemed truly shocked by that, but it's not my problem if they purposely blow their own minds by foolishly not expecting me – of all people – to deliver on my promises by obeying their orders as they required. They should know by now that when they say 'jump,' rather than bitching about some job description that I've never even seen before, I'm going to ask 'how high?' It seems to me like they are shocked in a negative way, but looking back at past discussions, my better judgment tells me and my common sense confirms it, that their being surprised is a good thing which can only serve in my favor," the young silently pondered as the disgruntled managers and supervisors ranted on and on about their expectations. When there was finally a moment of silence in which George was permitted to speak, he said, "Okay, well, I'm glad that you've noticed my progress and appreciate the seriousness of my dedication to this company, which implies your acknowledgment of the fulfillment of my end of our bargain. Now that it is your turn to fulfill your promise to me, how much of a raise are we talking about here?"

The room filled with silence and became so quiet that one could here a pin drop. George looked up at his managers and supervisors, all of whom stared coldly back at him with utter disbelief, shock and a hint of fear in their eyes. Their mouths gaped open with a sense of confusion, the complexion of their skin became slightly lighter and the veins in their necks began to protrude. When the head manager finally decided to resume speaking, she immediately experienced an intense difficulty in pronouncing words properly; she could not keep from stuttering due to her sense of shock. To remedy the situation, the supervisor began screaming at George for being disrespectful, sarcastic, arrogant, and called him a 'smartass' several times. When the young man explained that he was not being sarcastic at all, but that he was dead serious about receiving the raise he was promised, the assistant manager burst into a fit of a rage. "YOU DO NOT GET REWARDED FOR DOING YOUR JOB POORLY! WE ARE NOT SHOCKED DUE TO YOUR SO-CALLED IMPROVEMENTS AS YOU SO SARCASTICALLY THINK, WE ARE PISSED OFF AT YOUR SUDDEN DECLINE OF WORK QUALITY! GET THE FUCK OUT OF HERE! GO HOME, JUST GET THE HELL OUT OF THIS STORE, YOU GODDAMNED SMARTASS!" the assistant manager roared. So, George went home, confused and angry.

The next day, George returned to work and to his surprise, he still had a job with the company. He still did not understand what the problem was or why management refused to give him the pay raise that they had promised him, but nevertheless, he continued to do the job just as he believed they required of him. "George," the store manager said, "your still doing it. Straighten up your attitude and work like you used to." George looked at the woman in confusion, "excuse me, but I recall asking you for a raise not so long ago and you told me to be like everybody else. Well, I did that yesterday and I was yelled at and made to leave. What's the deal here? I am not in anyway trying to be a smartass; I just sincerely do not understand what it is that you want me to do. Can you please elaborate on that for me so that I can better understand your expectations of me?" The manager took a deep breath and slowly began to speak again, "son, I think you do know what we want from you, but you're young and naïve, so I'm going to give you the benefit of the doubt and just come right out and simply tell you what we expect. You see, we expect poor behavior from everybody else but not from you. You have always performed well and so we have come to expect that of you. In that sense, you've kind of screwed yourself over by showing us what you can do and what kind

18

of person you can be; you've set the bar too high for yourself and now we're kind of holding you to those lofty standards. We have different expectation for different people. Do you understand that?" The young man nodded, "yes, but what about the pay raises you promised me? I understand what you're trying to tell me, but I don't understand what you meant when you said that I needed to work like everybody else. I did that and you sent me home for it yesterday." The manager laughed and shook her head in amusement. "How old are you, George, nineteen, twenty, something like that?" "No ma'am, I just turned eighteen recently." "Well, see, that's why we're having this talk right now. You are young and naïve. You just don't understand how the business world works yet. You see, when a manager tells you something like that, like that you'll get a raise in time for working harder or something to that effect it's usually a lie. I really shouldn't be telling you this, but it's the truth. Managers are trained to tell people what they want to hear; we tend to be pros at saying one thing and doing another. Do you understand?" George looked up at the woman with a burning disappointment in his eyes.

"But that's dishonest; that's lying. You're a just a backstabbing hypocrite for doing things like that!" George sputtered in disgust to the smirking manager. "Yes, George, I know, but that's all part of the game. You don't get to be a manager by being nice to people and by coming to the workplace with this happy-go-lucky, positive, optimistic, tree-hugging attitude and with the mentality that the world is such a great place and everybody can trust everybody else. Okay, the ground is not made of marshmallows, flowers don't just pop out of the ground at a second's notice just because they feel like it, bees don't just fly through the air at ease aimlessly with nowhere to go and clowns don't dance around and make balloon animals for little kids just to be nice guys. Do you understand that? This is the real world, not a utopia where it's always fun time. I'm afraid to shatter your fairytale delusions of the world and to corrupt your innocence by telling you this, but the only way you get to be a successful manager is by being a two-faced, lying hypocrite. It's all about covering your ass. You have to be selfish and trust nobody but yourself and you have to do it well. In today's world, morality and ethics have no place in a business. Those things will just hold you back and put you at an unfair disadvantage. So, to sum it all up and to answer your question, we have no intention of ever giving you a raise. We just told you what we thought you wanted to hear just to shut you up. We have greater expectations of you and we hold you to higher standards, because you've demonstrated that you have such extensive abilities that we can take advantage of. Think about it, kid, you screwed yourself by coming in here with this positive attitude about how you're going to give the job your 110% best efforts, instead of just doing a half-assed job like every other normal kid your age. Now, we hold you to it because we know about it. You've given yourself no room to improve and no room to slack off. You only have yourself to blame, so get used to it. When management tells you something, they mean something else. You should know that by now and that is exactly why we called you a smartass for pretending that you didn't." By this time, George was disillusioned and absolutely horrified. "But why do you give the others raises then for doing way less than me?" he asked. "Because unlike you, they can improve, they just need some motivation. Money talks; raises are a good motivator. You are already working at your fullest potential. Why would we waste money by giving you a raise?" "Because I'll decrease my work output to give you a reason to motivate me. That's what I thought you meant when you said I should be like everybody else. So, I'll just do a better job of conforming then." "Then we'll fire you and make it miserable for you to get another job." "Well if you don't give me a raise, then I can always quit." "But you won't. Everybody else will but you've already been here an unusually long time for somebody your age. Face it, you won't quit; you're not going anywhere." "Well what makes you so sure that I won't?" "Because you're stupid. All the other kids come and go after only a few months. But you're still here. You let us take advantage of you. Accept it; any other person would've been long out the door already if I were to tell them even a small fraction of this stuff. But you're still here. You have no self-respect and no self-esteem, because you're an idiot. You won't quit. And besides, George, your parents won't let you. You must remember that they grew up during different times, back when your first job was your career. Back then, you didn't switch jobs unless you were laid off, because you certainly would never, ever, under any other circumstances quit a job. You just didn't do that back then, even if the pay sucked. You got a job and you were loyal to your employer, no matter how corrupt they were because your job was your career, end of story. And from what I gather from the few times that I've spoken with them, things have not changed. As far as they are concerned it's still 1955, so you go ahead and quit and then see how they react to your decision. You won't do it; you know you can't because you're just a gutless pussy who lives to let others walk all over you." "But I can always tell everybody else that you told me this stuff and then they'll quit and you'll be screwed! Then what will you do?" "Go ahead and tell them. I'll just deny it. Who do you think they'll believe: the caring, hard-working, reputable store manager or some snot-nosed, punk kid who's jealous that he's the only one not getting raises?" "Well, if I did quit, you'd be sorry!" "No, George, I wouldn't really care. I'd just replace you with somebody else. What, you think that would teach us a lesson? You're just a peon; you're absolute scum. We were in business long before you started working here and we'll remain in business long after you leave. By quitting, you'd only be inconveniencing yourself. But you won't quit," the manager said as she turned her back and walked away from the mortified young man.

A few years later, George realized that the manager was right; he didn't quit. He still worked for the corrupt, unethical company and continued to tolerate their discriminatory treatment towards him. He had since been transferred to the meat department, but his pay remained only slightly above the minimum wage. By this time, George had been working for the company for over six years and it was to the point where new hires right off the street were starting out at a few dollars more than what George made after those six long years. Despite his time at the store, he still remained the lowest paid employee as well as one of the hardest working employees. But nothing would ever change for him. Granted, the people changed; employees continued to quit as soon as they'd been hired; they would come and go, get hired and drop like flies – employee turnover was through the roof. Even the managers would come and go or get switched around or transfer from store to store like there was no tomorrow. It was like the company was playing an endless game of musical managers with no intention on ever stopping. But no matter who the managers were at any given time, they all had the same corrupt, selfish attitudes towards the employees who worked under them. Not surprisingly, this only led employees to stop caring about the company and many of them became negligent of their jobs by cutting corners and half-assing everything they could possibly get away with.

With this kind of morale in the store, it was not long before distrust, hostility and competition took its course among the employees who worked there. With management so hell-bent on cheating the store's clientele, they were thoroughly distracted by their efforts to what was going on between the employees. Therefore, many of the disillusioned, disgruntled employees began to steal, lie and cheat their ways through a typical workday. Many of the minority workers discontinued working altogether and would simply come to work to clock in and then leave right away. They would only return at the end of their shifts to clock out again. When they were actually at the store, they would spend their shifts hiding under display tables or sitting in the break room in the back of the store. When they were caught doing these things by management, they would simply get off the hook by pulling somebody else down with them; it became a common and highly effective practice to accuse their victims of racist and discriminatory behavior. For example, if one person was caught hiding under a table, he would just say that so-and-so made a racial slur and a terroristic threat against him and so he was hiding out of fear for his life. Somehow, it worked every time and because he was so tolerant of it; George was usually the victim of such a scam.

"They" and "should" soon became the words most widely used in the store. Such words always paved the way to such fine excuses for not working or for working improperly. It was always "they" want it done this way or "they" want it done that way or "they" said it had to be like this; "they, they, they, they." But whenever George asked who "they" was, he could literally hear crickets chirping in the background. Some claimed to know who "they" was but chose to not use names simply as a means of protecting themselves or as management liked to call it, "covering their asses." George, however, was not fully convinced of such a lame excuse from people who felt the need to constantly gossip anyway and decided for himself that the word "they" was used as a common placeholder by morons who had no idea whatsoever who they were referring to. And taking that notion into consideration, it was clear to the young man that his fellow associates were only using "they" for somebody to blame for the poor preparation of the workplace and ultimately as an excuse not to do their jobs. Perhaps what made it such a blatantly lame excuse was the fact that nobody even knew who "they" was. And to further compound the problem was how everybody had to formulate and hide behind a different and often conflicting set of "shoulds." All the word "should" ever really accomplished was to open the doors for unfounded opinions that really had no place in a business setting. It seemed that none of the employees could get it through their heads that how they thought things "should" be and how things actually were in reality was two entirely different things.

"I can't do anything right in this damn store because of how 'they' think everything 'should' be. I am always wrong, no matter what, even when I am obviously right, because of something 'they' think. Nobody will listen to me or take me seriously because 'they' don't want that to happen. 'They' 'should' be the dictators of the business. I know what I need to do; I need to become 'they.' Then, the only thing that will matter to anybody here is how I think things 'should' be," George thought to himself one day as he created a professional resume of his educational and employment history. He spent many hours on the document, trying to tweak it in every way possible to make it as good and as solid as possible. When he was finished he visited the company website and filled out an application for the open position of assistant store manager at the store where he was currently employed. Then he uploaded his resume and cover letter to the application and clicked the "submit" button. "When I become 'they,' I'm going to be making a few changes," the young man spoke aloud to himself.

Several months passed since the young man submitted his resume and application to the company. He had just turned twenty-two years of age when he was visited at work by the human resources director of the store's district. She had decided to pay the store a visit for the opportunity of interviewing the young applicant. She did just that and asked George many questions, all of which he answered thoroughly and honestly. "It sounds like if I gave you the job right now, George; you would make so many positive changes and bring sales to an all-time high, which concerns me," the woman said towards the end of the interview. "What do you mean? Is that not a good thing for both the store and the company?" George inquired. The woman smiled and let out a brief chuckle. "George, you've been here for how long?" "A little over six years." "And you didn't notice the course that the business has been going in since the time you started here?" "I am afraid I am unclear as to what you are asking me. Can you please elaborate?" "Okay, have you not noticed even in the slightest sense of the word that sales have drastically decreased, employee turnover has more than tripled and the customer base has been slowly diminishing lately?" "Well, yes, I have and that is why I am applying for this position. I believe that once I learn the duties outlined in the job description, I will quickly develop the skills necessary to turn this store around for the better." "Well, you see, George, that's precisely the problem. We don't want you to turn things around. We've worked very hard to run our business into the ground as far as we have, but we still have a lot of work ahead of us yet. Why would we hire you to come in here and counteract all of our hard work and tireless efforts?" George was now confused. "You mean all of the problems here have been created on purpose? All of the poor management practices in place here – you actually tried to do that?" The woman nodded, "yes, George, it's all part of the plan. We've been in business for over ninety-six years and we're ready to call it quits. We used to have a fine, highly profitable business but now the competition has become too fierce and the laws governing corporations have changed. Local ordinances have changed, the demographics of our customer base are constantly shifting and taxes are increasing all the time. We've decided as a company that its time to throw in the towel." Now George was angry. "Then why don't you just be honest and come right out and tell everybody that?!" "Because then they would all quit. We don't mean for this to happen overnight, but rather over a long period of time, let's say, five to ten years from now. But for that to happen, we first need to gradually run the business into the ground by making really bad management decisions. As a store manager, you would have to ask yourself 'what can I do to lose customers today?' You see, we want to slowly pull out of the business world; slowly put on the brakes and coast to a stop, not just slam on the breaks right away and come to a screeching halt. If we tell employees that we're doing this, they'll all quit and that will disrupt our plan. Also, this is a publicly-held corporation and if we tell people what we're up to, we'll just piss off our stockholders and people will stop investing in our company and more than likely, they'll file expensive lawsuits." "Well, what if I tell everyone about your evil plans myself? Then what will you do?" The woman seemed amused by this question as she smiled and giggled to herself. "And you really think for one second that anybody will believe you? If I didn't know any better and you told me this stuff, I would just think you're insane. Really, what kind of company intentionally goes out of business? Nobody will believe you and that's why this is the perfect plan!" There was a long pause while George took all of this information in. Finally he spoke his final words to his interviewer, "Fuck you," and then he left the room.

Later on, when George told everybody about the interview and repeated what was said to him by the human resources director, he quickly realized that she was right; nobody believed a word of it. He was laughed at and made fun of by the other employees and some of them even mocked him in sarcastic little skits: "look at me, I'm George! Attention everybody, aliens are coming to Earth to invade the store!" Other people claimed that he was just jealous that everybody else got raises and he didn't. Some voiced their opinions that he was just upset that he didn't get hired to do the job that he applied for and some yet even claimed that it was a conspiracy to piss everybody off so that they all quit and create a short-handed store. Then, George could just waltz in and save the day and management would feel obligated to give him a raise. "Give it up, George, you're a loser and we all know it," one stocker said as everybody walked away and left the room. But the room wasn't left completely empty: there, in the rear of the room stood three men. One skinny man stood on the far left, dressed in all black and covered in violent tattoos depicting zombies and skulls, another man, this one an extremely overweight fellow, stood in the middle, sporting an angered facial expression while he loudly cracked his oversized knuckles together and on the far right stood another man, this one slightly larger than the one on the left, dressed in tan and orange with an intense hate burning in his eyes as he wrapped a small piece of chain tightly around his clenched fists. "We believe you," the man in the middle said in a deep, raspy voice.

Slowly, the three men stepped forward and into the light. "My name is Rob," the large man in the middle began, "and these are my henchmen, Kermit and Jack." Kermit was the tattooed man in black and Jack was the man in orange. "What is this all about?" George asked. "We are a militia and I am the leader. I formed the group only two years ago after carefully reviewing the Constitution of the United States of America and finding that it is indeed my Second Amendment right to form such a group if I keep it well regulated. Our state also confirms our right based on numerous documents and quotes penned by George Washington, John Adams and Thomas Jefferson, three of our finest founding fathers. Today, we most closely resemble the A-Team from that television show, but we mean serious business. We dedicate our lives to fighting corruption, crime and greed. And, we also work here for a living, all three of us and like you, we've all been screwed over and taken across countless times. Now you tell us of their plans to make each and everyone of us jobless, instead of giving the notice that we need to find other employment opportunities. Can you imagine that? We'll all find out the day we come to work and see that sign on the locked door that reads, "OUT OF BUSINESS FOREVER. Then, we'll all have to compete against each other in an already competitive job market just to get a job to earn the money that we need to survive. But do they care? No, all they care about is being covered until their big day when they shut everything down. Well we're not going to stand for it. I've worked here for over twenty years, Kermit has been here for about fifteen years and Jack and yourself have been here for at least five years. Let's face it: this is where we work. This is our store. We've done everything in our power to keep it alive and thriving and now we find out that they've been counteracting all of our efforts all these years?! And how many times have we helped to repair different parts of the building to keep it in good shape, sometimes at our own expense even. This is our store, period. They may take their business out of it and they may take their resources out of it, but we own the building now and if they want to fight it, we are fully prepared to go to war. Besides, what about all of the money they saved by not paying us what we rightfully deserve? Well, this building will be our recourse because we are in need of a nice sized building to use as a compound to house our weaponry and supplies. This will be our headquarters," Rob roared with an intensity burning in his eyes of hate.

"Would you like to join our group?" Jack asked George. George nodded and said "yes." "Alright then," Kermit began, "then your job will be to start collecting guns and ammunition among other weapons. Don't tell anybody about it, though." George swallowed hard and nodded once again. "That's right," Rob spoke up, "collect supplies and speak to nobody about this, not even us. We must not be seen together because it may confirm us to be allies. This is a top-secret organization and a top-secret mission. The plan will be this: we will all continue doing our work as always, but then when the day comes that the store is closed and we cannot get in through the locked door, we will go to our homes to retrieve assault rifles and semi-automatic pistols. Then, we will meet back here and bust the door in together. The three of us will remain inside the building to secure the premises while Jack steals a tank from a nearby military base. We will wait for his return and then bust open a dock door, build a ramp with sturdy boards, and stand watch as he drives the vehicle into the store. Then we will secure the premises and stand guard, armed and ready to go. After that, we wait for the enemies and their forces to return."

George agreed to the plans and shook the hands of the three men, whom he would not speak to again until that faithful day.

As time went by and George continued to get screwed over by the company, he began building up quite an impressive arsenal of fine weaponry, including several different kinds of shotguns, rifles, and handguns. Everyday, he would purchase a brick of cartridges for the .50 caliber rifle as well as five boxes of shotgun shells for both the twelve and sixteen gauge models. On Fridays, he would purchase well over a hundred dollars worth of ammunition for .40 and .45 caliber pistols as well as ammunition for revolvers chambered in .357 magnums and .38 Special. On the first day of every month, he would also invest a few hundred dollars in armor-piercing ammunition designed for the AR-15 and AK-47 military-pattern assault rifles. Granted, the young man had to get a second job working part-time at a nearby gas station just to manage to pay for all of the ammunition, but in just a short time he had several hundreds of thousands of rounds for each of his guns stockpiled in the garage of his home. It didn't end there, however. The disgruntled young man even extended his arsenal to include several thousand different types of sharp combat knives, swords and even numerous weapons used by ninjas and by soldiers who had lived back in medieval times. He had Chinese throwing stars, nun chucks, bludgeons, flails, maces, brass knuckles, blow dart guns, crossbows, spears, throwing knives, battle axes and all kinds of other stuff. In fact, he even made it a point to stockpile the common self-defense weapons of the day as well as the common equipment carried by police officers; things like canisters of pepper spray, tasers, stun guns and batons. It was safe to say that George wasn't fucking around.

A few years later, as the store gradually became more and more abandoned by its once loyal customer base and employee turnover was higher than the number of workers hired in a year's time, George began to see the end in his sights. So, to be prepared for the end of the days at Turkowitz's Grocery Kingdom, the young man installed a cap onto the back of his pickup truck and tightly packed all of his arsenal and supplies into the back of the truck. In the passenger side of the cab, he even thought to cover the floor and seat with the chainsaws from his garage shelves. There was not to be a single instrument that could possibly be used in combat to be forgotten. The young man knew that when the militia invaded the store, there would be a full blown war between the city police, the National Guard, the ATF and any hired mercenaries or spies that the company hired to infiltrate the facility. The number of casualties would be extremely high as the militia would more than likely have enough ammunition to survive a five-year siege. But George believed that when the normal townspeople took notice to the great efficiency and dedication of the group, many of them would have a strong desire to join with hopes of settling their own personal vendettas. And with recruitment producing the numbers necessary to secure the compound, the fittest soldiers most suited for offensive combat could retreat from the premises to take on other missions. Sure, they would most likely be negatively referred to as terrorists in the beginning, but once the townspeople realized that one man's terrorist was another's freedom fighter, the numbers would bring in just the right quantities so that the group could feasibly take on other endeavors and in time, perhaps even a full-fledged revolutionary war against the United States government.

As the time began to approach, the days seemed to pass slowly. George would occasionally make eye contact with the other members of the militia whom he had not spoken to since their introduction in the break room a few years prior and he knew from the look on their faces that they were thinking the very same thoughts that he was. With the store shelves growing emptier all the time and the workers slowly disappearing, the store was only down to a few customers each day. The building was growing more and more into a ghost store with each passing week. The militia knew that the final day of the company's operation of the store could be right around the corner and they were all carefully prepared for the inevitable.

When the last day finally arrived, George was relieved. He knew that the company thought they were screwing him over by intentionally going out of business, but in the end he realized he was really screwing them out of a building worth around two million dollars. It also conveniently happened to be around this time that the young man came to expect the closing of the store to be some randomly approaching day that he began driving his loaded pickup truck to work. And that final day as he parked his vehicle, walked up to the store and noticed that there were no lights on in the building, he noticed that there was a sign on the door that read "CLOSED FOREVER." He tried the door only to find that it was locked and he instantly knew it was time to execute the plan.

"It's time," a deep voice spoke from the shadows. A startled George jumped from the unexpected sounding of the voice and turned towards the direction of the source. Then, the three other members of the militia slowly stepped forward from the darkness of the shadows and into the light where the young man could see them clearly. They appeared in front of him in exactly the same order in which they had when he had first met them in the break room just a few years before. Kermit, Rob and Jack, now fully clad in mercenary apparel; large black combat boots, heavy nylon pants with thick, plastic knee pads, long strips of large caliber bullets strapped across their chests in the shape of an "X" overtop of dark green vests and long-sleeved tan shirts, war paint on their faces, black fingerless, nylon gloves on their hands and black spiked military helmets from WW1, slowly pressed on towards the young man in the same fashion as before; the same dour demeanors, the same angry facial expressions and the same chain being tightly wrapped around Jack's knuckles. The only other differences were the increased number of morbid tattoos that adorned what was visible of Kermit's skin, the extra wrinkles upon Rob's face as time began to ravage his once youthful looks and the extra few inches that growth had added to Jack's already intimidating height.

"It's time," Rob spoke again, "It's time to take what is ours. Did you collect weapons as instructed of you?" George smiled grimly at the question as if it were a joke. "You better believe it, my fat, angry friend. Trust me; you will not be disappointed when you see the arsenal in the bed of that truck," the young man replied as he pointed to his parked vehicle in the parking lot. "Okay, well does everybody have what they need?" Rob asked the group. When everybody nodded to answer that they were prepared for the mission, Rob spoke again, "Alright then, let's do this," and then kicked in the front entrance door of the building.

"Everybody inside," Rob instructed as the four men shuffled into the vestibule of the store. Then, Rob and Kermit both simultaneously, as if planned, reached behind their backs and each produced a military-pattern assault rifle that they had previously strapped to the backs of their vests. Rob had an AR-15 and Kermit had an M-14. Jack then pulled out a .45 caliber pistol and a loaded clip of hollow tip cartridges and hastily jammed the clip into the weapon. Then he turned and walked into the store itself and George could see that he also had a rifle strapped to his back: a bayonet-equipped AK-47.

The other three men followed Jack into the abandoned building and switched on a light. The store look even more depressingly weird than it had before; the shelves were all completely empty, the cash register terminals remained but with the absence of the registers, the isle signs had been removed and stacked upon the front desk and old advertisement signs littered the dirty floor. The four men paused for a brief moment to look around the store and Rob began to speak again. "Bitchin'," he muttered as a grim smile of triumph took over his face. "It's ours," he said, "It's all ours. We finally have a suitable compound for our militia. This is perfect, because it's such a large building in such a strategic location! And those assholes up at the corporate office actually thought they were screwing us over! Wait until they find out that the four of us showed up to work today anyway and were not turned away by that dumb-assed sign in the window! They didn't want to give us any kind of notice at all that they were closing this store, which would have been extremely helpful because we all could have gone out and found other jobs well before today, but we showed up to work today anyway, like the loyal employees that we are only to discover that there is no work for us to and that we are all out of jobs. It's like they always told us before when they wanted us to tolerate their bullshit in screwing us over when they wanted more work done than any of us could possibly do in a shift's time, 'this is your store, you should take some pride in it.' And here we are at work on time and where are they? Sitting in the corporate office, probably laughing their asses off at how they just conveniently left us behind. Well, when they told us that this is our store, I know they didn't mean it literally," Rob paused as he cocked his gun, "but that's how I'm choosing to take it." Kermit smiled with amusement, "hell yeah," he started, "they always gave us that line of crap about how this is our store. Now here we are fulfilling our obligations as loyal employees at work on time but where are they? Out of business without the decency to have given us prior notice. But just because they went out of business doesn't mean that this is any less our store; they might not want it anymore but we do. We own this building now!" Then the three original members of the militia erupted into a fit of sadistic, morbid laughter.

   "So we're just going to take it?" George asked. Rob nodded. "But won't they try to break in and pull us out because the company is going to want to sell the building? Won't that be of interference to us when cops and military people show up to fuck with us? I mean, I know it will, I've given this a lot of careful thought but I'm really curious as to what you guys have in mind." "That's why we have the huge arsenals of weapons and ammunition," Jack answered, "we'll just kill anybody who tries to threatened our property and eventually in time they'll all get tired of being killed and fuck off." George scratched his head in thought. "In time?" he asked, "it will be a long time." "But where prepared for that," Rob answered. "That's right," Kermit added, "we are prepared for however long this takes." George smiled. "So, this really is screwing the company out of a lot of money, huh?" the young man inquired with amusement. "Sure is," Rob began, "because they want to go out of business, which means they will want to liquidate their assets, this building being one of them. Now they might try to sell it but as long as we are here, all they'll be selling is a meaningless piece of paper, the deed, but we're going to make sure that such a thing can't happen. You see, our goal here is screw over the company, not to allow them to conveniently pass this problem onto some other innocent company that did absolutely nothing to us. We don't want to screw over innocent people, just Turkowitz. So, we are going to call the corporate office and make it known to them that we are here and that this is our property now. Then, as you can probably guess, the very first thing those dumb-asses are going to do is call the police. The police will come here and be spotted by news reporters and this story will be all over the media. Then when Turkowitz does try to sell the building, nobody will want to buy it because they aren't going to want to be involved with what we are doing here. Do you understand?" George nodded and smiled grimly with approval.

"Okay, well let's do this. We've got to move quickly before the cops find out what were doing," Rob barked, "Jack, you get the tank. Kermit, go home and get the rest of your supplies. George and I will begin building the ramp at the dock door with the wood that I hauled here early this morning. When were finished building the ramp, George and I will drive our vehicles into the store where we will wait for Kermit to follow suit. We will then secure the compound and wait for Jack to return. When he does, we will have him drive the tank into the store and then immediately stand guard while the rest of us rip the ramp apart and carry the wood into the back room of the store. We then seal off the dock door and reuse the wood to cover up these big, glass windows in the front of the store. Now let's get moving!" George watched as everybody began scrambling about until he was interrupted by Rob's growling voice, "come with me." The young man immediately complied and followed the hefty man to the back of the building.

George and Rob worked fast to fulfill the plans of the militia. The ramp was built in record time and the two men then retrieved their vehicles and drove them into the back room of the building. Soon after, Kermit returned with a fully loaded pickup truck and a small trailer full of supplies. As soon as the trailer passed through the dock door, Rob slammed it shut and the three men ran to the front of the store to wait for Jack. "Where's your gun?" Rob asked George. "Oh, it's still in my truck," the young man answered to his less than amused, fat leader. Rob, rolling his eyes, then reached into a pocket on the side of his vest and pulled out a small 9mm pistol. "Well, use this for now," he instructed.

Eventually, the three men noticed Jack approaching the building with a military tank. "NOW!" Rob belted out and the three men dashed to the dock door to let Jack into the building. Upon opening the door, Jack began to traverse the wooden ramp but almost didn't make it as the wood bowed under the extreme weight of the vehicle, making creaking and cracking sounds as the persistent soldier drove forward. Fortunately, however, the tank made it inside just in time for police officers to arrive at the scene. Rob slammed the dock door shut and started screaming orders, "GEORGE, JACK, KERMIT! YOU GUYS ARE GOING TO HAVE TO OPEN THE DOOR AND GET THE RAMP INSIDE WHEN I SIGNAL TO YOU! I'M GOING TO GO ON TOP OF THE ROOF AND START SHOOTING AT THE COPS! WHEN YOU HEAR ME YELL 'NOW,' OPEN THE DOOR AND WORK QUICKLY! SHOOT IF YOU HAVE TO, BUT WORK QUICKLY! WE ARE NOT GOING TO HAVE A LOT OF TIME! ONCE YOU ARE DONE, CLOSE THE DOOR AND MEET ME ON TOP OF THE ROOF WITH GRENADES, RIFLES, AND PISTOLS! IT BEGINS NOW!" The excited man then picked up a box of hand-grenades and his AR-15 and dashed off in the direction of the stairs.

George, Kermit, and Jack stood silently near the dock door and listened as the sounds of several thousands of gunshots suddenly filled the air outside. Every now and then, the three waiting men could hear a grenade exploding but it was mostly the shooting that they heard. Eventually, the gunshots decreased until there was nothing but silence outside. "NOW!" Rob roared from the rooftop and the three men immediately flung open the dock door without a moment's hesitation. But as soon as the door was wide open, George was horrified at what he saw: overturned police cruisers all over the place, some on fire, guts and organs spewed about here and there and the lifeless corpses of what must have been close to forty police officers lying all over the place, all in a huge puddle of blood. The air reeked of death as the

32

young man's jaw dropped in horror, his widely opened eyes taking in the grisly scene of carnage. "GEORGE! HELP US DO THIS! WE DON'T HAVE MUCH TIME!" Kermit screamed at the hypnotized young man. Upon hearing the first few syllables, George snapped out of his trance and began helping to feed a thick, heavy chain through the holes in the bottom of the wooden ramp. Once the chain had been secured, Jack boarded the tank and started the engine. Kermit attached the end of the chain to a hitch on the back of the vehicle and a few seconds later, Jack drove forward and pulled the ramp into the building through the dock door. George then dashed out into the fiery carnage and as quickly as he could, he collected more than thirty handguns from dead police officers and their overturned cars and returned to the building before anybody could shoot at him.

Once all of this had been finished, Jack closed the dock door and Kermit ran off towards the stairs. "Now would be a good time to get some of your rifles," Jack said to the compliant George. A few moments later, all four members of the militia were reunited on top of the building where they watched police cars flood the parking lot as the sounds of loud sirens filled the air. "Should we just shoot them?" George asked. "Yes," Rob replied as the other men began opening fire on the still moving police cars.

Within seconds, Jack began firing his fully-automatic AK-47 into the parking lot, and George, fully amazed, watched as the empty casings littered the rooftop. Both Rob and Kermit quickly became busy with their tasks of sniping police officers with their semi-automatic AR-15s and occasionally throwing a few hand-grenades into the direction of the enemy. The loud noises of war filled the air as the young man stared in amazement at his three fellow militia members as they crouched down along the low wall and managed to aim and fire their weapons into the parking lot at the same time with such a high degree of agility. George, having slightly underestimated the level of the pending confrontation before making his way to the rooftop, had failed to pick the most appropriate weapon for the job; upon looking down into his hands, he noticed that he was holding a bolt-action 30-06 hunting rifle. "Oh, well," he thought to himself, "at least it's got an accurate scope," and then he was off to the other side of the roof where he noticed even more police cars arriving at the scene of the battle.

Just then, a smoke bomb landed next to his left shoe. The young man quickly picked it up, despite it severely burning his hand and heaved it back into the parking lot. It activated just seconds before landing, sending its thick clouds of toxic smoke into the entire area, giving George the short amount of time he needed to load his rifle. However, once loaded, the young man stooped to the very edge of the front of the building and hid behind a satellite without being seen. He then propped the barrel of his gun against the side of the satellite and as soon as the smoke cleared just enough for him to make out the figures of the coughing men in the huddled masses, he sighted them into the crosshairs of his scope and opened fire with the rifle, picking off the men one by one.

Eventually, the young man found himself really starting to get into the cause and hours flew by before he even realized what had happened. The young man shot and shot and shot, unknowingly shooting up hundreds of rounds rarely missing his targets as most of them were either headshots or shots directed at the fuel tanks of vehicles. The pungent stench of blood and smoke filled the air as the battle raged on; police cars were engulfed in flames and some even exploded as the entire parking lot of the building turned into a blood-soaked battlefield of chaos. But the young man continued on until he went to take a shot and heard a click come from his rifle. Instinctively, he reached into his supply bag for more ammunition, only to discover that he had run out for that particular gun. "SHIT!" he exclaimed as he listened to the gunfire continue down in the parking lot. He could see the hatch that he needed to get to in order to reenter the safety of the building, but as he watched the enemy's bullets bouncing off of and even penetrating the thick rubber of the roof between him and the hatch, the cold fear of dying corrupted his mind and began to rob him of his common sense. Now, with his war nerve fully struck, the young man believed that all he could do was run for cover no matter how dangerous the plan may have been. So, arming himself with Rob's semi-automatic 9mm pistol, George leaped to action and ran full speed towards the hatch while shooting several rounds randomly into the parking lot, but for some reason he chose to run in a squiggly motion, much like a rabid squirrel – an action that probably saved his life.

When George finally made it the hatch, he didn't even bother to descend the ladder; instead, he simply jumped down the hole, tripped on the stairs beneath, fell over the railing on the landing and somehow managed to land on his feet on the solid, cement floor twenty feet below. A slit second later, he noticed the other three men standing right in front of where he landed. George stood up straight and stretched his back, all while still holding the pistol and looked directly into Rob's eyes. "That was awesome," Rob complimented, "we all ran out of ammunition about a half hour ago and we called over to you to follow us but you were just so into it that you didn't even respond. And you've picked a great strategic attack point too, even though you put your life in grave danger to do so. Your choice of weapons was a bit strange but you handled that rifle like a professional assassin! You made that gun your bitch! Then you somehow managed to make it back to safety and came barreling down that hatch like something out of a James Bond movie. I must say, son, I am very impressed with your skill and dedication to our cause," the militia's leader spoke. Kermit and Jack stood silently, still holding their rifles by their sides and nodded in approval.

The four men began discussing their next strategy as they walked into the abandoned store. "RING, RING, RING!" the telephone relentlessly sounded. The men immediately stopped talking and froze in their footsteps. "Who would be calling the store now?" Kermit asked. "Should we answer it? Maybe it's the cops wanting to know what our demands are," Jack offered. "Fuck that," George began, "our only demands are to be left alone and you know there is no way they will honor that." Everybody looked to their leader in an inquisitive manner. "Well Rob," Kermit started, "what should we do?" Rob did not answer verbally, rather through his actions as he slowly approached the still ringing telephone. He then put his hand upon the receiver and with some hesitation he picked it up. "WHAT?!" the disturbed man barked into the machine. "Hello, this is the president of Turkowitz's Grocery Kingdom. May I ask what exactly the situation is where you are? What's this about the store being hijacked by disgruntled ex-employees? Is everybody alright? Did you catch them yet?" the concerned man on the other end bombarded Rob with questions. "Who exactly do you think you're speaking to?" Rob asked. "Uh, law enforcement?" the president responded. "No, moron, think again. You've heard that the building was taken over by disgruntled employees, right?" "Yeah." "So then you call the building and think you're talking to somebody who can't even get in through the locked and barricaded doors. I'll ask again: who exactly do you think you're talking to? Do you really think cops can make themselves invisible and walk through walls like ghosts or something?" "Oh my god! You must be one of the disgruntled employees! Why are you doing this? What exactly do you want?" Rob started laughing. "We don't want anything from you. We have everything that we need. We wanted the building, so we took it. Now leave us alone!" "But sir, you can't just take buildings that don't belong to you! That's our building and we want to sell it! Give it back!" "No. For years, you've treated us like shit and tried to justify it by saying that this is our store and that we should take pride in it. And then, without the decency to tell us that you were going out of business so that maybe we could have made other employment arrangements, you just close the store and take our jobs away from us. You didn't care how we got money to survive or where we tried to get jobs; you were just too greedy and only cared about your own monetary gain. Well, this is what you get. You're out of business now so you don't really need this building anyway." "But we want it! And besides, that's just how businesses work! Deal with it!" "Oh, I'm afraid we already have. You see, all these years you've told us that this was our store. Just because you went out business doesn't mean that this is any less our store. If you would have been honest with us and gave us some kind of notice that you were going to close the store down, none of this would have happened. But no, you had to be greedy and now we've dealt with the problem in a way that you didn't expect or for that matter, like. So, you deal with it, asshole!" "But you can't just take buildings like that! You had no right breaking in the way you did!" "Oh well, over the years you and your managers have done many things that you had no right to do but that didn't stop you, now did it? Look, it's out of my hands; it's your problem now. Okay, we showed up to work today only to find that there was no work for us to do. You may no longer need the building, but we do. You screwed us out of jobs so were screwing you out of a building. It's just a natural order of life." "But what you're doing is illegal! You're breaking the law! You won't get away with this!" "Are you retarded? Listen to me! All of these years you said this was our store. Now I know you didn't mean it literally, but that's just how I'm choosing to take it. We are not allowing you to screw us over like this by leaving us empty handed – not after all these years of dedicated service to your company. It's our building now and you're just going to have to accept that. Legal or not, it's ours. Deal with it!" "Deal with it how? In order to do what we need to do, you and everybody else in that building needs to leave so that we can sell the building and pay our investors. That is how a corporation works; when you go out of business, you need to liquidate your assets, but we can't do that if you just steal a building from us!" Now Rob found himself pissed off beyond all belief.

"Excuse me? Liquidate your assets? What exactly does that mean? Is it something like selling off good things that you have that other companies may have a use for?" Rob asked. "Well yes, that's pretty much the bulk of it. You sell what you can for whatever you can get for it and somehow get rid of everything else, usually by distributing it to other businesses," the president responded. "And you call this 'liquidating your assets?' Excuse me, but are good, hard-working, loyal employees not also considered assets? Your employee handbook often refers to employees as being assets. I'm sure you know of other companies that can use good employees, so why didn't you think to set up all the people you were laying off with these other companies? Why didn't you care enough about your employees to liquidate them by hooking them up with other jobs? Come on, how many other companies do you know of? You have suppliers, competitors, sister companies - the list goes on. But what about us? Aren't we assets too? Or is that just another lie?" Rob could hear the president chuckle in the background at this remark. "Look, how stupid are you? Companies just say things like that to get good employees and to keep them motivated. You're not an asset to us! We don't care about our employees! All of you, every single one of you – you're all scum. If you quit, it's not like you're teaching us a lesson or anything, because we'll just replace you. It's as simple as that. You mean nothing to us! Now get the hell out of my building and go liquidate yourself, you smartass! Just because you think you're so special and unique and that the world is made of rainbows and buttercups doesn't give you the right to invade somebody else's property!" Rob took a deep breath as he felt his temper growing more and more with every pulse of his increasingly speeding heart. "Fuck you," he began, "you may see us as scum and you've certainly treated us like scum over the years, but the simple truth of the matter is that we are very, very valuable scum. Without good quality scum like us, you cannot run any business. You need scum to make your company function. Scum stocked your shelves, scum ran your registers, scum unloaded your trucks and scum did everything else for you over the years. Whether you want to admit it or not, scum is your most valuable asset but you didn't care enough to liquidate it or to in anyway help it move on in the world. Instead, you just left it for dead. Well, I'll tell you one thing: I cannot for the life of me imagine somebody wanting to liquidate an asset of lesser value when they took no care whatsoever of their greatest assets of all. I guess it's all because you no longer need your scum, so you've chosen to simply leave it behind to fend for itself and to whither and die. But another thing that you no longer need is your building so I would advise that you just leave that behind too because it's ours now and if you come anywhere near it, we'll kill you and all of your shattered dreams, along with your miserable life, will fade away into nothingness. Think of it like this, ex-employees are in your ex-store, like an asset in an asset and you've just carelessly forsaken it. That's your problem, not mine. But you know that's okay; we'll be able to manage without you. You don't care about us anyway, you've said so yourself so this shouldn't even be an issue for you. In fact, what you should do is just move on in your life and forget all about this whole situation because there's nothing you can do about it and besides, you don't really even care anyway. You know you don't. You would rather be doing other things right now than talking to me. Like golfing for instance; why don't you just go out and play a few holes and forget all about your failed company and just leave us alone? You really don't care about the building anyway because we are in it right now and well, you've decided to go out of business and move on and in the process you've left us for dead. Now fuck off," Rob said as he hung up the phone. A few seconds later he took a deep breath, shook his head and walked away.

George, Kermit and Jack followed Rob to the back of the store. Suddenly, an angry Rob turned around to face his followers. "Look, we have a lot of work to do. The cops are getting restless out there. You guys need to barricade those big windows in the front of the building better than they are now and when you're done doing that, you ought to find a suitable room to use as an armory and then stock it with all of our weapons. I need to kill something right about now, so I'll just be up on the roof shooting at cops again," the leader instructed as he picked up his AR-15 and a box of loaded clips for the weapon. "Are we clear?" he asked. The other three men simply nodded in confirmation to the question.

When all of the windows and doors to the building were effectively locked and barricaded and the armory was set up in the old managers' office located in the back of the store, the three men decided that it would be a good idea to siphon the gasoline out of the fuel tanks of the vehicles to make fire-bombs, rather than just allowing the gasoline to go stale and be of no use for anything whatsoever. So, using empty glass bottles and pieces of cloth from cutting up old smocks and aprons, the three men produced a little over a hundred units. "Let's use them now before the gasoline evaporates," Kermit suggested as the men carried a few cardboard boxes full of the units to the staircase. Upon emerging on the rooftop, the men again immediately smelled the horrid aroma of death as they made their way toward a busy, rapidly-firing Rob. As the men peered over the rooftop and down into the parking lot, they saw more police cars and black ATF vans than they had ever before seen in their entire lives. Quickly, one by one, the men lit the cloth fuses of the units with cigarette lighters and threw them as hard as they could at the vehicles in the parking lot, completely fire-bombing everything in their sights. Smoke and flames filled the air as cars blew up and screaming officers lost their lives in the relentless blaze. Ashes began to drift in the up-currents of the extremely noticeable heat from the burning corpses that littered the parking lot below. Many of the law enforcement officers ran for cover as the fire scorched the battlefield, now burning the tar of the asphalt and emitting a thick black smoke and the dedicated, large militia leader continued firing as if completely oblivious to what was going on.

A few days later, the efforts of the militia grew with their experience in defending their compound. Each of the four men now dressed in the same attire, complete with the black combat boots and the spiked helmets. Each man was also heavily armed at all times, no matter where they went anywhere in the building. Even the most inexperienced of the men, George, carried eight guns on his person alone: a .45 caliber pistol on his boot, a .40 caliber pistol on his right hip, a 9mm on his left hip, a .38 special caliber derringer, as well as a .357 magnum revolver, both in concealment holsters in his pants, a .22 caliber revolver under his vest in a vertical shoulder holster, an AR-15 strapped to his back and a pump-action, sawed-off 12 gauge shotgun in his hands. In addition to these guns, George also carried an electronic stun-gun, a pair of brass knuckles, a big can of pepper spray, a bowie knife, a set of two Chinese throwing stars, a battle axe and a police style baton, all on his belt. Not surprisingly, the other members of the militia also carried similar equipment in much the same setups as George, the only difference being even more weapons. But the important thing was that everybody was prepared for everything imaginable, however, there was only one problem: the number of enemy forces outside the building was growing at an exponential rate with every passing hour. In fact, the National Guard had even arrived on the scene and it wasn't very long before they had the entire building surrounded.

The gunfire continued to rage on outside without there seeming to be any end in sight of the madness. George could hear the sounds of bullets hitting and ricocheting off of the brick exterior of the building as the enemy forces did everything in their power to weaken the structure and to intimidate the inhabitants inside. The shots were even louder up on the roof, obviously, because of the enemy's relentless efforts to defeat the militia's leader who was a true warrior at heart. George was a bit worried, however, not of the group's skill, but of the dwindling supplies. It was clear to the young man by this time that the police, ATF, National Guard, FBI, and SWOT teams were not going to succeed in taking down a man that the whole Viet Cong Army couldn't in the 60's and that nine massive heart attacks and four strokes couldn't since then. Rob was a true soldier who stood up for what was right; he was a dedicated freedom fighter who would stop at nothing. However, in the eyes of the enemy, Rob and everybody else in the building was a terrorist and that kind of association pissed him off to no end. He showed his distaste by spraying a constant stream of bullets into the enemy's direction and in the process, taking several bullets himself, but slowing down at nothing; he laughed in the face of death. But George was concerned about the eventual depletion of the ammunition supply. How much carnage and havoc could his fierce leader invoke without a gun? "Fear not, George. I have found death very hard to come by and if it should come, I am willing to pay that price by laying down my arms in death. Fear not the reaper; perhaps my life is testament that he fears me more," Rob attempted to comfort the young man. "Okay, but if you die, most likely we all will follow suit whether we like it or not," George said with grave concern as Rob shrugged his shoulders and smiled grimly. "George, a wise man once said that 'the tree of liberty must be refreshed from time to time with the blood of patriots and tyrants.' His name was Thomas Jefferson. Now, George, do you consider yourself a patriot?" "Yeah, well I guess so." "Fine, then stop your bitching. I know what I am doing and I'm telling you that everything will be okay. But if it isn't, oh well. We are all in this together and we all have to do what we have to do. If we die, we die," Rob said as he walked away.

The remaining militia men stood around in silence. "We need to get the greatest efficiency from our ammunition as possible," George said, "Somehow we need to be able to shoot higher than we are now. Rob could take out so many more people if he didn't have to crouch down like that." Jack and Kermit looked at the young man with confusion on their puzzled faces. "Yeah," Jack started, "but if he stands up, he'll get shot to death." "Well, what do you suggest we do then, George," Kermit asked. George thought about his idea for about fifteen seconds. "I know," he began, "we need to get all of those huge cardboard bales that are down on the dock up here. We can build a barricade with them. You know, like a wall all around the edge of the roof, like cops do with sand bags." Jack and Kermit both looked at each other as if George had said something really stupid. "George, you aren't referring to the compressed bales that we make when we unload the cardboard baler, are you?" Kermit asked. George nodded. "Those usually weigh a bit over three thousand pounds. Even the smallest ones we've ever made have got to weigh somewhere between two and three thousand. There are none down there that weigh any less than a ton. How the hell do you suggest we go about moving them?" Jack barked. Suddenly, George smiled with a clever gleam in his eyes. "We wrap a chain around them and feed it over the main support beam by the stairs. Then, we attach the other end to the hitch on the tank. We can hoist them up like that, and then once we have them all up there, we'll just slide them to the edge," the young man responded. "Sounds retarded, but it can't hurt to give it a try," Kermit offered as the three men began walking towards the hatch to go get started on the task.

At the end of that day, the three men had successfully completed the task to George's description. It was not by any stretch of the imagination an easy task, especially the sliding of the bales to the edge of the roof, but nonetheless, they got the job done to their satisfaction. Rob was extremely pleased with the improved shooting conditions and the heightened sense of safety that the bales provided him with. The leader commended George's ingenuity in realizing that there was a need for improved ammunition efficiency and in coming up with a working idea of how to achieve it. Rob, however, was very tired from shooting all day and asked that the other three men take over while he took a nap in the security of the armory. The three men complied and got to work shooting at the enemy. George used both his AK-47 and his AR-15 while the other two guys used similar weapons and threw hand-grenades at the enemy forces all throughout the night.

The three men were still restlessly firing round after round into the parking lot when the sun came up early the morning. George could not believe that the cops and military officials just kept coming and coming in greater numbers all the time. It seemed like for every person he killed, five more came, and so far the militia had killed close to a 500,000 people. But the men continued on in their efforts until Rob emerged on the scene. "Come downstairs. We need to discuss a new strategy," the leader spoke to his men.

"Look," Rob began speaking, "maybe you guys haven't noticed, but the enemy just will not leave us alone. They're just going to keep coming and unlike ours, their ammunition supply is unlimited. Since we've been here, we've used up more than half of our supply. Maybe you've noticed that we have to wade our ways through empty casings just to get to the edge of the roof where we shoot from. So, I think what we need is a surprise attack. That tank is equipped with one hell of a destructive cannon that we haven't even thought of using yet. I mean, come on, we've been using it to tow everything. So, this is what's going down. The people outside are obviously retarded because it hasn't occurred to them yet to just blow up the building. So, what we're going to do is trick them into coming into our building where we will kill them in greater numbers without the use of a single bullet." "And how do you propose we pull that off?" Kermit asked. "Simple," Rob started, "Jack will drive the tank full force through the barricaded front windows into the parking lot where he will mercilessly run over the enemy and shoot the cannon at their vehicles. The sudden surprise of this happening will cause many of the people outside to run into the building without thinking, just to find cover. When it dawns on them that they have just infiltrated our compound, the very first thing they'll do is start searching for the rest of us. Luckily, they don't really know what we look like in any great detail, so we'll hide behind the customer service desk and wait for them to realize that they *really* are inside the compound. Then, when it dawns on them and fear begins to set in, we will run as fast as we can past them and into the back room. They will be too shaken to think of shooting at us but they will follow and in large numbers too. We'll have cardboard cut-outs of men from old displays set up in that huge walk-in freezer in the back. The door will be open and right inside the door will be an opened oil drum full of bleach. When we get into the back, we will quickly hide behind the freezer door and wait for them to all run into the unit. Then, we slam the door shut and park a huge pile of wooden skids in front of it among other stuff." "Okay, then what happens?" George asked. "Then Jack will drive the tank back into the compound and use it to block the hole he made in the wall. He will then stand guard with a gun in case

42

somebody tries to get in. The rest of us will climb to the top of the freezer with a drill and make a hole right above where the barrel of bleach is. Once we do that, we will pour as many containers of liquid ammonia through the hole and into the bleach as we can. Then we will seal the hole and there you have it: a make-shift gas chamber. Then we'll climb back down and make it a point to hit the power switch for the freezer in order to make it even more miserable for those captive inside. Just think: the lights will go out and the fans will turn on. The assholes inside will quickly become asphyxiated and die of suffocation. And their corpses will freeze solid for our uses later," the leader explained. "Our uses later?" George asked. "Hostages; if they're dead, they'll pose no threat to us, but if we can somehow preserve them in their life-like forms, we can pretend that they are hostages to keep the enemy from blowing our compound up," Jack offered. The leader nodded in approval. "Let's do it," he ordered.

George watched as Jack drove the tank to the front of the compound, rolling loudly on its tracks as it ripped up and cracked the floor tiles. George stood by the customer service desk with Kermit while Rob was busy setting up the freezer. The tank was steadily traveling at a very slow speed as it drove towards the front barricaded windows. Finally Rob reappeared and gave the thumbs-up sign to Jack, who immediately acknowledged the sign by going back down into the vehicle and closing the top hatch. George could feel his heart beginning to race as his palms grew sweaty from nervousness. "What if we all die? What if the enemy gets into the compound too early? What if I get shot when I'm running towards the back of the building? What if the trap doesn't work? What if the tank breaks down or runs out of fuel?" all the "what-if" thoughts of nervousness bombarded the young man's nervous and frightened mind. "Are you shaking?" Rob asked. George nodded and said that he was a bit uncomfortable with the plan. Just then, Rob became infuriated with the young man and began screaming at him to not be so afraid. "WHY ARE YOU SCARED, GEORGE, WHY?! THERE IS NO TIME FOR FEAR! EVERY SECOND COUNTS! GROW SOME FUCKING BALLS! THIS IS WAR! NOT A LITTLE GIRL'S TEA PARTY! THIS IS WAR! NOW GET WITH THE PROGRAM!" The young man swallowed hard as Rob scolded him for his cowardice and then returned his gaze towards the tank.

Jack slammed the vehicle into the full-throttle and sent the tank flying into the barricaded window. This action made a tremendous noise that made George jump slightly, but within seconds, Jack was busy running people over, crushing police cars and blowing up all the ATF vans, fire trucks, ambulances and other large vehicles that were present on the scene. Rob, Kermit, and George watched as Jack brought death and destruction to the already chaotic parking lot, crushing and shooting everything in his path. Then, suddenly, six military helicopters swooped in and began shooting at the tank with 50 caliber machine guns. The three men inside the building watched as Jack leisurely adjusted the cannon to aim up at the helicopters and then within seconds, shot them each out of the air. The ground shook as several huge, heavy chunks of flaming metal hit the asphalt of the parking lot and in most cases, crushing their allies in the process.

Suddenly, just as planned, several hundred people dashed into the building through the hole in the wall. They carefully and nervously huddled near the hole to watch the tank continue to destroy their vehicles and supplies. "NOW!!!" Rob roared as the three men sprung up from behind the customer service desk and ran as fast as they could into the back of the building. This seemed to take everybody by surprise but within just a few seconds, all the people were screaming and running after the three men. "GET THEM! DON'T LET THEM ESCAPE!" the people yelled as the three militia men made their way to the freezer and hid behind the door and other nearby obstructions, like large towering skids of boxes. "WHERE DID THEY GO?! FIND THEM!" the screaming got louder as the people got closer. "THERE THEY ARE!!! GET THEM!!!" one man screamed as all of the people ran full speed into the freezer and began tackling the cardboard cut-outs to the floor. Then as quickly as he could, Rob slammed the door shut. "HEY! THIS WAS A TRAP! LET US OUT OF HERE! YOU WON'T GET AWAY WITH THIS!!!" the muffled screaming from inside the freezer continued. The three men held the door shut with all their weight and strength until an unknown hooded man came running into the back towards the militia.

"OH NO! WHO THE FUCK ARE YOU?!" Rob roared in fear as the unknown man dashed towards him. "I TOLD YOU WE WERE GOING TO DIE!" George shouted at Rob. Kermit was speechless. Finally the man stopped, looked around and then dashed off into another direction. The militia didn't know what to do, but they also didn't have the time to think about it either because their intruder returned a few seconds later with an electronic pallet-jack loaded with the heavy skids that Rob had planned to use to barricade the freezer door. "ROB! GEORGE! KERMIT! WHEN I SAY 'NOW,' GET AWAY FROM THAT DOOR!" the man yelled to the confused militia as he hastily swung the machine around to haul the skids in front of the freezer door, skid first. "NOW!" the man belted out as the three men still holding the freezer door scattered out of the way like cockroaches. A split second later, the man had crashed the skids up against the freezer door and then just parked them there. The door was sealed.

"You...you...you...helped us. Why?" a nervous and confused Rob stuttered. The man remained silent but answered by stepping into the light and removing his hood. "Bruce! Man! How did you get in here?" Rob happily exclaimed. "I heard about some pissed-off ex-employees invading the store and going on a rampage on the news a few nights ago and I just figured it had to be you guys. And I just wanted to join your group because I really hated Turkowitz's myself. That's all," Bruce answered. "You do know you can't leave now, right? You're stuck here with us and if we ever get caught, you will be in as much trouble as us because they'll consider you a member of the militia. Do you realize that?" Rob calmly asked as the muffled screaming from inside the freezer behind him continued. Bruce nodded. "Sure, I realize what I'm getting involved in here, but I've got some serious bones to pick with this company as well and you know that old saying: a man's got to do what a man's got to do?" the young, skinny man responded. "Alright then," Rob spoke, "you may join our militia. What type of weaponry do you prefer?" Bruce smiled morbidly. "I prefer all kinds of old fashioned, obsolete stuff that ancient people used long, long ago to cause their victims as much pain as possible. I wouldn't think you guys would have anything like that, would you?" "What do you mean," George asked, "like old ninja shit and stuff like that?" Bruce nodded. "Yeah, I always wanted to kill my enemies with weapons that they used back in medieval times, you know, like in the movies and in video-games?" "Well, you're in luck because we have a lot of that stuff in our armory," George responded. "Okay, then, Bruce, you will be our ninja and we'll put you on compound security detail. Your job will be to defend the building from intruders. Obviously, we can't put you outside because you'd be shot in a second. Is that cool with you?" Rob asked. Bruce smiled and nodded. "I'll be the official militia ninja and arm myself with the weapons of old!" he responded. "Right," said Rob with a slightly raised eyebrow.

Just then, Jack arrived with another man who had gotten in from outside. "Ryan, is that you?" Kermit asked. "Sure is, my friend. I'm ready for war!" "Damn it! How did you guys get in here?!" Rob demanded. "Jack left us in when he was parking that badass tank in that hole in the wall up front," Ryan answered. "Oh, okay then," Rob said as he climbed to the top of the freezer and began pouring container after container through the small drill-hole that he had made in the top of the unit. "AAAAAAAHHHHHH!!!!!" the screaming and banging noises from inside the freezer boomed as Rob covered the hole up and dropped back down to the floor. "NOOOO!!! WERE GOING TO SUFFOCATE IN HERE!!! YOU BASTARDS!!!!" the screaming continued as Rob then flipped the power switch on the freezer to the "on" position, only to piss off the people inside even more.

As the muffled screaming continued, Rob began leisurely walking away from the freezer area towards the armory. The other five men followed, talking excitedly amongst themselves about all the different kinds of weapons that they had access to. When the group finally made it to the area of the armory, they entered the tiny room and closed the door behind them. "All of our weapons, ammunition and battle supplies are stored here when not in use," Rob explained to the two new members who stood in awe at the wide array of artillery, "We have everything you could ever need in here and more. You may help yourself to any of the weapons you see in here as we will not be able to take any of them with us when and if we ever leave the compound for any reason at all. Beyond concealed handguns and knives, all of what you see here must remain. The only rule is that you return unused weapons to this room when you are finished with them instead of just letting them scattered all over the building. This is necessary for the next guy who comes in here for a weapon and it is also common sense to keep track of your stuff in case the enemy should manage to break in. Are we clear?" the leader spoke with authority. "Yes," the other men simultaneously responded. "Now arm yourselves," Rob ordered the newest recruits.

Bruce and Ryan studied the various weapons in absolute amazement. It was not very long before Ryan begun strapping all different types of holsters to his body and loading them with pistols and revolvers. Then he stuffed his pockets with as much ammunition as possible and picked up a semi-automatic 16 gauge shotgun. Bruce, on the other hand, was busy studying all of the different kinds of swords and medieval weaponry. He seemed to be almost in a trance as he sorted through all of his various options, but then a smile spread across his face as he picked up an old flail. Slowly, he lifted the wooden handle with his right hand and touched the metal ball with the other hand to check the sharpness of the spikes. Apparently they passed the test and met the young man's criteria because one of the spikes drew blood from his index finger when he touched it. "Hot damn!" he exclaimed with a smile of satisfaction as his blood hit the floor in small drops. "A true relic of the bygone era," the entranced soldier began in a pure sense of amazement as he stared at the spiked ball still swinging on its chain, "it will finally rise again in modern times but this time to further our cause as it is one of the few weapons the enemy will never expect us to have." The young man then tucked the flail into his vest and quickly started arming himself with several other weapons as well, including many knives, sabers, a spear, a pair of brass knuckles, a set of Chinese throwing stars and a large, heavy battle axe strapped to his back. Then he picked up a large sword with one hand a spiked helmet with the other. "I'm ready to do this thing, bitch!" Bruce snarled with determination. "Yeah, well, just in case the ninja stuff doesn't work out for you, you should probably have a gun on you as a backup weapon, don't you think?" Ryan asked. "Fine," Bruce muttered as he picked up a .38 caliber pistol and shoved it into his vest pocket.

When the two men emerged from the armory, they found only Jack sitting at a table eating canned fruit with a spoon. "Did you guys find everything that you needed in there?" he asked. Both Ryan and Bruce nodded. "Cool. Well, the others are on the roof shooting at cops again. George thought it would be fun to shoot the gas tanks, windows, and tires out of their cars with a .22 caliber rifle, since he had something like 10 or 11,000 rounds for it and since that particular gun isn't exactly the best to use in combat or even as a sniper rifle. Kermit, well, he's using my fully automatic AK-47, while Rob, on the other hand is up there with a .50 caliber rifle that he used to hunt with. Now he's hunting bear with it!" Jack said as he started laughing to the two silent men. "Don't you get it? Bear? On the CB radio, the word 'bear' is used as a reference to cops," he tried to explain. "Oh," Ryan said, "well, what should we do for now?" Just then, the lights in the building went out and the three men found themselves in total darkness. "Well I guess you can fire the generator up," Jack replied.

A few minutes later, the lights were back on again and all six men reunited in the armory. "We need a new plan," Rob informed the others. "But what?" Ryan asked. "I know," Kermit offered, "we'll fuck with them. We'll haul as much perishable goods and shit that we don't need, like salad dressing in glass bottles and jars to the roof and chuck the stuff at the cops. Two of us will continue shooting while the rest of us throw as much shit at the enemy as possible." "And what will that do?" Rob asked. "Three things," Kermit said, "it will piss them off, it will help clear some space in the compound and it will make things extra miserable down in the battlefield." "Yeah and I'm a good shot too. If I throw stuff just right so that it hits people in the faces or in the temples, it could knock them out or even kill them, either way, rendering them useless," Bruce added. "It's worth a try," Jack offered. "Alright, well then get to it. George and I will shoot from both ends of the building and the rest of you can throw as much shit into the parking lot as you want. Have fun," Rob instructed with a hint of uncertainty in his sarcastic voice.

A few hours later, Ryan, Bruce, Jack, and Kermit had thrown thousands of expired and perished products from the roof at the enemy. There was angry screaming from below as disgusted cops and other law enforcement agents dodged flying objects from all directions. And in most cases, when they would dodge a flying jar of mayonnaise or something stupid like that, they would get shot by with Rob or George. The four men were having the times of their lives as they raced back and forth from the hatch, chucking as much junk at the people below as possible. Rob wasn't too surprised when he noticed that the men had gotten a bit carried away; they began launching huge loads of rotting meat at the enemy and Kermit even made it a point to roll a full helium tank off the edge of the building. It landed with a thud and then the valve broke off from all of the pressure inside, sending the heavy canister flying through the air like a balloon, killing two people in the process. But perhaps the most disturbing effort was when Jack had decided to take the orders of throwing shit at the enemy literally; the young man decided to hook a pump up to the sewer, attach a fire hose to the pump and drag the hose up onto the roof. When he had everything functioning to suit his devious plan, he began spraying hundreds of thousands of gallons of stagnant sewer water loaded with piss and liquefied shit over the side of the roof into the parking lot and all over the enemy forces, much to their great distaste.

"WHAT THE FUCK!!! WHAT IS THIS CRAP THAT THEY'RE SHOOTING AT US NOW?!! IT'S SOME KIND OF RANCID SLIME!!! OH MY GOD!!! IT'S SHIT!!! WHAT SICK BASTARDS SPRAY SHIT AT PEOPLE?! IT REEKS!!! LOOK AT ALL OF THIS SHIT EVERYWHERE!!! WHAT'S THEIR PROBLEM?! AHHGG!!! A TURD JUST HIT ME IN THE FACE!!! IT STINKS SO BAD!!!! WHY SHIT?! OF ALL THINGS WHY THIS FUCKING SHIT?!!!" the horrid screaming sounded from the parking lot below as Jack continued to pump a seemingly endless supply of sludge from the sewer that ran beneath the building. But eventually that section of the sewer ran empty and Jack aborted his disgusting and perhaps, misguided mission. The other five men briefly peered down into the parking lot and had a difficult time believing their eyes; the lot was filled with thousands of rotting corpses, overturned vehicles, blood, guts, shit, flaming cars, the two military helicopters from before, now completely destroyed and still on fire, rotting meat, perished grocery products and garbage, among many other horrid sights, completely covered in sewer sludge. The air was thick with stench and black smoke in addition to all of this, but yet the enemy forces continued to pour onto the scene in greater numbers than before. "There's just no stopping these guys," George observed as the six men climbed down through the hatch and reentered the backroom of the compound.

"Your absolutely right, George," Rob responded, "It doesn't look like they are ever going to give up and leave us alone. And if they can't just fuck off and accept the fact that we own this building now, then we're going to end up fighting them until we run out of supplies and have to surrender instead of being able to do the work of a militia which is why we came here in the first place. We might have to just give up." An awkward silence filled the room for several minutes. Finally, Ryan spoke up: "but then that means that they win. How can we allow that?" Rob nodded in acknowledgement of what he believed to be a legitimate concern. "Look, we might not win, but we sure as hell aren't going to lose. We may break even in the deal but nobody is going to win, especially not Turkowitz's. We may have to blow up the building and that's okay, because if we can't have it then neither can anybody else. I mean, if we can't even use our own building, then why should we allow anybody else to? That is the only way we can truly lose out in this deal." The men listened to their leader speak with careful thought but Bruce seemed a bit worried about the whole

49

situation. "What's wrong, Bruce?" Rob asked. "Well, it's nothing really, but hasn't it at all occurred to you guys that we're probably going to either end up in jail or dead for doing all of this?" The other five men started laughing morbidly with amusement. "No, that's not going to happen," Rob began, "that would be a fine example of losing and we're out to win. But by the looks of it we might not be winning this battle, but we sure as hell aren't going to be losing either. We'll find a way out of here one way or another – you just wait and see."

The six men then started walking through the backroom in silence. Eventually, they made their way to the freezer, which was also silent. "Do you think they're dead?" Kermit asked. "Yes, I'm pretty sure that they are. I'd be quite impressed if anybody in that freezer was still alive," Rob answered. "So now what?" Bruce asked. Rob just looked at the sword-armed man and then at Ryan, the man armed with the semi-automatic shotgun. "You two guys are on defense, so you should be up front where the tank is so that you can kill anybody who tries to crawl into the building through the hole. Jack and George, who are insanely obsessed with blowing things up should have already realized that they could be making bombs out of the propane canisters and then throwing them off of the roof at the enemy. Kermit and I will set another trap, this time involving the fryer grease from the old deli department and a net. We'll grease up the floor in front of the main entrance of the building and string up a large net that I have in the armory. We'll roll the net out flat on the floor in behind the grease and string it up through the ceiling rafters. We'll then hook the ends of the ropes to the old electronic pallet-jack so that when the machine is driven towards the back of the building, the net will pull up and capture the people who were walking and tripping over it." Rob replied. "But how do you think your net idea is going to work exactly?" a confused Kermit inquired. Rob smiled cleverly. "It's all quite simple, my friend. We'll grease up the floor and set up the net. Then you un-barricade and unlock the main door and with a piece of white cloth, wave it to the cops outside. They'll think we're surrendering and come barging in, slip on the grease and fall down onto the net. Then when I yell the word 'now,' you slam the door shut and re-secure it. I'll pull the jack back as fast as it can go and there you have it, a net full of captured cops." Kermit was now smiling at this plan. "But then what do we do with them all?" he asked. "Easy – we'll just tie the net shut and cut it down. Then we'll drag it with the pallet-jack to the backroom and somehow without them grabbing onto us, we'll just pick up the whole net and throw it into the cardboard baler. Then we'll do it again and again until they wise up and stop falling for it. But until that happens, we'll just keep crushing them. It's okay if any of them get away; that's what Bruce and Ryan will be prepared for on defense. So, now we all have jobs to do, so let's get to it!" the leader barked as everybody scattered in their own directions.

In almost no time at all, George and Jack had made their way to the roof with all of the propane tanks that they had managed to convert into deadly bombs. There were about forty in all and it didn't take very long to use them up. Jack would ignite them and George would heave them as far as he could out into the battlefield. Within seconds, they would explode with a very loud rumble that shook the ground and the whole building. The noise of the explosion was almost deafening as it caused the two men's ears to ring. Aside from the explosions, all that could be heard from down below were the sounds of violent screaming, loud sirens, and rapid gunfire. But when all of the bombs had been used, the two men slowly stood up from the bale that they were hiding behind and looked down into the parking lot. To their utter amazement, the bombs had blown large craters in the asphalt, as well as having killed many enemy soldiers. Just then, the two men had to drop back down quickly behind the bale to avoid getting shot from the cops below. Behind the bale, they stayed as still as they could but George could still feel the impact that the bullets had when they hit the tightly compressed cardboard. And then a gas grenade landed right in front of the two crouching soldiers. Quickly, Jack picked it up and tossed it back down into the parking lot. A few seconds later, the sounds of loud coughing filled the otherwise silent air.

Slowly, George and Jack made their ways down into backroom of the store. There they met up with Rob and Kermit, who were busy trying to shove a huge net full of writhing, struggling and screaming enemy soldiers into the opened baler. Instinctively, the two bombers dashed over to the baler to assist their leader. The four men got kicked, punched and scratched, but together they managed to get the net full of their enemies into the large, green compressor. Then, almost immediately after, Bruce and Ryan arrived with another net full of screaming and thrashing men. "That was way too easy," Ryan said, "even easier than fishing with a net." The six men laughed together as they piled the second net into the machine and slammed the door shut. Rob then turned the key, sending the machine into operation.

51

The six militia members stood in awe as the top part of the machine started descending towards the victims, who were screaming in terror. Slowly, the machine compressed lower and lower as the screaming became louder and louder. And then, the sick sounds of breaking bones filled the backroom as the screaming became silent. The machine continued to go lower and lower, making the most sickening squashing sounds as body organ became crushed from all of the pressure. The floor in front of the baler quickly covered up with a thick, heavy, dark-red blood as the now-familiar stench of death filled the air. George felt sick to the stomach as the baler had reached it limit and began moving in the upwards direction. Slowly, inch by inch, the machine opened up, bringing the gate with it. The top part had returned, covered in blood and guts, with a long intestinal tract stuck fast to it. George threw up.

Suddenly, the sound of alarms echoed through the building. "INTRUDERS! BRUCE! RYAN! MAN YOUR POSTS! NOW!" Rob roared as he pulled out his .45 and started running towards the front of the building. Bruce picked up his sword and Ryan retrieved his shotgun and the two young men dashed to their posts in record speed, where they found close to fifty SWOT team members breaking in through the wall. Ryan and Rob began shooting as fast as they could while Bruce came up from behind and mercilessly started running the enemy soldiers through and beheading them with his sword. The SWOT members fired off many rounds, but missed their targets every time due to their fear of the sudden onslaught. A few seconds later, the other four militia members appeared with shotguns as the killing continued. Disturbingly enough, Bruce seemed to be truly enjoying himself as he slashed open body after body with his sword, spilling the enemy's blood and watching it run down the long, sharp blade and all over his hands. Then, to his dismay, he accidentally dropped the weapon but fortunately managed to replace it with his flail. "WHAT THE FUCK?!" one enemy soldier screeched as he saw the medieval weapon just seconds before Bruce cracked him in the face with the spiked ball and then proceeded to run and others through with a long, sharp spear. Eventually, Bruce noticed that he was the only militia member fighting; the others were watching in amusement as the young man took life after life just by using his primitive weapons. Before too much longer, Bruce was the only living man, now soaked head to toe in the enemy's blood, standing in the middle of an area covered with mangled corpses. "Wow, that kicked ass," Kermit said, "with that skill, we might never have to leave." Rob shook his head with disagreement, "you know we can't stay here forever," he said.

A few days later, the militia thought it would be a good idea to show the enemy soldiers who were shooting at the building from outside what could happen to them if they didn't give up. So Rob opened up the freezer where the first invaders were killed and stood in the doorway in pure amazement. Apparently, the bodies froze solid before they could ever begin any of the stages of decomposition, so the corpses were perfectly preserved with the same tortured facial expressions that they had made during their horrible deaths. "This is perfect," Rob said to himself, "we can use these things to serve as examples of what we're all about." So the leader had his men carry the frozen corpses to the roof one by one and when they were all up there, all six men started tossing the corpses at the enemy soldiers down below. "OH MY GOD, IT'S RON! AND DAVE! AND JOE! WHAT SICK ASSHOLES DO STUFF LIKE THIS?! THEY'RE FROZEN SOLID!" the screaming from below sounded to Rob's grim satisfaction.

Unfortunately, the effort did not work. All throwing frozen corpses did was piss off the enemy even more. Worst yet, the generator ran out of fuel. This upset Rob because he had planned on mutilating enemy soldiers in the old meat room with the band saws. Now there was no electricity to power the saws. So each of the six men, including Bruce, gathered up guns and ammunition and carried it to the roof where they shot relentlessly. But the enemy just wouldn't give up. The six men could see from the rooftop that all of the roads around the area had been barricaded except for one that was being used by military and law enforcement. And the enemy soldiers just kept coming with no end in sight. All the militia could do was shoot and hope they didn't run out of ammunition – but then half an hour later, that was exactly what had happened.

By this time, there were empty casings everywhere but not a single live round for any of the guns that the six men were armed with. But the shooting outside continued. "It's over," Jack said. "NO IT'S NOT!" George scolded as he grabbed a case of lighter fluid and a cigarette lighter and scampered to the roof. From the hatch, Rob watched as the young man lit all of the cardboard bales on fire and pushed as many of them as he could over the edge down into the empty parking lot. "TAKE THAT, ASSHOLES!!!" George screamed with rage as he flew back to the hatch. Then, as he was closing it, he noticed the military helicopters coming in. "I guess it really is over," the young man said to his leader.

"What do you suppose they'll do to us when we're captured?" Bruce asked nervously. "Nothing," Rob responded, "because they're not going to catch us." The other five men looked down at their feet in disappointment. "Come on, Rob, give it up. We're done. There is nothing we can do. They're going to catch us and that's it. There is nothing we can do about it," Ryan said. "Yeah, man, really, he's right," Kermit started, "we've fought an impressive battle, but now it's time for the end. I mean, you had to know we would eventually run out of ammo." Rob shook his head in disagreement. "Quitters," he said, "we are far from being finished here. Now there are shovels in the armory. We're going to tunnel out of here. Get to work." All of the other men just looked at each other with doubt in their eyes. "NOW!" Rob roared, so the men got to work.

"Rob, can we stop now," George whined, "we're never going to make it anyway." Rob said nothing but gave George a shock with his taser. "No. Keep digging," the leader growled as the men mined away at the floor at the far side of the building in what used to be the dairy department. "FASTER!!!" Rob roared.

"Come on, man, we're working as fast as we can! Give us a break!" Kermit complained. "I'm warning you all: one more word and you're dead. I'm not above stabbing any of you to death. Keep working. I'm going to try to keep everything secure the best I can and then I'm going to build the most powerful bomb that I can with the limited resources that we have left," the leader said as he walked away.

The men dug as fast as they could and piled the soil into the building. It was a difficult task, because their only source of light came from battery-powered camping lanterns. But the men worked as fast as they could anyway; the sweat poured down their faces and painfully stung their eyes, huge blisters formed on their hands, their hearts pounded speedily – it was pure hell. But they knew it was only a matter of time before the circling helicopters would land on the roof and the men didn't want to end up in prison, nor did they want to die if they defied their leader, so they dug for their lives. Meanwhile, Rob constructed a bomb with dynamite and other items that he could scrounge together in the pitch-dark compound that was powerful enough to obliterate the entire building and everything in it.

A few hours later, Rob had finished his work on the bomb and mounted it in the very middle of the building, right next to the main load-bearing support column. He returned to the hole where the other five men were diligently working on the tunnel only to find that they were not even half way done with their project. Rob peered down into the narrow shaft to see the men tiring as they slaved away and warned them to continue relentlessly until the job was done. But just then as Rob was inspecting their work, he heard a familiar voice through a megaphone outside: "GUYS! GEORGE, RYAN, ROB, KERMIT, BRUCE!!! WHY ARE YOU DOING ALL OF THIS?! YOU GUYS HAVE TO STOP! WE CAN WORK THIS OUT BEFORE ANYBODY ELSE GETS HURT! THIS IS DIANE, YOUR STORE MANAGER! LET ME IN AND WE'LL NEGOITIATE! ROB, I KNOW YOU'RE THE RING-LEADER HERE! I KNOW ABOUT YOUR SECRET MILITIA AND I KNOW YOU'RE IN CHARGE; YOU PUT THESE GUYS UP TO THIS HORRIBLE BULLSHIT! ROB, I HAVE LISA FROM HUMAN RESOURCES AND FRED, THE PRESIDENT OF THE COMPANY HERE WITH ME! LET US IN AND WE CAN NOGOTIATE WITH YOU! THE POLICE WILL NOT TRY ANYTHING FUNNY WHILE WE ARE WITH YOU, SO YOU CAN TRUST US! WHAT DO YOU SAY, ROB?!" Rob just stood by the opening of the hole and quietly scratched his chin in careful thought. "Kermit and Jack, come with me. The rest of you keep working," he said. Then the three men walked off into the dark building.

Kermit and Jack followed their leader to the front of the building near the main entrance. When they arrived at the door, Rob stopped dead in his tracks and turned around to face his followers. Saying nothing at first, Rob allowed Kermit to speak. "Rob, what's going on here? Are we giving up? Are you going to surrender? What about the tunnel? Why are the other guys still working?" Rob smiled mischievously. "No," he began, "didn't you hear that bitch babbling a little while ago? She said the police won't fuck with us while we're 'negotiating.' So, we invite them in and use them as hostages. That way, we'll have all the time in the world to work on the tunnel. Get it?" Kermit nodded with his consent.

"But wait a minute, why do you need the two of us to be here with you when we could be digging? I mean, the sooner the tunnel is finished the better, right?" Jack asked. Rob smiled grimly and let out a little morbid chuckle. "My dear Jack, do you really think we're going to let these assholes live after what they did to us? I mean, come on, we killed thousands of other jerks for less than what this stupid bitch manager has done to us, so do really think we're going to let them go free once they're in our custody? Fuck no!" the leader responded. "Well yeah, Jack," Kermit added, "you always said you'd love to get your hands on the enemy for what she did to you. Now's your chance." "So, what, swords again?" Jack inquired. "No, no. Jack, what is the number one thing you've always treasured and tried to live up to in your life? Is it not the very same thing that this bitch has used against you since she became our manager? What about all of the times she has discriminated against you by not giving you off to go to church or to celebrate religious holidays with your family? What about all of the insensitive and cruel jokes and remarks that she had made towards you for believing in your chosen faith? And what about all of those times when she would take off on the days you requested just so you had to work when all the time you knew there was no way in hell she was going to use those days in the same ways you would have? You yourself have often complained of her pillaging you and discriminating against you by not allowing you the time off you require practicing your faith. And then, on top of it all, while you miss out on all of these holidays, you get to hear her brag to other employees about how she went to the movies or slept all day or did something she could have done on any other day but she chose the days you wanted off instead. What about that, Jack, and what about how you said you would often hear her telling the customers how religious she is? Well Jack, how did the Romans punish such blasphemy, intolerance, contempt and disrespect to the state religions back in their day?" Rob asked. "Well," a now angered and hot-tempered Jack responded, "they used crucifixion." Rob nodded. "Right, now the two of you go in the back and find those six long wooden beams and some hammers and a box of nails and start hauling all that shit up to the roof. Then somehow create what you feel fit and then go help the other guys finish the tunnel. I'll let our guests in to 'negotiate.'"

The two men scattered like cockroaches as their fearless leader stepped toward the door and opened it. "ALRIGHT, LET'S DO THIS!" he barked outside to summon the manager and the other two jerks that accompanied her. They began walking towards the open door in an almost reluctant manner but made their ways inside the building quickly enough to satisfy the leader. Rob locked and barricaded the door and then turned to face his company. He saw the selfishness and the greed gleaming in their eyes as they stared back at him with a sense of anxiety. Rob's eyes focused on each one of his guests, studying their facial expressions and trying to read their thoughts in an effort to determine their motives. He looked at the president, Fred, and then at Lisa and back again. Both appeared hardened with greed as their eyes were glazed over with an anticipating facial expression seeming to reflect nothing more than selfish thoughts of how they could profit from the situation at hand. Then Rob looked into the eyes of his former manager and saw the devil.

She began to speak, "why are you doing this, Rob, why?" "You know why, you stupid bitch," he answered. She looked confused but said nothing. Rob spoke again, "you know why. I told you countless of times in the past about the unacceptable behavior of both you and the company but all you did was laugh about it, like I made a joke. But I was being serious and you knew that and you laughed anyway. You had this arrogant attitude that you could do whatever you wanted because you're the employer and so you're entitled to your stupid draconian policies about how every little thing has to be your way. But then when I told you that employment is a two-way street, a contractual agreement between two mutually consenting parties and that I can have my own policies as well, again you laughed in my face and told me that what works in theory and what looks good on paper rarely pans out in real life and if I had a problem with that, I could just quit. But instead I suggested to you that maybe you could meet me half way because a productive workforce is a content workforce founded on both open communication and compromise; one that feels its needs are being met and its concerns are being heard by an employer who cared. But then you looked me in the eyes and do you remember what you had the nerve to say to me at that moment? You told me that we reside in an 'at-will' state and so you could fire me at anytime you wanted for no reason at all. That's what you said and then you walked away. And then there were other times when I told you that this bullshit system of how the world thinks it has to cater to employers would one day end and I said this in hopes of reaching some kind of mutual agreement with you concerning the fair and efficient management of the staff and again you laughed in my face and walked away. And since then, all you've ever done was go out of your way to counteract all of our hard work. You would make us redo our work, you would make us do the work of other employees, you would make us help other departments, but you would never allow anybody to help us even when it was crucial to getting the job done. Then you would impose impossible time limits and quotas for getting the work done and base annual pay increases on them. Since you've been here, not only has it been a first for me to not get any raises but it's also been a first for me to experience decreases in my pay. Never has it been this bad where I found myself doing more work than ever before and my pay ended up going down. Meanwhile, you're giving yourself big raises and bonuses to do absolutely nothing and then you have the nerve to brag about it." "Uh, Rob?" Diane interrupted, "are you going anywhere with this?"

Rob was pissed off by this comment. "You don't even care, do you? All this time you've been firing people, getting people to quit, not replacing anybody and all of this extra work gets put onto my shoulders and you have the audacity to cut my pay for not getting the work of ten full-time jobs finished in addition to my own work load? And then we all have to hear about the new plasma television that you purchased with your so-called 'managerial bonus?' And then you ask me if this is going anywhere? Look, bitch, it's like this: I've had it with your bullshit. I've had it with you illegally deducting time from the payroll, I've had with you not allowing me any breaks or lunch hours, I've had it with your nasty, disrespectful ways and now this whole situation. Who the fuck do you assholes think you are to just go and deliberately run the business under without telling the employees? Oh yeah, you wanted to make it real smooth so you would have staff until the very end and so that the stock holders would never suspect foul play. You didn't care who you were hurting in the process, you only cared about yourselves." Rob continued. Then Fred yawned with boredom.

"Do you think this is funny, asshole?" Rob snapped at the man. "Look, why are you doing this? You never did answer that question?" Fred asked. "Well, asshole, it's quite simple really. My men and I are doing this because despite the way your company has treated us, we've still have always taken pride in our work. And in the past, it seemed that whenever something went right, you jerks would take all the credit for it. But the minute something was wrong, then it was our fault and you didn't want any credit for it; you refused to take the blame and own up to the responsibility when bad shit happened. And then that line, over and over and over and over again: 'this is your store; you should take pride in it.' Yeah, well, it's funny how it's our store when it's convenient for you hypocrites to have it that way. But then the

58

second you want to make some big decisions like this or to sell the buildings, well, then it's not our store anymore. The minute we would potentially benefit by being included as part of the team, we get cut off. But, you see, there is only one problem. We have been told that this is our store so much, that we have come to believe it and just because you want to go out of business, lay off all of your employees and sell the store, well we feel that all of that doesn't really make this any less our store, so we've simply taken it over. We've figured since you're going out of business, you really don't need this building anymore, so we've claimed it for our own. We've taken what is ours. You could have just let it go, but no, you had to make a big fucking deal out of it by getting all of these police and military groups involved and by having FBI agents trying to constantly break into our building and well, we're just fighting back; we're defending what is ours. Does that answer your questions, asshole?" Rob asked.

Fred's jaw dropped in reaction to Rob's response. "Uh, excuse me, young man, but were you just born yesterday? Everything you've just described that has been going on in this store during your time as an employee here, well, that's all just completely normal stuff. Managers are supposed to make more money in one year than you will ever make in your entire life and you will always be expected to do more work in one day than they do in one year. The main function of a manager is to just walk around wearing a white shirt and tie with a cup of coffee in their hand, like they own the place, telling employees what to do. Managers are not supposed to actually work; they coordinate your efforts and that is why they are able to take the credit for your work. And if you fuck up, it's probably because you didn't listen, so that is why you are still given the blame." Fred said. Rob was furious at this comment. He could feel the vein in his neck pulsing with rage. "Oh, is that it?" he spat out, "so the manager can take the credit when work is done well, but then deny all responsibility of an error when somebody needs to take the blame? How convenient! Well, how about this, asshole, it should be the other way around. The manager takes the blame for shit that goes wrong and the employee takes the credit when things go right, because after all, the manager is already making more money than God! What the fuck do you have to say to that?!" Fred shook his head in disappointment. "You really are slow, aren't you?" he asked Rob.

"Look here," Rob started again, "I know how the real world works and it's not anything like this. Sure, most managers do tend to be lazy, overpaid, inexperienced, underachieving, credit-sucking, arrogant jerks, but nowhere I have ever been has been so terrible as this company. You are all just a bunch greedy, selfish, lying, cheating, money-grubbing, snot-nosed hypocrites who make horrible management decisions without even realizing it because you are so evil and stupid that you let your asinine sense of pride and selfish greed get in the way of good judgment. Look, I've seen my share of corrupt businesses in my day but you scumbags take the cake. I swear I've never, ever before in my entire life encountered such a disgustingly high degree of bullshit anywhere else that I've been. True, a certain amount can be expected but this is just way too much; it's ridiculous. And I'll tell you another thing: this is not in anyway or in any capacity how a business works. This is not how you run any kind of respectable business. And you have the nerve to ask me if I am slow? Look into a fucking mirror, you damned jackass!" "ROB! NOBODY TALKS TO FRED LIKE THAT! HE WORKS HARD FOR THIS COMPANY!" Diane chimed in. Rob noticed the appalled and offended looks on his guests' faces, especially Fred's. "Oh, well, it sure must have been a shocker for you since you let me get it all out without even a single interruption. But, I must ask, why are you all so shocked? Is the truth really that surprising and offensive to you? And another thing, I know how hard Fred works. Last year he made a whole $4,664,594.36 to sit on his ass and do absolutely nothing but dream up even more greedy schemes to rip people off. I've seriously done more work in one day than this bastard has ever done or will ever do in his entire life! But I can't be given raises. No way; you all tell me that you can't afford it because business expenses are too high. Well I'm not retarded. I know the real reason you can't afford to give me a raise is because this fucking asshole thinks he needs to be paid millions of dollars to do absolutely nothing but roll around in his huge piles of embezzled money while thinking about how to make even more, as if what he's got just isn't enough. Yeah, I know how hard Fred works. It's apparently hard work to do nothing and act like your shit doesn't stink!" Rob responded. "NOW THAT IS ENOUGH! WE WILL NOT HAVE YOU BASH OUR FINE BUSINESS MODEL!!!" a terrified and quivering Lisa managed to squeak out in a trembling voice. Rob looked over at her in disgust. "Who the fuck asked you? Who said you could speak? I wasn't talking to you. I have nothing to say to you since what you've done to me in the past. I remember our stupid little interviews where you told me what you thought I wanted

60

to hear just to take advantage of me and my efforts. And then that one day I'm out on the sales floor stocking shelves and decide to take a break, which the company handbook said I was entitled to. So, I walk over to George to speak with him for five minutes and then your fat ass wobbles by and sees me. George and I didn't scatter like cockroaches like everybody else does because we were not doing anything wrong. So I said 'hello' to you and smiled very politely and you just kept walking without saying a word to me. I still remember that dirty look you gave me that day and still remember what happened immediately after that: you went straight to Diane and had her come reprimand me for standing around and not working. What was that all about, bitch? Am I not entitled to a five minute break once in awhile? And if you had such a problem with it, why didn't you just tell me yourself? Was it because you're a spineless pussy or was it because you're just too fat and lazy to hold a simple conversation? Or perhaps it was because you were offended when we didn't scatter in all directions and run around like chickens with our heads cut just to appease you; perhaps you get off on that like it somehow makes you feel important or something to see people fear you and run around to kiss your ass. You're probably so used to that nonsense that when we didn't do it for you, it offended you and made you feel like you're not as important as you think you are; like you're not special. Well, you know what? You're not special at all. You're just an overpaid, overfed, lard-assed bitch with you head shoved so far up your own ass that you're totally blind to reality. Perhaps this issue goes deeper than that. Are you insecure and emotionally-challenged with mental problems and so low self-esteem that you need to have your ass kissed by the employees to confirm the opinions that you would like to have of yourself? Perhaps that's also why you are so fucking fat!" Rob grilled her. By this point the woman was shaking with fear and had tears rolling down her chubby, makeup-painted, mascara-running face. "Wipe that shit off your face right now! You look like a fat-assed, goddamned whore!" Rob continued lecturing the crying woman. "You're not going to get away with this!" she whined.

"WHAT'S THIS ABOUT?! JUST WHO DO YOU THINK YOU ARE, YOUNG MAN?! DO YOU THINK YOU SOMEHOW REPRESENT THE EMPLOYEES HERE OR SOMETHING THAT YOU HAVE THE RIGHT TO STAGE SUCH AN UPRISING AGAINST US LIKE THIS?!" Fred roared at Rob. Rob turned around to face the screaming president. "YOU ALLOWED US IN HERE TO

NEGOTIATE! SO WHAT THE HELL IS THE STORY?! ARE WE GOING TO TALK OR ARE YOU JUST GOING TO INSULT US ALL DAY?!" Fred continued. Suddenly Rob struck the man with a backhanded slap to the face. "OUCH! WHAT WAS THAT FOR!" he demanded. "You don't talk to me like that. You are in my domain now. You don't ever, ever, ever, under any circumstances, raise your voice to me. Do you understand that?" Rob scolded. "THIS IS MY STORE! I'LL DO WHAT I WANT! YOU CAN'T TELL ME WHAT TO…" the man continued yelling until he was interrupted by Rob's brass knuckle-clad fist in his mouth. "Oh, and to answer to your question, yes, I do represent the employees. You wouldn't allow them to form a union, so they appointed me to watch out for their job-related business interests. Who do I think I am, you ask? Why would I need to think about it? I know who I am. I'm just not so severely retarded like you that I actually have to sit around trying to remember my own name. But, you know what? Somehow I suspect that these were rhetorical questions that you asked just to serve the purpose of being a smart-ass and you know I don't tolerated that kind of bullshit," Rob said just before striking the man a second time, this time knocking him unconscious.

"Okay Rob, fine, let's talk about this. What are we negotiating about? What are your demands?" Diane managed to ask in a civil tone. "Oh, I don't have any demands. Letting you come in here to negotiate was just an excuse to keep the police from attacking. We actually ran out of ammunition and needed some hostages. You three will serve that purpose quite nicely." "Okay Rob, you do realize that you can't stay in here forever, don't you? Why don't you just call off your agenda and let's talk; let's negotiate. You might as well so we can end this thing as peacefully as possible at this point and maybe they'll go easier on you when this is all over. I mean, don't you realize how crazy and ridiculous this all is? You're mad at Fred because he makes so much money? Don't you realize that his salary is comparable to what CEOs and presidents of other corporations make?"

Rob scratched his chin as he listened to what Diane had to say. "Listen," he started, "you know I'm not going to get caught. I know what I am doing here, so there really is no need to negotiate. You are in my domain now and I regard you all as my personal property and I will dispose of you as I wish. And you mentioned Fred's salary as being normal, well about that: I realize that what you say is indeed the truth but it doesn't justify the corrupt and greedy actions of that scum-sucking weasel over there. It just doesn't. And while his salary may be comparable, his work ethic most certainly is not. Now I realize that other people in his position with other companies don't do much work either but he is the epitome of greed, selfishness, corruption, lowness and laziness; he is the embodiment of worthless shit. What I mean is that of all the corporations in the world, I am sure that he probably does the least of any other president or CEO. So even if he were in anyway the least bit honorable or respectable and actually did something constructive for this company, you still couldn't justify his corrupt, self-serving actions even if you wanted to. And on top of that, I have always been skeptical of large corporations. While I respect the right of the people in a capitalistic society to determine and act upon their own business needs and to make their own decisions regarding investing and starting companies, I fear that corporations that have grown too large and too powerful may become corrupt enough to find themselves making shady deals with the government. You see, corporations are taxed at a very high rate so the government profits tremendously from their existence and under most circumstances, it does not want to see them fold. So there have been several cases where the government would overlook illegal activities that a corporation was involved in and the corporation would help the government out in return. Both parties would then enter into secret illegal agreements, conflicts of interests and conspiracies that all had to do with money. It's like 'you scratch my back, I'll scratch yours,' but in an illegal, unethical way. I fear that the results of such conspiracies tend to lead only to a socialist society in that large corporations benefit from the existence of government assistance programs. The more disposable income the consumer has, the more profitable corporations are able to become. And when a company is already being taxed at a very high rate, it is not likely to be affected by slightly increasing taxes. The taxes that pay for socialist programs pale in comparison to the profits those corporations are able to make as a direct result of there being more money in the economy. Anyway, I believe that your company is one of the those corrupt corporations and all I can say to that is that I hope you burn in Hell for the rest of eternity for the sins that you have committed against your loyal employees," Rob lectured the woman.

"Alright Rob, I just asked a simple question. I didn't ask you to ramble on and on about your crackpot conspiracy theories, okay?" Diane responded. "They are not conspiracy theories, bitch, this is reality. I think you already know about all of this stuff, but if you don't, just open your eyes because it's really not that hard to see," Rob answered. "Oh its reality, is it? Well I didn't know it was such common knowledge, Mr. Know-It-All!" "You're absolutely right, I do know it all, but you can call me Rob. Thank God, though, it's about time somebody took notice to my supreme omnipotence! But seriously though, bitch, don't ever refer to my explanations of the world as conspiracy theories because this stuff is, or at least should be, common knowledge. You're just a stupid bitch who doesn't know her ass from a hole in the ground." "Oh, I see how it is. Well, if this bullshit is such common knowledge, then elaborate on it for me. Give me an example or quote somebody credible on this issue. Let's see you scramble for words now!" "Look, I don't really know what you want me to say but for what its worth, Thomas Jefferson warned of this very issue almost two hundred years ago; he acknowledged the problem of corrupt and overly powerful corporations by saying 'I hope we shall crush in its birth the aristocracy of our monied corporations which dare already to challenge our government to a trial by strength, and bid defiance to the laws of our country.' How's that, bitch?" "No way! There's no way he said that! You just made that up! That doesn't count!" "No, I really didn't make it up. Jefferson really said that, word for word. But how convenient it would be for you to not know that? You obviously want to make me look like a fool in front of your cronies. But the joke is on you because if you are truly that stupid and uneducated that you can't even remember quotes from one of the greatest thinkers of all time, well I don't know whether to laugh or to cry."

"Alright, whatever, enough of this nonsense; I am now fully convinced that you are an idiot who has lost his mind. Okay Rob, I'll ask you again and this time I want you to answer with simple language instead of trying to avoid the question by complicating everything. You do realize that you can't stay in here forever, don't you?" "Simple language? Why, because that's all your small retarded mind is able to comprehend?" "JUST ANSWER THE FUCKING QUESTION!!!" Diane barked at Rob and then there was a brief moment of silence. "You don't speak to me like that. I'll tell you what I told Fred. Under no circumstance do you ever raise your voice to me," Rob said just before he slammed his brass knuckle-clad fist into Diane's mouth. She fell to the floor, screamed in pain and then quickly held her hands over her injured mouth. Soon there was blood running out of her mouth, through her fingers and down the front of her scarf and blouse. Fred was still passed out and Lisa sat against the wall while holding her folded thighs up against her chest with her arms and hiding her face in her thighs and shaking violently. Her crying was muffled but still barely audible as she hid her face. Diane glared up at Rob from the floor. "Do you want to try speaking to me again?" he asked. She nodded.

"Excuse me, your majesty, may I have permission to speak now?" she said in a sarcastic tone of voice. "You may proceed," Rob responded. "You do realize that you can't stay in here forever, don't you?" "Yeah, well, I've got a plan, so you don't have to talk to me like I'm retarded." "Oh, and what's this brilliant plan of yours?" "Well, it is brilliant actually. You see, while you are in my custody, the police will not try anything stupid. Also, this entire time that I spent telling you how I feel about you and why I am doing all of this, my men were digging a tunnel out of here. I've successfully managed to stall you and everybody else long enough for my men to dig my escape route." "Oh, how lovely, Rob. And you don't think we'll just tell the police as soon as you make a run for it? What are you going to do with no ammunition? I guess you didn't think of that, did you?" Rob smiled grimly at his ex-manager. "You'll see what's in store for you. I'm going to kill all three of you in my own special way, without the luxury of a fast-acting weapon like a gun. Believe me, as the three of you are dying slow and painful deaths, you'll wish somebody would shoot you just to put you out of your misery. But that's not going to happen because you're a stupid bitch who had to get authorities involved to trespass on my property. Oh well." Rob explained as he noticed an intensified increase in Lisa's crying and fearful shaking. Just then Fred came to, spewing blood from his mouth full of broken teeth, jumped to feet and while screaming loudly, began charging towards Rob. When the man was almost about to run into the brave, militia leader, Rob pulled out a stun-gun and shocked the man with a straight one million volts of electricity. Then he also shocked his other two guests until all three of them were rendered unconscious.

Shortly after this flawless initiation of Rob's brilliant plan, the other five members of the militia appeared at the scene. They all appeared dirty and exhausted as they proudly informed their leader that the tasks had been completed. The tunnel had been dug through the floor, under the parking lot, across the street, and it lead into a dense patch of shrubbery in a nearby resident's backyard. The three crucifixes had also been built to completion on the roof in the front of the building facing the parking lot. All the men needed to do were set the heavy wooden structures in the upright position, leaning them against the charred remnants of three cardboard bales. Rob was pleased to see his plans coming together.

"Help me carry these assholes up to the roof," Rob ordered. Kermit, Jack, and Ryan promptly complied and each picked up an unconscious enemy and carried it to the roof. Once Rob made his way to the roof and saw the crucifixes lying in a row, he ordered that Fred be position in the middle with one woman on each side. George positioned the unconscious bodies on the crosses and Bruce began pounding nail after nail into their limbs and clothing. Then Jack appeared with a spool of copper wire and used it to wrap tightly around the entire set ups, to keep the bodies from becoming free of the crucifixes. All six men then pooled together to set up the three crucifixes against the cardboard bales and finished off by dumping buckets of the remaining delicatessen fryer grease all over the wire-bound bodies. The men continued doing this until the bodies were dripping with lard and a dense mixture of thick, fatty, oily grease.

Meanwhile, Rob had made his way into the store and pressed the activation switch on his bomb. The timer had become active and displayed a time of only twenty minutes before the total destruction of the building would occur. But even knowing that time was short and of the essence, it was all the man had left to pull himself away from his awesome creation. He wanted to run away as his eyes studied the tiny LED screen, gradually counting down, second by second in glowing red digits. He wanted to embrace the device but at the same time he knew he needed to move; twenty minutes was not enough time to begin with and now the timer indicated a little less than fifteen minutes. But there was just something about the combination of his pride of accomplishment and his fear of the reality of what he was doing. It was a morbid sense of satisfaction and glee with a shallow undertone of the sadness one feels at the end of an era. But Rob did what he needed to do for both himself and his men and now he knew it was time for them to finish what they had started. His knowledge of the coming time gave him the necessary strength and so he found himself more than able and willing to pull his fixed stare from the device as he turned and dashed to meet his men on the roof.

When Rob met up with the rest of his unit on the roof, he was very pleased with what he saw leaning against the charred bales before him. All three of the enemies were now conscious, though quite disoriented, confused and frightened, but their eyes widened in terror as Rob approached. "W-W-WHAT'S GOING ON?! ARE WE CRUCIFIED?! WHAT THE FUCK?!" Fred spat out as Rob stood before him with authority. "Why yes you are, asshole. Welcome back to reality. Did you have a nice slumber?" Rob asked the crucified man tauntingly. "WHY ARE YOU DOING THIS?! WHY?!!" "You know why. All of these years you've treated us like shit and paid us brutally low wages and told us it was because you couldn't afford to give us raises. Then I found out what you make in a year to do nothing. Perhaps if you weren't so goddamned greedy, your employees could live above the poverty line, don't you think? But when one works for you, it is hard to imagine a wage that covers the basic costs of living because on top of your already disgusting salary, you think you also need constant raises and bonuses. As if what you have already isn't enough, you think you need to cut costs to increase your own profit margins; to increase your salary. One of those main costs that you've always cut was the payroll expenses. Perhaps the reason you could never afford to pay us what we deserved was because you were too concerned about padding your own salary." "SO YOU'RE GOING TO KILL ME OVER THIS?! WHAT THE HELL DON'T YOU UNDERSTAND?! THAT IS JUST HOW CORPORATIONS WORK! THERE'S NO NEED TO KILL PEOPLE JUST BECAUSE YOU DON'T UNDERSTAND HOW THINGS WORK!!!" "Oh I understand alright. All of these years you've been exploiting people who just wanted to make ends meet and people who just wanted to make an honest living by using capitalism to further your leftist agenda of achieving socialism. You've obviously been engaged in illegal government alliances for your own personal gains because in all of your speeches and newsletters, you've always seemed to advocate collective and government ownership and administration of the means of production and distribution of wealth. You've always seemed to oppose most private property and you've always hinted towards your wishes for a system of society in which every aspect of industry is controlled by the state and ruled by a coercive government that maintains a total gun ban. Why? Because deep down, you are secretly a communist." "WELL HOW THE HELL DOES THAT MAKE ANY SENSE?! IF EVERYTHING IS RUN BY THE GOVERNMENT, HOW AM I SUPPOSED TO GET RICH?! EXPLAIN THAT ONE, SMART-ASS!!!" "What's to explain? You know damn well what I am talking about. You think you can make friends and bribe people in high places to allow you to run your businesses anyway under the guise a government owned operation and then you'd give your friends a cut of the profits to keep quiet. You'd have no competition because there would be no private industry and you'd make higher profits because of that and because of the fact that there would be more disposable income in the economy due to unnecessary government assistance programs. It's all a conspiracy and you thought you would get away with everything that you've done. Well, today is the day you die, asshole!" "YOU CAN'T PROVE ANYTHING!!!"

"FINE!!! IT'S ALL TRUE!!! DIDN'T WE TELL YOU ENOUGH ABOUT HOW WE RUN OUR COMPANY?!!! BUT YOU JUST HAD TO PUSH, DIDN'T YOU?!!! WELL IT'S ALL TRUE!!! ARE YOU HAPPY NOW?!!! YOU CAN LET US GO NOW!!! YOU'VE GOT THE INFORMATION YOU WANTED FROM US!!! NOW LET US GO!!!" Lisa shrieked while still crying her eyes out over the situation. "It's too late. You've had plenty of opportunities to do the right thing but you had to be selfish and stubborn. Now your time has come. I'm afraid it is too late to save you now," Rob morbidly responded.

Diane, hardened with hate, selfishness, hypocrisy, dishonesty and greed, was still completely unfazed by the situation. She looked Rob directly in the eyes and said, "oh, how cute Rob. You've managed to crucify us. How original; what a great plan! But you know you'll never, ever get away with this. You're just too weak-minded, fat and stupid to actually pull this off. You'll get caught by all of those cops down there in the parking lot and they'll lock you up and throw away the keys. You will never see the light of day again, I promise you that." Rob stood there in silence, jaw dropped and completely baffled at total lack of concern for her safety and for the safety of her two companions. It seemed that even in the face of death her greed remained strong and unwavering; she just did not and could not appreciate the seriousness of the situation she was in. "Don't worry, buddy," Rob thought quietly to himself, "this will be over soon enough and she'll finally be in Hell where she belongs." But then she spoke again and disrupted Rob's thought process, all in completely obvious efforts to foil the whole operation and to stall for time. "You know all of you guys are going to Hell for this when you die, right?" Diane gently spoke.

Rob was totally pissed off at this sudden comment because it was too similar to his own thoughts of Diane; if what she spoke was true, it would surely counteract his efforts to be eternally free of the cursed bitch because he would have to deal with her bullshit for the rest of time. "FUCK YOU!!!" the man screamed as he looked down at his watch. It was then that he realized the militia only had eight minutes before the building was destroyed. "MEN, GIVE THIS BITCH WHAT SHE'S GOT COMING TO HER! SHE HAS PISSED ON ALL OF YOU IN THE PAST, FIGURATIVELY, AND NOW IT IS TIME TO LITERALLY RETURN THE COURTESY!!!" Rob ordered as each of his five men filed in line and unzipped their pants. Kermit was the first to whip out his cock and then the others followed; simultaneously however, they gladly shared the moment by showering Diane's face with their large amounts of collective piss.

The disgusted woman cringed as the warm, yellow liquid drenched her ugly, makeup covered face and became soaked up in the stupid-assed clown scarf that she wore around her neck. After spitting piss out of her mouth, she began to speak. "You are all going to Hell," she said again. Rob looked down at his watch and noticed that they only had about four minutes to evacuate, but being told his thoughts of the bitch were true of himself bothered him too much to leave before settling what would be the final score. So, the angry man turned to face his enemy and made eye contact with her as he stood before her crucifix. "NO! YOU ARE GOING TO HELL, YOU STUPID, FUCKING BITCH! YOU ARE THE ONE AMONG US WHO SHALL PERISH AND BURN AS YOU ATTEMPT TO STAY AFLOAT THROUGH FUTILE EFFORTS IN THE LAKE OF FIRE! THERE AND ONLY THERE SHALL YOU MEET YOUR MATCH; YOUR EQUAL IN THE KINGDOM OF THE UNDERWORLD! AND WHEN THE END IS UPON US ALL YOU WILL BE THE FIRST ONE WHO EMBRACES THE DRAGON, FOR AT THAT TIME WILL BE THE FULFILLMENT OF THE PROPHESIES TELLING US THAT MEN WILL WORSHIP THE DRAGON BECAUSE HE WILL GIVE AUTHORITY TO THE BEAST WHO WILL ARISE FROM THE SEA! YOU SHALL BE THE ONE WHO SITS UPON HIS BACK, BEHIND HIS SEVEN HEADS AND TEN HORNS AND TEN CROWNS; YOU ARE THE SCARLET PROSTITUTE WHO SOLD HER SOUL IN HER ENDEAVORS OF GREED UPON THIS EARTH! YOU ARE THE ONE WHO SOLD THE LIVES OF YOUR EMPLOYEES SHORT AND CHEATED THEM EVERY CHANCE YOU'VE HAD AND YOU'VE DONE ALL OF THIS ONLY TO PURSUE YOUR OWN SELFISH GRATIFICATION!!! FUCK YOU!!! FUCK YOU, YOU STUPID

BITCH!!! YOU ARE THE ONE WHO IS GOING TO HELL AND YOU'RE GOING THERE RIGHT NOW!!!" Rob screamed in her face. "Nice little speech you've got there, fatty," she replied, "but your own stupid morals and values and all of the self-righteousness in the world cannot compare to my to unparalleled powers." "OH YEAH?! WHAT THE HELL DO YOU THINK YOU'RE GOING TO BE ABLE TO DO ABOUT ANYTHING RIGHT NOW?!" Rob pressed as he noticed her lips begin to move in an unnatural manner. He slowly took a step back and watched in horror as the bitch began chanting something slow and eerie in a raspy voice in the unspoken Latin language. It became louder and louder as black storm clouds began to roll in and fill the sky, making the day look like the dead of night.

Her voice switched back to the English language as she looked to the sky and smiled grimly. "TELL ME, CREATOR, WHO THE EVIL ONE AMONG US IS! WHO AMONG US WILL JOIN THE RANKS OF THE DAMNED?! MAY YOU STRIKE DOWN THE EVIL ONE WITH YOUR DEADLY LIGHTNING! KILL THE EVIL ONE AND THE DISCIPLES OF THAT UNHOLY HEATHEN AND SEND THEM TO HELL!" Diane shrieked at the sky in a blood-curdling, bone-chilling voice. Rob, now totally terrified, kept slowly backing up, while never taking his eyes off of the bitch or blinking, until he was reunited among his militia. All six men then jumped as the loud rumbling of thunder shook the air. Then lightning flashed across the sky and the air was quickly filled with the sound of Diane's evil, high-pitched laughter. "YES! YES! STRIKE DOWN THE EVIL ONE! STRIKE DOWN THE EVIL ONE!" she shrieked excitedly. Suddenly a large, bluish-white bolt of lightning flashed from the sky and struck the copper wire that held the bitch to the crucifix and ignited the thick fryer grease, setting the entire structure on fire. A few seconds later, similar lightning bolts also struck the other two crucified assholes and the darkness was lit up by the bright fire of the three flaming crosses bearing the enemies as they screamed in pain, agony and torment.

"THEY TOOK THE NEGOTIATORS HOSTAGE AND THE HOSTAGES ARE DEAD!!! THE HOSTAGES ARE DEAD!!! MOVE!!! MOVE!!! MOVE!!! MOVE!!! MOVE!!!" sounded a voice from down below in the parking lot and a few seconds later the air was once again filled with the familiar sounds of gunfire. "WE'RE MOVING IN!!!" the voiced bellowed again as the rooftop vibrated from the evident smashing of the barricaded doors and windows just below where the militia stood. Again, Rob glanced down at his watch and nearly panicked when he realized that he and his men only had fifteen seconds to evacuate. "LET'S GO, NOW!!! WE ONLY HAVE FIFTEEN SECONDS!!! MOVE OUT NOW!!!" the determined man barked as he and his men dashed as fast as they could down into the store and towards the tunnel entrance.

Just then the doors and windows from all directions burst open as thousands of soldiers and police officers rushed inside of the building screaming and shooting as fast as they could at the escaping militia. With only three seconds on the clock, Rob jumped into the tunnel and lurched forward with all of his speed and strength. His men followed suit and just as George brought up the tail end and managed to move away from the entrance of the tunnel, the bomb exploded and obliterated the building, killing everybody in it.

The sound of the explosion was more than Rob had expected and the force was so great that it shook the ground and caved in most of the tunnel just behind the frantically running men. Luckily, no part of the tunnel yet to be traveled was badly affected and so the men continued until they reached the other side that exited into the shrubbery. The only bodily damage they suffered was a slight ringing in their ears; otherwise all of the men were still in perfect physical condition as they moved slowly to the exit of the tunnel and peered out over the side. Slowly, one by one, each of the men climbed out of the tunnel and into the dense bushes and underbrush. When they were all out of the tunnel they managed to meet up in a small hollow under a large bush. They stood side by side and peered through the vegetation at their former compound. The building they had been in just a minute earlier was now nothing more than a smoking crater in the ground. Surrounding the crater were huge piles of debris and rubble of what used to form the store itself. The parking lot had also been badly scorched from the intense fire and heat of the explosion as a result of the bomb's force blowing outward in that very direction. Destroyed vehicles, debris and thousands of fried, lifeless corpses and skeletons were all that remained.

"It's all gone," George broke the silence, "it was supposed to be our compound. We were supposed to be prepared for attacks but we ran out of ammo. You guys told me that we would be so prepared for this that the military and police officers would give up after they became tired of getting killed. But then we ran out of supplies first because no matter how many we killed, they just kept coming and

71

coming and coming. We had to resort to destroying the compound just to get out alive. But that's just it: destroying what we were trying to protect in our efforts to protect it. It's so ironic that all of these people had to die for a building that no longer even stands. I guess we failed our mission." A few seconds of silence went by before Rob spoke up with a glare in his eyes. "George, listen to yourself. We in no way even came anywhere close to failing our mission. Sure, our main goal was to takeover the building but we knew what we were going to be up against. We thought we might be successful in our defense of the building but from the very beginning we had a backup plan in place just in case exactly what happened was to occur. Do you understand that? Yes, we wanted the building and we were willing to fight for it but we were not willing to die for it or to go to prison for it. The whole plan was to just try and if we were unsuccessful in taking over the building, then we would find a way to completely destroy it so that the company couldn't have it and then we would find a way to escape without getting captured or killed. And that was exactly what we did; the forces against us were too strong and persistent, so we set a bomb and baled without getting caught. After all the shit we've gone through, especially at the point where you just wanted to give up, how can you possible think we failed? We simply did what we had planned to do. Sure, I would have liked greatly to have been able to use the building as a compound but look at it this way: we fucked over a corrupt company by destroying their precious building, we killed its president and human resources director and we overthrew a tyrant. Never again will she be able to hurt anyone and all of the money she made from their little going out of business scheme, well it won't help her now, not in Hell. Men, even though this didn't last as long as we had hoped, I still see this as a great victory for us. With Turkowitz's gone and Diane, Lisa and Fred all burning in Hell, we have ended their reign of terror. Men, we truly are heroes. Not too many other people would be willing to put their asses on the line in an effort to provide a very valuable community service like we did," the militia leader spoke to his men with pride.

"But what about all of the innocent law enforcement people that died trying to stop us? They could not have all known of the great corruption that we fought against. They could not have possibly have seen us as freedom fighters. They probably thought they were doing their jobs by fighting against terrorists," George inquired of his leader. "George, I see your point but we did what needed to be done and all they did was get in the way and interfere with our operations. They should have just minded their own business but instead they had to stick their noses where they didn't belong. All they did was get in the way and make things difficult for us. So we simply defended ourselves. Don't you understand that all of those jerks who thought they were going to save the day were either appointed by the government or worked for the government? What business does government have trying to endanger a state-recognized militia in an effort to counteract its purpose? And what business does government have trespassing on private property? Look, we did what we needed to do and for that we are heroes. Do you understand?" George smiled to this comment. "Oh well since you put that way, I see what you are saying. It does make sense. I guess we really are heroes, aren't we? Wow that just feels so good to know that I was a part of something that made the world a better place to live and work!" Rob nodded in confirmation, "maybe it was no revolution, I mean, we didn't exactly get to overthrow the government but we did the best we could. I'm very proud of you guys. You see, it is without a doubt that the true bravery, such as ours, that lives in the hearts of patriots, rekindles the flame of liberty for future generations to enjoy. I know Jefferson would've been proud," Rob said as a tear rolled down his cheek.

"What do we do now, boss?" Kermit asked. "Well, you all know we can't stay here because sooner or later they're going to be looking for us. We obviously have to leave the country and go somewhere where the heat is off and take a short vacation before it will be safe to return, you know," Rob replied. "Oh, like the time we did that job in New York and then went to Canada for a month?" "Right, but this time let's go somewhere new, somewhere we haven't been already." "What, like Chicago?" "No, I'm thinking Mexico this time. We really should leave the country for awhile and after all, we all deserve a nice vacation after what we've done for this ungrateful, unappreciative society that will surely try to hunt us down like dogs. Let's go somewhere tropical like the Gulf or Tijuana." "Sounds good to me," Kermit replied.

"Alright, well let's go," Bruce said to the militia. Rob turned to face all of his men. "Is Tijuana cool with everybody?" he asked. When everybody smiled and nodded to show their consent, Rob pushed his way through the thick vegetation and stepped out into the open lawn. The others promptly followed his lead and the group of proud, triumphant men began walking up the street, side by side with the site of the smoking rubble still burning behind them. Eventually they came to a stop sign and watched as a mini van pulled up and slowed to a stop. Rob casually walked up the van and opened the driver's side door. The startled driver looked at the large man with confusion in his eyes. "GET THE FUCK OUT OF THE VAN!!!" Rob barked at the driver as he threw the clueless victim into the street with just one swing of his powerful arm. Rob climbed into the driver's seat and waited as his men quickly boarded the rest of the vehicle. "Alright, Tijuana it is," Rob said as he pulled away from the stop sign and began the long drive to Mexico.

A few days later, all six men were lying on a sunny beach, drinking margaritas and smoking Cuban cigars. As they were enjoying their pleasant tropical paradise they could not help but to think of the events of the past few weeks. They also thought of all their ex-coworkers who were at home doing things by the book and searching for new jobs, never with any intentions of ever seeking their own revenge against the company that betrayed them and left them all behind. Of course the betrayal still hurt but then it became quite obvious to the militia that they would not be where they were at that very moment had things not gone the way that they did. Instead, the alternative would have been unloading trucks and stocking shelves forever. It was then that the six men realized that sometimes it was good to be left behind.

MICHAEL R.
PLANKTEN
MAY 16, 1975
JAN. 22, 2003
ALWAYS IN OUR HEARTS

One day during a slow shift at his job as an auto mechanic, Mike looks out the window and sees a male cardinal with beautiful red feathers. When Mike innocently makes eye contact with the bird, he falls under its evil spell and eventually ends up in a mental institution. Traumatized, Mike has no idea that the demon-bird plans to haunt the rest of his tortured, miserable life.

2

THE CARDINAL SIN

The Cardinal Sin

It was a cold fall day and the skies were colored with a dull shade of grayish-white. The sun was hidden behind dense clouds which drastically hindered its ability to light the earth and as a result the daylight was dim. The combination of the cold air and the dark, shadowy earth created a very dismal atmosphere and was enough to make anybody want to crawl into a hole and die. All around, people and animals alike were finding themselves distracted by the weather as night was slowly beginning to creep in. Clearly, it was an intense battle of the sun, the moon, night and day as the clouds dominated the sun and cheated the day by cutting it short. It was only late afternoon but the sun was evidently losing its struggle as the daylight became dimmer with every passing minute.

Mike stood frozen in his position over the archaic carbureted engine of the car that he was working on. He was tired from a long shift at the auto garage where he was employed and more than ready to go home for the day. There was only one more hour in his shift, but as he stared into the distance, he found it impossible to get any work done. Mike watched as dark clouds filled the sky, slowly robbing it of its light and as the trees stood like soldiers in the background. All but a few leaves had fallen from each of the trees and the young mechanic was becoming more and more lost in his growing state of depression as he watched a great deal of the vegetation die a little more with the end of each day.

As placid as everything seemed, Mike had the feeling that he was not alone in his belief that all was not right with the atmosphere. It seemed that all of the animals were in hiding; there was not a rabbit on the ground or a bird in the sky. Not a single person walked on the sidewalks or drove an automobile on the streets; it was like a ghost town. "This is strange, there has to be some life somewhere besides me," the young man thought to himself as he scanned the land and the sky and everything within his range of site, but what initially seemed to be an impossible task ended when a streak of red zipped across the sky. It was a lone, male cardinal bird.

Mike watched as the cardinal flew around in circles and hovered perfectly still in other places; within the depths of his own mind, Mike had often wondered what it was like to have such a keen ability to hang, suspended in mid air as the cardinal did. In a way, he was envious of the bird because it did not have any responsibilities, only free-time to fly and frolic. It was not that Mike wanted to be a cardinal, so much as it was that the bird could share its gift if only for a few minutes. "Oh well," Mike sighed as he watched the bird land on a low tree branch close to the window that he was watching it through. The small bird calmly rested upon the branch as it puffed up its ruffled, scarlet feathers with a strong sense of pride, most likely in an effort to stay warm. The little bit of remaining sun light glistened on those shining red feathers as the bird sat still as a statue, its wings tucked inward and the crest making up the tallest point of its body. Mike studied the bird in great detail in its state of solace and noticed the only movement to be the occasional parching of its dark orange colored beak against its black facial background. The bird did not seem to have a care in the world as it sat upon the branch, unrivaled by any other animal in its immediate area. This struck Mike as odd; he knew that there was something seriously different about this cardinal, but what? The young man could not determine whether the actions and the lack of concern of the bird was a direct result of bravery or of ignorance. Which ever it was did not matter much, because either way, Mike was fascinated by the creature and in a way, he liked the cardinal.

"Pretty, isn't it?" a deep voice interrupted Mike's trance, completely derailing his train of thought. The startled young man slowly turned around to see his boss standing over him with frustration burning in his dark eyes. "Listen, son, I'm not paying you to stand here and look at pretty birds," the boss scolded as Mike now nervously fidgeted with his greasy, dirty fingers. "Sorry, boss, it's just that I…" "You nothing, now get back to work before I fire you!" Mike's heart was beginning to race just as it always did during such intimidating interactions between himself and the boss, but the rest of his body was just too tired to process the situation and as a result, his fatigue interfered with his thought process, ultimately making the chore at hand a much more daunting and tedious task, but Mike tried anyway. He picked up a hammer and approached the car engine. "Wait a minute! Just what are you going to do with that?" the boss excitedly bellowed at the young man. "I'm going to change the spark plugs like you asked," Mike slowly and quietly replied. The boss shook his head as he snatched the tool away from the tired young mechanic.

The boss took a long and careful look at Mike as if studying him; his eyes seemed to burn a gaping hole deep into the young man's soul. Mike watched as the anger slowly faded from his boss's face and was replaced with concern. "Michael, are you okay? You really don't look too good right now. You went from bright red to a pasty-white; you're so pale right now. Why don't you just go home early today, son, you seriously look like a corpse. Go home and get some rest, I'll take care of the car. Go," the boss said with sincerity and with that, Mike walked home and went to bed.

All night long, Mike's mind was haunted by frightening and grotesque nightmares and morbid images of the cardinal. The young man watched the cardinal taunting him from the tree branch as his dead-end job sucked his life away and did nothing more than to secure a dismal future full of failure and heartbreak. That entire night, the cardinal tortured the poor man's soul for some unknown reason, but it was not long before a loud crash in his bedroom window suddenly ripped him from his deep, troubled sleep. "Thank God, it was just a dream," Mike thought to himself, "But what was that noise?" Mike looked around the room trying to locate any possible culprits for what could have caused the sound – and then it happened again. The startled young man spun around as fast as he could and rushed to the window to see what had hit the glass hard enough to cause the annoying sound. And there on the window sill sat the cardinal.

Mike carefully studied the features of the bird in close detail and was able to quickly identify it as being the same exact bird from the tree branch the day before. But why had it followed him home? Mike was baffled by the situation and took a few more steps toward the window to get a closer look, but when the bird saw this, it flew away. The young man did not know what to think as he drew in a deep breath through his mouth and slowly exhaled through his nose in an effort to calm himself down. He stood perfectly still in his tracks for a few minutes before he could bring himself to move again. "Well, at least it's gone," Mike wishfully thought, but just then, the cardinal returned and slammed itself into the window with full force. The young man was deeply confused by this fiasco as he watched the bird fly away again, only to return to the window a minute later.

Mike decided to leave for work early that day to escape the torment of the cardinal. However, when he arrived at work, he noticed the same bird sitting on the same tree branch as the day before. It had obviously followed him again. "Whatever, I'll just work inside and keep my back to the windows as much as possible," Mike decided as he entered the garage.

"Michael! You're early today! How are you feeling?" the boss greeted as Mike walked into the office to pour himself a cup of coffee. "Oh, I'm doing alright. I still have a lot on my mind, but I'm rested enough to do my job today," Mike answered as he sipped at his cup of strong, black, aromatic coffee. "Glad to hear it, son, but can I ask what exactly is bothering you?" "Well, boss, do you remember that cardinal that I was looking at yesterday? It followed me home last night and has been flying into my windows all morning and now it has followed me back to work. See, there it is on the tree branch, staring at me. I find it annoying, that's all." The boss began laughing with a menacing look on his face. "You mean to tell me that your problem is with a bird? That's great! You're quite the joker, son." "No, I'm serious. I'm not joking. That cardinal is out to get me." The boss continued laughing hysterically, but when he noticed that Mike was not even cracking a smile, the laughter slowly stopped. "You're serious, aren't you?" the boss asked. "Yes, I am," Mike responded. "Oh. Well. Grow up, Mike! Now get to work!"

As Mike worked that day, the cardinal continually flew into the window nearest to where Mike was standing. It was chirping loudly as it slammed itself into the glass window pane, over and over and over again, relentlessly. The cardinal proved to be such a distraction to Mike that it took all that he had to complete his shift that day, but when he had, he ran all the way home in hopes that the cardinal would not follow him. Once concealed within the safety of his home, he ate a light dinner and went to bed. Again he slept well, but the only problems were the nightmares of the cardinal and the rude, early-morning cardinal-induced wake up call as the same red bird slammed itself repeatedly into Mike's bedroom window – again. Because of this, Mike chose to leave for work early again that day, but it did no good, because the cardinal followed him to work so that it could fly into the garage windows again that day as well.

As the months passed and the cardinal was still haunting Mike's daily life, Mike became more and more distracted from his responsibilities. Being awaken at all hours of the night and harassed at every possible moment throughout the day, Mike was finding his internal clock to be disrupted and thrown off, because the cardinal was getting gradually worse with each day. As a result of this, he was showing up late for everything and constantly missing deadlines. His bills were getting paid late; he was showing up for work late, and even missing whole doctor appointments. He was not getting adequate amounts of sleep at night and his health was beginning to suffer. In fact, everybody who saw him told him that he looked like crap, with his heavy eyes and unshaven face. When asked what was wrong or what his excuses were for being negligent in his responsibilities, he always blamed the cardinal, even though nobody but him had ever witnessed the cardinal attacking windows like Mike so often claimed.

The cardinal was ruining Mike's life, but nobody believed him, so the day eventually came when all of Mike's friends, coworkers, and family members set up an intervention to try to help the poor young man deal with his "imaginary birdie friend." They tried telling him over and over again that there was no cardinal, but each time he swore that there was, even though nobody wanted to listen. When the intervention proved to be unsuccessful, Mike was taken to a mental institution tightly bound in a straight jacket, while kicking and screaming about how much he hated the cardinal.

At the mental institution, Mike was given a room with a window and a bed. Nothing else was in the plain, tiny, white room. He was given intense counseling sessions to help him overcome his fear of cardinals, but nobody would listen when he tried to tell them that the cardinal was real. Instead, everybody simply treated him as if he were insane and would lock him in his room for the better part of the day so that he would be able to relax and calm down. But every time he was in his room alone, the cardinal would appear on the window sill and repeatedly fly into the glass. When Mike would scream for help and summon the doctors, the cardinal would disappear, only to return when they left Mike in the room alone again.

Mike nervously sat on his bed, staring at the window. The cardinal repeatedly flew into the glass panes, only stopping to stand on the window sill to look in at Mike and taunt him with a series of loud, high-pitched chirps. Nobody would come to help the troubled young man if he called for it and worse yet, nobody would believe him. So, Mike just sat there on his bed, watching as the cardinal pecked at the glass and chirped in its annoying, condescending manner. It seemed to be making a fool of him. "I HATE YOU," Mike said aloud to the cardinal as it stared in the window at him before flying away.

"Maybe it will leave me alone now," Mike naively thought. His mind was so frazzled and exhausted and haunted by the cardinal. He saw the cardinal even when he closed his eyes. His mental health was suffering terribly to the point where he found it extremely difficult to hold even a single thought for more than a few seconds at a time. He even forgot his own name, but Mike believed that there was hope for him. He tried to stay positive and think pleasant thoughts, but just then, the cardinal flew into the window with full force, completely destroying that small sense of harmony that Mike strived so hard to achieve with his thinking of serene settings. That loud crash in the window was the straw that broke the camel's back and Mike completely snapped.

The young man jumped to his feet and began running around the room, screaming obscenities at the top of his lungs about how much he hated the cardinal. In a fit of rage, he flung his bed across the room and dashed to the window where the cardinal was sitting and with all the strength and speed that he could muster, Mike attempted to kick the taunting bird off the window sill, but only shattered the glass instead. The cardinal flew away as the doctors came rushing into the room to restrain Mike. "The cardinal was here, it was sitting on the window sill," Mike told them. "Yeah, sure it was. Now let's get you a nice straight jacket so that you can't hurt yourself," one patronizing doctor replied. "NO!" Mike challenged the doctor. "I'M NOT WEARING ANY STRAIGHT JACKET! LEAVE ME ALONE!" "Okay, fine, not a problem. We can do this the hard way," the doctor said as he pulled a pistol out of his lab coat and fired a tranquilizer dart into Mike's neck. Soon after the dart hit him, the young man became so dizzy and tired that he collapsed in a heap on the floor.

When Mike came back to consciousness, he was tightly bound in a white straight jacket and sitting upright with his back leaning against the wall of an all padded room with a high ceiling, one door, and one tiny window located just below the ceiling only for the purpose of letting daylight into the room. Mike did not see the window at first because it was positioned on the wall that he had his back to, but before long, he was made fully aware of its presence by the cardinal, who decided to fly into it repeatedly. Mike tried to ignore the sound, but the sharp repetition of the crashing sounds went through him like nails on a chalk board. He could not hold his ears because his arms were restrained by the straight jacket and he could not hum or whistle over the noise, because the bird was just too loud to be blocked out. "I just can't do it; I cannot live in this world with the cardinal. Nobody believes me anyway; the cardinal has stripped me of my dignity, though he'll never take my pride!" Mike thought out loud as he watched the bird slam itself into the window over and over again.

Just then, the door to the room opened and an elderly woman walked in carrying a tray of food and of course, the cardinal disappeared. "The doctors say I must remove the jacket now and you may eat," the woman said to Mike as she placed the tray on the floor and carefully undid the straps on the jacket and removed it from the young man's body. Mike's initial response was going to be to thank the woman, but he knew that as soon as she left, the cardinal would return. He just could not continue life anywhere the cardinal would find him. He knew he needed to escape. Wanting his problematic life to end so desperately, Mike suddenly acted on impulse and punched the woman in the face, knocking her out cold. He then ran out of the room, slamming the door behind him, and took refuge in an opened janitor's closet located just down the hall. Once inside, he closed and locked the door and turned on the light. When the tiny, dirty room flooded with light, the young mental patient looked around and noticed nothing more than a bunch of brooms, mops, buckets, cleaning supplies, boxes, and an orange extension cord. He studied the objects in the room to determine whether or not any of them could be of potential use to him, but when his gaze fell upon the extension cord again, he froze. Mike had an idea.

The young man picked up the cord and unraveled it. It was long and durable, which suited his purpose for it nicely. Slowly, he fed the cord through his hands until he reached the end of it and then as carefully as he could, he tied it into a hangman's noose. Then he found the other end and threw it up at the light fixture, catching it and pulling it down to his desired length, and then fastened it by tying a loop and a knot into it and pulling the noose down so that it hung just a two feet above his head. When this task was completed to his liking, the young man picked up a piece of paper and a pen that was resting on top of a box in the corner of the room. On it, he wrote: "I have chosen to take my life because of the cardinal. I am really very sorry that it had to come to this, but nobody believed me when I told everyone about the cardinal haunting my life. I just cannot take it another day. I hope that you all will forgive me and learn to cope with my death in a calm manner. Please don't grieve for me, but instead be happy for me, because now my existence can be cardinal-free, for I hate the cardinal so very, very much. With that, I bid you all farewell. Sincerely, Michael." The young man then placed the note on the floor right inside the door and quickly stacked the boxes in the room just below the noose. Then he climbed upon them, put his neck through the loop in the cord, took a deep breath, and jumped.

As all of his body weight pulled the cord tight against his neck and snapped it, Mike felt his life fading away. He felt comforted and proud to realize that he was finally able to experience the one thing in life that he had always wished for: hanging in the air; the slightest bit of dignity he had left at that point. So, Mike hung with pride and although the pain was intense, the young man felt happy to have finally escaped the cardinal and as a result, he died with a smile on his face.

Nearly a month later, after the discovery of Mike's lifeless corpse hanging in the janitor's closet and after all of the funeral arrangements had been made and the planning and mortuary work had been done, Mike was interred in the local cemetery by his family, friends, and members of his church. The funeral was short, sweet, and sad, but still nobody believed that the cardinal even existed. Everybody simply thought that the young man had been driven insane by the pressures and stresses of the modern-day society in which he had lived. Mike's perceived mental illness concerned many and as a result, his funeral had a good turnout of folks wanting to pay their last respects and to show support for the family. When everything was finished and the last words had been said, the mourners all left the cemetery to allow its employees to fill in the grave with soil.

When all was said and done and Mike was dead and buried and said to be at rest, the cemetery became a quiet and still place once again, just as it had been prior to the funeral. There was no wind or sunshine; it was just the dead of winter with nothing but the still, frigid air. There were no signs of life anywhere in the immediate area and the skies looked a stormy-gray as dark rain clouds rolled in. Yet, the air was still and cold with the absence of precipitation and completely lacking even the slightest and quietest of sounds. Not a single vehicle passed on the street and not a single person was out walking or riding a bicycle. Just as it was the day that Mike first encountered the little red bird that drove him to his suicide, it was now.

As his dead, lifeless corpse was left to undergo the many stages of decomposition six feet beneath the earth's surface, Mike found his spirit to be in a very dark place of uncertainty and confusion. He knew that what he did was wrong; he had allowed pride to get in the way of good judgment, even though he had been provoked and tormented to the point of insanity. But given the circumstances, he did not know whether or not he would be held accountable for his actions and could only hope that everything would work out for him in the very end. However, until then, Mike could only try to relax to allow his spirit be at rest – if it was possible.

The rain clouds continued to roll in with a great haste, but at that very moment, it was the calm of the storm. Everything was still and serene as a dark solace filled the air of the desolate wasteland and it seemed that nothing could possibly disrupt that restful state - but just then, a streak of red flew across the cold, cemetery air, landed on Mike's tombstone and eagerly decorated it with an abundance of its watery and repulsive bird shit, which ran down the front of the freshly-carved stone, putting a series of disgusting white lines through the epitaph. As it proudly ruffled its flee-ridden, scarlet feathers to prepare its body for a nice, long and rejuvenating slumber to rest from its flight, it had shattered the tranquility of the cemetery and anybody passing by could see that there on Mike's tombstone, sat the cardinal.

Copyright 2008 by Anthony G. Roof

Charlie is the happiest man in town. He shares a loving home with his wife, son, and their cherished pet dog, Fluffy. Charlie loves the dog more than anything else in the whole world and tries to do anything he can to make her happy. But one day, when the jolly old man moves the dog house too close to a fence, Fluffy climbs up on top of her house and tries to jump over the fence, hanging herself to death on the end of her chain. Charlie slips into a deep state of depression and falls in with the wrong crowd. It isn't long before he begins a life of crime and develops a morbid obsession with death.

3

RIGOR MORTIS

Rigor Mortis

One warm summer morning as the sun was rising and the birds began to chirp for a new day, Charlie awoke to the tantalizing aroma of a fresh pot of dark roast coffee brewing downstairs in his kitchen. Yawning, the happy old man slowly climbed out of bed and kicked on his slippers. As he made his way downstairs, he greeted his wife and took a seat at the kitchen table. "Good morning, Brenda," Charlie said to her as she poured him a big hot cup of fresh coffee. "Hey, Charlie, did you sleep well last night?" she asked him. Charlie smiled and nodded as he took a deep sip of his coffee. "Sure did, my dear, and how about you?" Brenda put down her cup and responded rather cheerfully, "well, yes, I must say that I did. So what are your plans for the day? I'm thinking about going shopping later this afternoon and maybe if the weather permits, I might take a walk through the neighborhood." "Well, my dear wife, I was planning on taking Fluffy out for a walk today. I want to see how far she can go today and hopefully she can beat her record from the other day." "You sure love that dog of yours, Charlie. Well, I'm going to clean up here for a little while, so you have a good walk," Brenda said as she exited the room.

A few moments later as Charlie was getting dressed for the day, he thought about how much fun it was going to be to spend the whole day with Fluffy. He buttoned his brightly colored flannel shirt and slipped on his shoes, all in an excited rush to get outside where his beloved dog was waiting for him. As the jolly old man emerged from his house and attached the leash to the frantically jumping dog's collar, he unhooked the chain and gave the dog a hug. "Hey there, Charlie!" his neighbor called out and waved as he drove by. Charlie just smiled back as he climbed to his feet and began walking with Fluffy.

As the happy old man and his excited dog walked through the neighborhood, many, many people waved, said hello, and stroked the dog's soft fur. It seemed that everybody in the neighborhood loved Charlie and knowing this made him happy and grateful to be alive. He felt comforted to know that he was constantly surrounded by his friends, people who admired him and young children who looked up to him. In fact, Charlie was the happiest man in town and a legend in the eyes of many. People would go out of their ways to talk to Charlie and just about everybody in the neighborhood would bend over backwards to help him if he needed it. Young children would often walk with

Charlie and Fluffy to ask him questions about his life. They were always fascinated by his war stories and by the tales of his truck driving days. It was definitely true that everybody held a high degree of respect for the old man, but amongst the townspeople, it was also common knowledge that Fluffy was the main source of his extreme happiness and ultimately, his greatest weakness.

In the beginning of that summer, the days were long and hot and as they passed one by one, Charlie and Fluffy never missed a single day of walking, except for when there was rain and thunderstorms. It was about mid August, however, when the weather became too hot for taking longs walks everyday, so Charlie spent more time with his wife and allowed Fluffy more time alone to sleep in the shade and the shelter of her dog house. The only problem was the fact that Charlie loved Fluffy so much that his efforts to protect her when he was not around were too dedicated that they were to a default; he had several tags on her collar, twenty eight of them being duplicate name tags, she was locked into a fenced-in section of the yard, and she was also secured to the fence with a long chain. The old man certainly meant well, but his over-protective nature was so strong that it got in the way of good judgment; Charlie could not understand the idea of either chaining the dog up or fencing it in, but instead, he thought that both would only make the dog safer.

So, one day, Charlie and Brenda sat in the kitchen talking and drinking coffee. Brenda shared her stories about what she did that day and all Charlie could talk about was how great Fluffy was. Brenda was pleased that her husband had such a great friend in the family pet because it made him happy and pleasant to be around. She did not mind that Charlie seemed to be obsessed with the dog, because as strange as it was, animals made him happy and more appreciative of the world around him. "Well, Charlie, I'm glad you love Fluffy so much, but I really don't think you should have her both chained up and fenced in. Really, what's the point in doing both?" Charlie's smile faded as he answered the question, "Why, Brenda, our beloved Fluffy needs to be safe, you know. It's the fence that keeps her in, but you know sometimes fences break or dogs dig under them. The chain is simply a backup device. Besides, if the chain should break, the fence is still there. Why, what's the problem with caring?" "I'm just a little concerned that it might be overkill. You see, Charlie, there is such a thing as doing too much and it's called negligence. You could be creating a hazard for the dog by putting so many obstacles in her way.

Didn't you ever hear the old saying 'where there's a will, there's a way?' If she wants to get out, she will, and all of these restraining devices could only hurt her. I'm just saying you should choose one or the other; the fence or the chain." "But, Brenda, Fluffy needs both! I love her!" "I know, Charlie, but that's the problem. Well, you should at least move the dog house away from the fence. Didn't you ever read any of the brochures about proper pet care that I brought home for you? They all clearly say that you should never have the dog house right up against a fence like that." By now Charlie was beginning to get upset. "But Brenda, Fluffy likes to be near the neighbor dog, Thorp! How can she do that if she is chained in the middle of the yard?" "Look, Charlie, if you put the dog house in the middle of the yard and get rid of the chain, she'll be able to do that." "But I like our arrangement just the way it is!" the now red-faced old man shouted as he rose from his seat and stormed out of the kitchen.

As Charlie walked into the next room while looking down at the floor and muttering about how unreasonable he thought his wife was being, he nearly walked into his son, who quickly got his father's attention to avoid the collision. Looking up and seeing who it was, Charlie greeted his son. "Oh, hello, Billy, how are you?" Charlie asked while he studied his son's dour facial features. "Bad," the son finally answered. By now, Charlie was concerned. "Why bad, Billy, what's wrong? What happened?" Looking back up from staring at his feet and making eye contact with his father, Billy began to speak with a slight quiver in his voice. "It's Fluffy," he began but was not able to finish.

"FLUFFY!" Charlie shrieked in a state of panic and fears as he pushed his son aside and went racing outside through the front door as fast as he could. With his heart pumping like there was no tomorrow, the old man dashed around the house and into the backyard where Fluffy was kept. When he finally made it there and frantically looked around, he was absolutely mortified at what he saw: there, over the section of fence above the dog house, the carcass of fluffy hung by the chain attached to the collar on her neck.

Crying, the old man slowly walked around the back of the fence and into his neighbor's yard. With a great sense of hesitation, he made his way to the section of the fence where the dead dog was hanging. With tears running down his face, he cradled the still warm, dead animal in his arms and carefully unhooked the chain from her collar. Slowly and painfully, he worked his way back into his own yard and onto the back porch, still cradling Fluffy in his gently shaking arms. Then he looked up and saw Brenda and Billy staring at him. As his tears began to form a puddle on the cement porch, he looked at his wife with resentment burning in his eyes. "So, I guess you're going to say that you told me so?" he barked at her. "No, Charlie now is not the time for criticism and blame. Why don't you just sit down and try to relax? Billy, help your father." Brenda said as Billy quickly grabbed a chair and brought it to his father. Slowly, Charlie sat down on the chair and continued to cradle his beloved dog.

"I'm so sorry, dear. Would you like to bury her in the yard? I'll help you make a nice little grave for her so that you can be reminded that she is off in a better place now. She'll never suffer again, ever. What do you say Charlie, should we help you say goodbye?" Brenda asked. Charlie looked up from his dog and at his wife. "No, thank you, I think I need some more time to say goodbye. In fact, I would like to be alone if you don't mind," Charlie answered. "Okay then, come on, Billy, let's go inside and give your father some privacy," Brenda said as she and her son walked into the house through the back door.

Slowly, the old man climbed to his feet and walked into the middle of the back yard where he had found his dead dog hanging over the fence. Then he looked down at the pained expression on Fluffy's lifeless face and noticed that her body was beginning to stiffen up. "No," he thought to himself, "her body cannot undergo any more changes; I'm simply not ready!" But rigor mortis continued to set in anyway. "WHY, GOD, WHY?!" the old man screamed at the top of his lungs while shaking his clenched, white-knuckled fist at the sky. And then he buried his best friend.

As the days went by after the loss of Fluffy, Charlie found himself slipping deeper and deeper into a severe state of depression. He never went to bed, but when he did actually sleep, it would easily be for days at a time. He discontinued grooming, ate very little food, stopped going to church, no longer took walks and became anti-social. When he was awake and out and about, he wore all black, listened to death metal music, did hard drugs and drank heavily. He spent most of his time out of bed sitting in bars and going to concerts. He even got a tattoo of a flaming skull on his left arm with a red banner beneath it that read "Life Sucks," much to Brenda's disapproval. Also, he no longer went by 'Charlie' anymore; his new moniker of choice became 'Chuck' and he would answer to nothing else.

With his deep state of depression still raging on, Chuck found himself heavily addicted to alcohol and crack cocaine, among many other drugs. He had traded in his car for a motorcycle, joined a street gang, and even became a violent and notorious criminal that everybody in town feared. In a sense, Chuck had become almost like a spider, with his web being the city at night. His outrageous behavior caused him to lose all of his true friends and made him estranged to his family and neighbors. Everybody who had once respected him now hated and despised him. Before long, he found himself with huge gambling debts and constantly involved in gang wars and street fights with other criminals and gangs. Chuck was out of control.

Chuck often spent his nights in the cemetery located on the top of the hill behind his house. Since the demise of his beloved dog, the old man had found himself obsessed with death and so the cemetery felt like a comfortable place for him to lurk. What seemed like every night, if the weather permitted, Chuck would get drunk and stagger up the hill to the cemetery with a bottle of bourbon and a pack of cigarettes. He would guzzle the entire bottle of bourbon while sitting on a tombstone smoking a cigarette. Then, he would piss on a different grave every night, in order from the first one in the first row to the last one in the last row, until he'd pissed on each one and then he'd start over. Then, after his ritualistic urination, he would often throw himself on the ground in the middle of the cemetery and pass out with a cigarette still burning in his mouth.

Twenty years later, this was all still going on. Chuck was still suffering from his severe depression, doing drugs, drinking heavily, wearing all black, riding his motorcycle, gambling, committing violent crimes and sleeping in the cemetery – except during the cold winter months when he slept in a casket in his dark, damp, and dismal basement. Billy had long since grown up and moved away and Chuck and Brenda no longer spoke. However, Chuck still mourned desperately for Fluffy.

Then, one day as a then very old Chuck was sitting at the kitchen table drinking black coffee and preparing to shoot up heroin, Brenda spoke to him for the first time in about twelve years. "Charlie, why do you spend so much time in the cemetery?" she asked, but Chuck just ignored her. "Charlie, why do you spend so much time in the cemetery?" she tried again, but only to be ignored again as well. "Charlie? Are you listening to me? Charlie?" she continued, but with still no answer. And then she remembered what he wanted to be called and rolled her eyes with disgust before attempting yet another time to communicate with him. "Chuck?" she began. The old man looked up

93

from what he was doing and made eye contact with his wife. "Yes?" he answered. "Why do you spend so much time in the cemetery? Really, it's been like eighteen years now since you've started this sick trend of yours and" "Twenty; it's been twenty years," Chuck interrupted her. The now thoroughly disgusted woman rolled her eyes and continued again, "yeah, twenty years, whatever. Look, it's been a long time since you've been normal. Why do you spend so much time in the graveyard; what's so great about it? What about it appeals to you so much that you have to spend every night there?" Chuck simply shot her a morbid smile. "It's where I feel I belong," he answered. "Well how do you know that it's been twenty years? Do you actually keep count of the time or something up there?" she continued to interrogate her husband. "It's been twenty years since Fluffy died," he told her. Brenda rolled her eyes again. "Oh. Well doesn't this just figure. This is a Fluffy thing and it has been since the beginning. When are you going to just get over this nonsense already and accept that fact that your damn dog is dead because you were stupid and wouldn't listen to me?!" the frustrated woman snapped at Chuck.

"What did you say?" the angry, bitter, old man slowly asked in a steadily deepening voice. "You heard me, Charlie; it's time to grow the hell up! This is bullshit! You need to get your act together!" "You bitch; you don't talk to me like that! First of all, you will refer to me as Chuck from now on, secondly, don't tell me what to do because I'll do what I want, and finally, don't you ever let me hear you disrespect Fluffy like that again!"

That night, Brenda called the city police to report her husband and all of the illegal activities that she knew of him being involved in. Then, she called a lawyer to schedule an appointment to discuss divorce proceedings. She had decided that she just couldn't tolerate being around her husband another minute. Chuck was just too far gone for her.

As Chuck was walking up the hill to the cemetery later that night, he found several police officers waiting for him. "Mr. Charles Johnson, we know it's you! We know about your crimes and sick lifestyle! We have a warrant out for your arrest! Surrender now and we won't shoot!" one officer called to him through a PA system in a patrol car. "ARGH!!! THE NAME'S CHUCK!!! AND FUCK THAT!!!" the drunken, cigarette smoking, old man roared out as he turned around and went running at full speed down the hill with the

94

sound of gun shots and sirens blaring after him as he made his get away.

When Chuck finally made it to the bottom of the hill and could not see the cops coming after him when he looked over his shoulder, he quickly jumped into a large bush at the very foot of the hill. A few seconds later, he could both see and hear and the cops running on foot and driving patrol cars down the side of the hill and by the bush that he was hiding in. When they were all long gone, Chuck emerged from the bush, ran into a dark alley and climbed through the window of an old, abandoned building. Once inside, he found a suitable hiding place on an old, rickety loft and hid back in the farthest, darkest corner he could find. There, in the corner, he found an old, dusty tarp, which he carefully pulled over his body to hide even more thoroughly, exposing nothing but his face. As the old man sat all huddled up in his dark corner he experienced nothing but angry thoughts. "Those assholes, how dare they call me 'Mr. Charles Johnson;' that's not my name anymore! That was just a label that society branded me with so that they could more easily identify me from everybody else in their superficial plastic planet joke of a world! It was all just some kind of liberal government conspiracy to track my every move in life so that they could rob me of my hard-earned money and call it taxes! Fuck that! Fuck their pathetic, candy-assed, conformist ideals; they need to cut the crap and just live their lives instead of caring about what everybody else thinks of them and instead of catering to every stupid-assed, sugar-coated trend that comes around just so that they can fit in like sheep, surrounded by false friends sporting fake smiles and promoting shattered dreams! Well, whatever; let them be conditioned by names and numbers on some asshole, suit-and-tie wearing politician's chart while they dwell in their precious, leftist utopia of false optimism! But I won't join them; no way! So there won't be any more 'Mr. Charles Johnson!' I go strictly by 'Chuck' now; no proper names or last names, just plain-old, simple, fucking CHUCK!!! Why can't people just get that through their close-minded, society-loving, thick-headed skulls?! It's not rocket science! If Aristotle, Plato, Hippocrates, and all of these stupid-assed pop singers like Madonna can just simply go by one name, then why the hell can't I?! And further more, why the hell are they after me now?! All kinds of cops, the sheriff, and even the damned deputy try fucking getting me?! What the fuck is this all about?!!!" Chuck thought to himself out loud in a screaming volume as he huddled in the dark, dusty corner, lit a

95

cigarette and began greedily smoking like there was no tomorrow. After that, he sat in silence, watching large rats scamper about on the floor and eventually fell asleep, only to be haunted by his dismal memories of Fluffy.

The next morning, Chuck awoke to the sound of sirens blaring in the streets as patrol cars raced throughout the town. The old man slowly worked his way across the rickety, unstable loft towards a small window and peered outside at the town. There were police officers everywhere. Just then a sudden voice roared throughout the building, "FREEZE!!!" it shouted and a few seconds later, Chuck could feel the cold metal touch of a handgun barrel. Without hesitation, the old man complied and put his hands up in the air. "Now, slowly, turn around and keep your hand in the air where I can see them!" the voice spoke loudly in the old man's ear. So, Chuck complied and slowly turned around, only to face another criminal, one who he knew as a member of his street gang. Realizing who it was and smiling, the criminal pulled back the gun and laughed. "Chuck! It's only you! Oh, thank God! I thought for sure you were another cop! Man, am I glad to see you!" Chuck did not smile. "Okay, so what's with all the cops – what's this all about?" he asked. "I don't know, man, but I'm afraid they might be after me, so I'm hiding. I guess you're in the same boat, huh?" Chuck scratched his head with curious thought. "Yeah, I guess you could say that. They were after me last night so I came here to hide. But I have no idea what all this is about today. I don't know if they're still after me or if this is something new." Suddenly, the sirens got louder as the patrol cars were passing the building outside. A voice on the PA system in one of the cars that had been talking the entire time now became audible to the two men, "MR. CHARLES JOHNSON, COME OUT WHERE EVER YOU ARE! WE WILL FIND YOU EVENTUALLY! I REPEAT, MR. CHARLES JOHNSON, COME OUT AND MAKE IT EASIER ON YOURSELF! WE ARE THE POLICE AND WE HAVE THE ENTIRE TOWN SURROUNDED! COME OUT WHERE EVER YOU ARE!" The two men just looked at each other. "Does that answer your question?" the criminal asked. "DAMN IT, THE NAME'S CHUCK!" the old man shrieked.

By now, the criminal had a confused look on his face. "Uh, yeah, Chuck, let me get this straight. We are surrounded by cops who want to catch you and take you away and you're more concerned about being referred to as 'Chuck' instead of 'Charles?'" Chuck said nothing and simply nodded.

"That's it," Chuck began, "I'm just going to have to kill myself. Hell, I'm eighty six years old so I've lived a full and productive life. I'm just so sick and tired of all this bullshit." The troubled criminal put his hand to his chin with careful thought and scratched his head with his other hand during a very brief moment of silence. Finally, he pulled out his gun and handed it to Chuck. "Okay, well, here you go then. You can use this if you want to. I have to say I'm really sorry to see you go like this, but I fully understand where you're coming from, I mean, life aint easy, man, so I just want you to know that I respect your decision," the criminal said in a noticeably saddened voice. Chuck just stared at the gun for several seconds without taking it before he smiled and spoke again, "Aw, Jose, you're probably the best friend I've had in nearly fifteen years. You've always been there for me and about the gun, well I greatly appreciate your generosity, but I'm afraid that I have other plans for how I want to go. You see, Jose, I have some unfinished business to attend to first." Jose smiled and nodded. "I understand, Chuck, I understand."

Outside, the sirens continued to echo through the streets. "MR. CHARLES JOHNSON, COME OUT WHERE EVER YOU ARE!!! WE ARE THE POLICE AND WE HAVE YOU SURROUNDED!!!" the amplified voices outside continued. "DAMN IT, DAMN IT, DAMN IT, DAMN IT, DAMN IT – AAAARRRRRGGGGGHHHHHH!!!!!! WHAT DON'T THOSE BONE-HEADED MORONS UNDERSTAND?!!! MY NAME IS CHUCK!!! JUST CHUCK!!! NOT MR. CHARLES JOHNSON, NOT CHARLES JOHNSON, NOT CHARLES, NOT MR. JOHNSON, NOT JOHNSON CHARLES, NOT MR. J, NOT CHARLIE JOHNSON, NOT CHARLIE, NOT C-DAWG, NOT CHARLIE J OR CHUCKY J - JUST PLAIN-OLD CHUCK!!!!" the old man flipped out. "Dude, Chuck, calm down, you're going to get us caught for sure with all of your yelling and carrying on. Damn, just relax, alright?" Jose attempted to subdue the panicking, hypertension-suffering man. "NO, JOSE, THESE FOLKS HAVE TO REALIZE THAT I AM CHUCK, I AM FEAR, I AM AN UNDERGROUND REPRESENTATION OF WHAT THEY ARE ALL INSIDE BENEATH THEIR SUPERFICIAL, SOCIETY-LOVING MASQUERADES!!! I AM CHUUUUUUUUUUUUUUUUUUCKKKK!!!!!!!!!" Jose rolled his eyes as he watched the still screaming, black-clad, tattoo-covered, old man rip his shirt off like the Incredible Hulk as the amplified voices outside once again spoke the words, "MR. CHARLES JOHNSON, WE WILL FIND YOU!!!"

"THAT'S IT!" Chuck barked as he dashed across the unstable, gently swinging loft towards the tiny, dust-covered window on the far wall. Then, he forcefully pushed it open and stuck his head outside. As he watched the police cars driving beneath him, he shouted at the very top of his lungs the words, "THE NAME IS CHUCK!!!" Suddenly, the car beneath him came to a sharp halt and within seconds, the entire building was surrounded by police officers on foot, aiming AR-15 military-pattern assault rifles at the old man's head.

One police officer began speaking to Chuck through a megaphone, "MR. CHARLES JOHNSON!!! OR 'CHUCK,' WHATEVER!!! WE HAVE YOU SURROUNDED!!! SURRENDER OR WE WILL SHOOT!!!" "NEVER; I WILL DIE BY MY OWN TERMS!!!" Chuck shouted back to the police as he quickly pulled his head back inside the building and threw himself to the floor. The sounds of loud gun shots filled the air as he did this and when he looked back up at the horrified Jose, Chuck smiled and gave him the thumbs-up sign. "CHUCK! WHAT THE HELL IS YOUR PROBLEM?! WHY DID YOU DO THAT?! NOW YOU BETTER HAVE A FUCKING PLAN TO GET US OUT OF HERE OR I'LL KILL YOU AND YOU'LL NEVER HAVE THE CHANCE TO DIE ON YOUR OWN TERMS!!! HOW WOULD YOU LIKE THAT, YOU STUPID OLD MAN?!!! HUH?!!!" Chuck laughed as Jose cocked his gun and put it to Chuck's head.

"Jose, relax, of course I have a plan," Chuck began as he pushed the gun out of his face, "follow me." Carefully, the old man climbed to his feet and walked to the ladder of the loft. Then, he slowly and carefully descended the ladder and walked the perimeter of the building until he found a manhole cover. "Well," he started as he looked at the still-armed Jose, "put that gun away and help me lift up the cover," to which the desperate criminal complied. "Okay, let's just set it here for now, okay, just like that, and now, down you go," Chuck instructed as Jose obeyed the orders and climbed down into the hole, closely followed by Chuck. When both men were down, Chuck pulled the manhole covered back over the hole and finished descending the ladder to join Jose in a deep puddle of foul-smelling, stagnant water. "Now what?" Jose asked. "Now we make a torch and find our way out of here," Chuck answered as he broke off the bottom ladder rung which was weak from rust, removed his tattered shirt and wrapped it around the chunk of rusted metal. Then, he produced his cigarette lighter and lit the shirt on fire, flooding the immediate area with a flickering, orange light. "See that long, black-water filled tunnel ahead of us, Jose?" "Yeah." "It most likely runs parallel with Main Street, which means it probably leads to the quarry right outside of the town. That would make sense, right, since after all, this sewer seems to be filled with mostly rain water anyway?" "What of it, Chuck, come on, because we don't have much time?" "Well, my friend, now we run for our lives." "But what happens when the torch goes out?" "Then it goes out. We don't necessarily need light to run in a straight line, I only lit that to see where we were and what the situation was." "Alright, well, let's do it." And the two men were off, running down the tunnel as fast as their legs could carry them.

"Alright; you were absolutely right, Chuck! How did you know it would lead to the quarry?" an ecstatic Jose asked as the two men swam across the water-filled hole towards the sides to climb out to freedom. "Well, I guess when you've lived somewhere for eighty six years, you just pick up on a few things, I would think." Chuck and Jose then climbed out of the quarry and shook hands. "Hey, listen, Jose, I'm sorry for putting you through all that; I was just so pissed off is all," Chuck said. "Oh, it's okay, Chuck, I realize you have a lot on your mind right now with everything that's going on in your life and I'm sorry about all those disrespectful things I said to you back there. I didn't mean a word of it." Chuck smiled. "I know you didn't. You were distressed. I taught you well. So, buddy, I guess this is goodbye. By this time tomorrow, I'll be dead." "I'll miss you, Chuck! I mean, this is going to be hard for me. You've taught me everything I know and yet, there's just so much left to learn. Who will teach me that, Chuck, who?" "You'll get through this buddy, I know you will. You'll find many teachers along the way, but before long, when you get to be of my age, you might one day have the joy of teaching another young, aspiring criminal our fine trade. You see, Jose, when I first met you, I knew just by the way that you were stabbing me and by the look in your eyes that you had that special flame inside of you; that glowing beacon of hope. You've always been a quick learner and a good student. I know that after I'm gone, you'll continue to make me proud." A tear began to roll down Jose's cheek. "I love you, Chuck," Jose stuttered. "And I you, my son, but listen, we can't have anymore of this nonsense. You've got to be strong like all of the greats before you. You've got to be stoic, because you know, Jose, a wise man is one who is free from passion, unmoved by joy or grief, and submissive to natural law. And one thing I'm sure you've found out by now on your own is that in nature, only the strong survive. So, you must simply accept who you are and not carelessly turn yourself into some king of emasculated, metro-sexual pussy in some pathetic attempt to communicate your feelings. You've got to be yourself or the world will just chew you up and spit you out like yesterday's news." "You see, Chuck? You're just so full of wisdom; you've got so much to offer. I'm going to miss that." "Jose, don't worry about it. You'll pick this stuff up on the way. But as far as all of the big lessons in life, I'm afraid that I've taught you all I can. Now I'll tell you again, son, dry those tears, you're a hardened criminal, not a wimpy, emotional, tree-hugging pussy!" Jose smiled and let out a slight chuckle. "I'll always remember you, Chuck. Every time I rob a gas station or cut weed like you showed me to, I'll think of you. It's just going to be an adjustment, you know, since you've always been my best friend and mentor. But maybe someday, we'll meet again." Chuck nodded approvingly. "That's right. I've lived a full and productive life and you need to do the same. And then someday, when you kill yourself, maybe we'll meet again in Hell." "Thank you for everything over the years, Chuck." "Don't mention it." Then the two men smiled, shook hands, and parted ways – forever.

That night, Chuck went back to his house for what would be the last time in his life. It was late and Brenda had long since gone to bed, so the tired old man sat down on the couch and turned on the television to watch the news channel. He was curious as to whether or not the police were still after him, because he wanted to be able to say goodbye to the world without any kind of interference whatsoever. As Chuck flipped through the channels and decided upon one to watch, the first thing he noticed was a large picture of himself smoking a cigarette on the screen. The news reporter spoke, "Police are still searching for local man, Charles Johnson, who had been in hiding since being encountered in the cemetery last night. Apparently, Mr. Johnson prefers to be called 'Chuck' and will not answer to anything else." "Damn right," Chuck said out loud. The television screen now featured a police officer who was speaking about his encounters with the wanted criminal. "Well, we knew there was a lot of crime going down in the city but we never knew who was behind it all. The street name 'Chuck' kept being thrown around, but nobody ever knew of this man's last name. We would pick up inmates and ask them what possessed them to do whatever they did and we always heard about this mystical 'Chuck' character. So, last night when we got a telephone call from Mrs. Johnson saying that her husband, Mr. Charles Johnson, was this man Chuck, and that he liked to spend many of his nights in the cemetery, we set up a sting there. And eventually, along came Chuck." The television screen then went back to the news reporter. "That's right; the suspect is apparently only going by the name 'Chuck,' as evidenced by this police video footage shot earlier today. Then the screen featured a shot of the abandoned building surrounded by police cars with the sound of the PA system calling out for Charles Johnson. Suddenly, the window in the building flew open, Chuck's head came out and the sound of him screaming, "THE NAME IS CHUCK!!!" filled the air. "Damn right," Chuck said again.

Then Chuck changed the channel to another news report. A woman on the screen was also speaking of the old man. "The wanted felon known as Chuck is still currently on the loose. Police tried to capture the eighty six year old man in the cemetery last night, but where unsuccessful as Chuck simply yelled at them and ran away. Police ask that if anyone has any information of Chuck's whereabouts, to please contact them immediately." Chuck changed the channel again, but only to see another news reporter. "Police tried to catch Chuck last night in the cemetery, but after apparently becoming offended that they called him by his full name, the suspect yelled at them to call him 'Chuck' and then ran away. In sports news tonight, the results of the local race where…" Chuck interrupted the reporter by changing the channel yet again. This time, the new channel featured a police officer. "We were waiting in the cemetery when along staggered Chuck. As you all probably know by now, he got away and we encountered him in an old, abandoned building on Main Street today when he once again yelled at us to call him 'Chuck'. We asked him to come out, but when he refused, we entered the building and he was not there. It's actually quite embarrassing because we have no idea whatsoever as to what happened to him." Chuck smiled as he changed the channel again. On this channel, he noticed a large border on the bottom of the screen that read "BREAKING NEWS" and the word "Live" at the top of the screen. The news reporter was in the middle of a sentence when the old man turned to that channel, so he listened to get an idea of what the big deal was. "And so, police assure us that Chuck is most likely armed and should be considered extremely dangerous." Chuck turned off the television and sat in silence for a short while. "What the hell did I do now that everybody is so obsessed over?" Chuck asked himself out loud.

"Well, I do believe that my time has come, because I'm sick and tired of being surrounded by retards and self-righteous fools who feel it necessary to get on my shit about everything all of the time and also, I am eighty six years old; I've lived a long and frustrating life, so the joke is on everybody else if they think for one second that I'm just going to continue putting up with their bullshit," Chuck said out loud as he rose to his feet. "Hmm, how should I do this? What is the most morbid way possible so I can leave a permanent mark on society? I know. I'll leave a suicide note for Brenda telling her where I am and to come alone so she can watch me die. And I'll do it in my favorite place, the cemetery, since it is symbolic of death anyway and has all the tombstones and old, twisted trees to supply the dark imagery. And as for my companion in death, since every great and notable suicide seems to include such a sick concept – who shall that be? Oh, I know; Fluffy. For it was Fluffy who provided me with the climax of my happiness in life and it was Fluffy who killed my spirit; in fact, when she died, a huge part of me died with her. And now, we shall be reunited in death," Chuck thought as he slowly walked through the living room of his house towards the back door.

Once outside, Chuck picked up a shovel, the very same shovel he used to bury Fluffy, and proceeded to dig her carcass up. He had expected to find a skeleton when he began this morbid task, but to his amazement, he found a still-intact, fully recognizable, slightly adipocere-covered, rigor mortis-stricken, mummified dog body. "No way," the old man gasped, "she has been uncorrupted by time! Only now, twenty years after her gruesome death, has the true decomposition stages begun. In fact, she's still in... She's still in... Could it possibly be? She's still in rigor mortis, one of the very earliest stages of the decomposition process. Rigor mortis – over twenty years later! She's an incorruptible! This is a sign. Her spirit has perfectly preserved her body so that she may rot with me. She shall be my companion in death," Chuck quietly spoke to himself.

Slowly, Chuck picked up the dog and cradled her in his arms for the first time in over twenty years. Tears filled his eyes as he gently stroked her soft, dead fur with his aging hands. It was then that he realized that even though time had ravaged his once youthful looks, it had done nothing to his beloved dog; she still appeared the same way she had twenty years ago. "Oh, Fluffy, I missed you so much! Why? Why did you have to leave me when you did? My life has not been the same since that horrible day twenty years ago! Not a single day has gone by that I didn't think of you. But don't worry, I'm coming. Soon, I will join you in death and we will be together once again! I'm going to kill myself soon and its going to be like a huge celebration as I say 'fuck you' to the world and laugh at all those morons who couldn't catch me as my life fades away at those very last seconds! And you'll be there with me and it will be glorious, like fireworks on the fourth of July…" Chuck's voice trailed off as he gave himself an idea.

Carefully, the old man put the dead dog down and scampered into his garage where he had stored a huge and illegal bottle rocket-like explosive device that he had built from an empty oil drug, gun power, and all of the other ingredients one would find inside the projectile part of a bottle rocket. Slowly, he rolled it onto rollers and with a great pain, managed to work it all the way up the hill and into the very middle of the cemetery, where he then set it up and prepared it for launching. Then, the old man ran back to his house and found a piece of paper and a pen. On it, he prepared his suicide note. It read: "Dear Brenda, as you know, my life has sucked royal donkey balls since the time of Fluffy's untimely demise. She died young but died none the less. Now it is my turn to join her in death and I would like you to be there so that I can say goodbye to you and to the world through you. Immediately after reading this note, you will come to the cemetery and you will come alone or you too, will be joining us - your husband, Chuck." Then, Chuck walked into his bedroom where his wife was sleeping, put the note on the nightstand, and set the alarm clock to go off in fifteen minutes. After completing that task, Chuck quietly left the room and crept outside to fetch a coil of heavy-duty rope and of course, the rigor mortis-stricken carcass of Fluffy.

With the rope on his right shoulder and the cold, dead dog cradled in his arms, Chuck walked up the hill towards the cemetery. He briefly thought about what he was about to do and felt a strong sense of pride and excitement. Strangely enough, the old man did not even have an ounce of fear in his body. His thoughts came to a halt however when he reached his destination. It was time to put his plan into action.

Articulately, Chuck positioned his body so that he was leaning against the rocket and then stuffed Fluffy's body down his shirt so that only her head was exposed, sticking out of the shirt collar alongside Chuck's head. Then, with both his arms, he picked up the rope, tied one end of it to his waste, and began wrapping it around, tying himself and his dog to the rocket. When he got to the other end of the rope, he simply tied it to his left leg just above the knee so that he was now completely bound to the rocket with rope except for this lower legs, feet, arms, and head. All that was exposed of Fluffy was her head, which now was positioned in such a way that it looked like Chuck had two heads. Then, Chuck lit a cigarette and waited for Brenda to arrive.

When his wife finally did arrive a few minutes later, Chuck smiled as he took a long drag of his cigarette. "Hello Brenda, I've been waiting for you," he told her. "Chuck, what are you doing?" she asked him. "I'm killing myself," he responded. "How, by shooting yourself into a black hole in space or something? And what the hell is that thing by your head?" the tired and bored woman asked without amusement. "This here is the remains of Fluffy and we're going to blow up in the sky like a firework to celebrate my freedom from this cold world." Brenda rolled her eyes. "What does all of this have to do with the dog?" she asked. "Brenda, if you recall, there was a time when my name was Charlie. I was a legend in this town because everybody knew and loved me. It was a good life and I had Fluffy to thank for that. Well, when Fluffy died, I was heartbroken and my life just spun out of control. It was like I was dead inside, you know, when she died, a big part of my spirit died with her. I just couldn't cope with the huge void in my life caused by the hollow emptiness of solitude. So my life just became a downward spiral of drug and alcohol abuse and before too long, I found myself to be a hardened street criminal. I broke the law that I once defended, but it wasn't that idea that scared me the most. You see, I was always a perfectionist, you know, and when I became a criminal, I was determined to be the best, most notorious criminal that this town had ever seen. What scared me was that when I had achieved that goal, it wasn't so much that I was breaking the law anymore; it was more of the idea that, in my own mind and in the minds of my followers, I became the law. Simply breaking the law proved not to be enough anymore, so I became the law in a sense by becoming the master criminal and most feared and respected gang leader in town. It was then that my will and principles, or doctrine as some called it, became the law that would govern all of the criminals of the streets. I allowed such illegal activities to become a part of my lifestyle because it just worked; everything seemed to fit together nicely. Others apparently thought so too, because they became my students and in time, my loyal minions and henchmen who watched my back and defended my honor in times of peace and my life in times of war. I taught a lot about the lifestyle over the last several years, but I also learned far more than I could ever teach. But the education changed me forever and only upon reflecting on my life did I fully begin realize that Charlie was long dead. So now, as you know, my name is Chuck and everybody hates me except for my small, but loyal underground following. But recently, I found that because of you, not even they are enough to defend me; because of you, the police, and the townspeople - everybody is after me. I'm not sure why or what they think I did, but what I do know is that this has become a regularly occurring theme, one that just gets worse with every incident, and I'm just getting way too old for this bullshit. So, you know, I stopped to think yesterday and I realized that everything bad that has happened in my life over the past twenty years was a result of losing Fluffy. So, you see, I have decided to just end it and go and join her before the police actually do catch me and lock me away somewhere forever. I just can't allow them to win this battle. They didn't know Fluffy; they have no idea what all of this is about. So, now, I'm afraid that my time has come." Brenda just stood there idly by with her arms crossed across her chest and yawning. "Why do you have to be such a drama queen, Chuck, okay, this is nonsense. Get off of that thing, now," she said.

Chuck shook his head. "No, I won't be doing that. You see, as you so thoughtfully pointed out to me once before, Fluffy died as a direct result of my being a negligent pet owner. So, I let her down by putting her in an unsafe environment. But I'm sure she understood that it was a mistake and that I meant well; I'm sure she still loved me anyway despite the great pain she must have been in as she died. In fact, I'm absolutely positive that her spirit is right here with us now, watching over me lovingly. You see, when a body dies, it rots. A corpse undergoes many interesting stages of decomposition, but for some reason, Fluffy's corpse has not. It is still in the stage of rigor mortis, as it was the moment when I buried her. Her corpse has stood the test of time and has been rendered uncorrupted by the elements. Only now, being exposed to the open air is she beginning to show signs of rot. Don't you see? It's a sign that she waited for me, to rot with me, to be with me once more. And so, you see, if I bail on her again, I would be letting her down again. I'm not going to betray her like that yet another time. This is what has to happen. And then our bodies will rot together, but in pieces, of course. We'll blow up and rain to the earth where we will fester and decay and it will be ever so glorious." Brenda shook her head in disgust and confusion. "What the hell are you talking about?" she asked.

"Decomposition," Chuck began, "when people and animals die, they decompose." Brenda nodded, "well, yeah, I know that, but what of it?" Chuck smiled and started again, "you see, the heart is a very important organ in our bodies. The heart, as I would imagine you know, pumps our blood, our life fluid all the days of our lives. It is such an important organ, that it has been honored and revered by millions of people since the beginning of time. That is where we get our metaphoric imagery involving the heart and the role that it serves. You see, the heart has become symbolic of the feelings, emotions, beliefs, values, morals, and convictions that govern our lives on this earth. But it is still also a word used in reference to the organ that pumps our blood, keeping us alive so that we may feel these concepts that govern our lives. Without the physical heart, there can be no metaphorical heart that represents who we are inside. When Fluffy's physical heart stopped that one horrible day over twenty years ago, my metaphorical heart stopped as well," Chuck said as he paused to light a new a cigarette.

Brenda looked thoroughly confused, even more so than before. "So, what does the heart have to do with decomposition process of a dead body?" she asked. "Well," Chuck started again, "the stopping of the heart is the first stage. When the heart stops beating, all of the blood in the body begins to settle into whatever parts are closest to the ground. This is why when you see a corpse their exposed skin always appears to be so waxy and pale. And then livor mortis sets in, which happens within the first hour and seems to occur for about up to maybe twelve or so hours later. This is the stage where the skin discolors into a purplish-red appearance and the fingertips, toes, ears, and the nose begin to turn blue. This is also about the time when the eyes begin to flatten. You have to also keep in mind that the body temperature is cooling at a gradual rate every hour, making the very sense of death seem even more real. It is then that the muscles relax for a very short period of time before they stiffen into what we call rigor mortis, which is where Fluffy is currently at in the process. But in the more advanced stages of rigor mortis, the stiffening of the muscles becomes most evident in the face even though it exists all over the body, but it really doesn't matter, because eventually, in most cases the muscle fibers will begin to break down and decompose, which creates a softening effect of the muscle tissue. Usually, by this time, the corpse starts to experience a greenish discoloration of the skin as it putrefies; the greening typically begins somewhere in the lower abdomen but does, in time, spread to effect the entire corpse, leaving the face so puffy and swollen that nobody could even begin to recognize it. And as the body swells and turns green, the foul, putrid odor of death occurs because of the bacteria that is at work destroying the body; in fact, the same bacteria like that of the intestines that by this time is busy producing foul-smelling gases that have been known to bloat the corpse, turning the skin black, while causing the eyes and tongue to protrude as the intestines themselves are busy being pushed out through the rectum. After all of those lovely things, the skin usually blisters, comes loose from the corpse, and bursts open, exposing the internal organs to experience the same fate. Soon after that, the organs liquefy, leaving the rapidly rotting corpse to leak from all orifices. But it all begins with the stopping of the heart."

Chuck paused to light yet another cigarette. There was no doubt in his mind that Brenda was thoroughly disgusted with everything that he had just told her. Finally, with a nervous and disturbed quiver in her voice, she spoke again. "Uh, Chuck, what is all of this about? What does any of it have to do with you killing yourself? Wouldn't those things happen anyway when you died, whether you killed yourself or not?" Chuck then took a deep drag of his cigarette and began laughing morbidly as smoke puffed out of his mouth and nose. "My dear wife," Chuck said, "don't you get it? Everything that I just described to you are things that I learned from spending so much time here in the cemetery. What, did you think that I would spend so much time here and never get curious enough to actually dig people up to see what they look like? How naïve can you be? I'm Chuck! But really, to answer your question, this is all about Fluffy. You see, it is normal for a corpse to decompose in such a gruesome manner, even while sealed inside caskets and burial vaults. But Fluffy, well, she was buried in the open soil, completely exposed to the earth and at the time of her exhumation, she had very little signs of decay. In fact, she is still in rigor mortis as we speak. How can this be? Incorruptible corpses are extremely rare – but they do exist and being that they do, it makes me a bit uneasy as to how they are able to defy the biblical concept of 'ashes to ash, dust to dust.' Well, I don't have all the answers and I really don't know what has happened here, but I do know one thing: if our hearts can be symbolic of our feelings for one another, then the stiffening of our muscle tissue can also be symbolic of the same kinds of feelings, because the true physical heart is really nothing more than muscle itself. In this case, Fluffy's body tensed up when she died and has remained that way to this very moment. So have my deeply profound feelings for her – don't you see? I have always felt that I was completely alone in my state of grief after Fluffy died; I didn't think anybody felt the same way I did. But when I dug her up earlier today and witnessed her still intact rigor mortis-stricken corpse, I knew then that I wasn't alone all these years after all. So, you see, I need to join her now, so our bodies may finally rot together, which can be symbolic and represent the joining of our eternal souls in the spirit world."

By this time, Brenda just looked at Chuck in disbelief. She simply could not comprehend what she was seeing and hearing. "Look, stop babbling about nothing! You still didn't answer my question. Why are you killing yourself when your body will just decompose anyway? What's the point in all of this, because I'm not buying it! Incorruptible corpses not turning into dust and ash – don't you think those things ever take time?" she asked. "They do take time and what a concept time is. We can either decompose naturally or accelerate the process with fire. We can either kill ourselves or die by nature's hand, but does any of this really matter? Time makes all of these things irrelevant because you know the world will still be turning when I'm gone. My corpse may take time to rot on this planet while my spirit goes so high that it actually breaks the time barrier. But time is time and to answer your question as to why I am killing myself, I must tell you that my time has come," the old man responded.

"Is all of this for real, Charlie?" she asked. But the old man did not answer. He just stared at her. Rolling her eyes, she tried again, "is all of this for real, Chuck?" "Yes, Brenda," Chuck said, "I am afraid that all of this is really happening, right before your very eyes. You see, I didn't want to just kill myself without explaining my reasoning to you, because I was concerned that you would misunderstand my intentions and my logic. Those things often manifest themselves as my word, which I give to you now. You must understand that a man's word is all that he has in this world. I didn't want you to be lead astray by all of the crap they're slandering my name with on television; I saw that garbage and its all complete bullshit. I wanted you to know the truth so that you may say 'goodbye and fuck you' to the world for me after I'm gone. I'd gladly do it myself, but I obviously cannot get too close to the public without getting nabbed. So that's where you come in. I know you'll do what is right. And with that, my dear wife, I bid you farewell," Chuck said as he took one final drag of the last cigarette that he would ever smoke in his life.

"WAIT!" Brenda shrieked. "What am I supposed to tell people when they ask? That you killed yourself because your dog was in rigor mortis?" "Yeah, pretty much," Chuck answered, "tell them that my time has come and when I discovered a symbolic resemblance of Fluffy's corpse to my feelings for her, I just knew what I needed to do. Also, you need not just wait to be asked, but rather proudly volunteer that information." Brenda scratched her chin thoughtfully as she watched her husband smile while his still-smoldering cigarette butt continued to burn closer and closer towards his fingers. "You know you're a coward for doing this, don't you Chuck? You used to be a tough, hardcore, working-class man with strong, working-class, conservative values. But now you're just a pussy whose running from his problems in life like every other suicidal, spineless idiot in the world, only you're so self-conscious that you think you have glorify your deed. But to me, you are still nothing more than a coward." Chuck laughed at her. "You know, I can see why you might think that. However, I am eighty six years old. I have nothing to run from. I wouldn't live much longer anyway, so why wait around for death? I'm just choosing to say 'fuck you' to death by dying on my own terms, my own way. So, with those things considered, I believe that your opinion of me may be misguided. Perhaps rather than criticizing me, you should be applauding my self-determination. You call me a coward and a pussy, but would a coward or a pussy have the balls to take their life into their own hands? I think not. As for being suicidal, the definition of the word is 'suggestive of suicide;' I've never once in my entire life suggested to anybody that they *should* take their own life. Just because I have chosen to go this way does not mean that I am telling anybody else to do it. What, do you think this is a game of monkey-see-monkey-do? Just do as I say, not as I do. Got that? And furthermore, I am not as self-conscious as you may believe; you may not realize this now, but I don't really care what people think of me and that includes you. And as far as my conservative values that you cite, I must point out that your argument is grossly flawed. You think that nobody with such a mindset should have the capacity to do something like this?" Chuck said and Brenda nodded to answer his question. "Well, you must understand that at its core, conservatism is about the responsibility of the individual and not so much the collective. I realize that despite this, society as the collective tends to tell people who are suffering, whether emotionally or actually terminally ill that they have no right to take their own life into their hands. This is wrong because it's just another way that the government tries to undermine our individual freedoms when we should be living in a democratic society. I mean, just the very idea that society knows better than the individual is a communist concept that has no place in this nation. So, as far as I am concerned, to think that your self-righteousness is more important than my fundamental right of self-determination is totally asinine."

Brenda was speechless. It seemed that everything that she said to deter Chuck from his deed had failed. All of his answers flowed right out of his mouth as if they were scripted and there seemed to be nothing she could possibly say that he did not have a deeply thought out, almost intelligent answer for. After a few seconds of silence, she tried one last time. "So all of this, you really want to glorify this? Because that was the one thing I said that you did not argue with." Chuck nodded. "Yes, you see, death is a beautiful thing. Especially when it is planned, controlled, and self-inflicted so that the person it is happening to may feel more like the recipient or the winner of the prize rather than like the victim. When you think about it, it's really no different from planning families and planned childbirth, which we did for Billy. And so, with that said, I finally bid you farewell," the old man said as he reached down to the fuse of the rocket and pressed his smoldering cigarette butt against the fuse, lighting it.

As the fuse rapidly burned, shooting sparks in all directions as it became shorter and shorter, Chuck laughed morbidly and uncontrollably while rubbing his hands together greedily. When the fuse finally disappeared into the rocket, the ground began to shake. Then, suddenly, with an extremely loud whistling sound and a tremendous speed, the rocket flew up into the air while Chuck was still laughing. Brenda watched in amazement as the device became a small spot in the sky and exploded with an incredibly loud bang. Very shortly after the ground-shaking explosion, large chunks of steaming metal and flaming body parts came crashing down into the cemetery. To her right, a big chunk of the oil drum landed nearby and to her left, she noticed one of Chuck's arms; the one with the "Life Sucks" tattoo on it. And finally, not too far in front of her, Brenda noticed Fluffy's flaming skull.

After standing still in the very same place for several minutes, having not moved an inch since her conversation with her now late husband, Brenda finally shrugged her shoulders. "Oh well, you don't see that everyday," she said to herself out loud as she calmly turned around and walked home like nothing had ever happened, feeling comforted to know that Chuck and Fluffy were finally reunited again – in Hell.

Copyright 2008 by Anthony G. Roof

THE

CENTIPEDE

When Elizabeth notices a common house centipede scampering across the floor in her living room, she becomes frightened and wants to kill it. Her mother, however, advises against this desire claiming that centipedes help to control the home's insect population. Elizabeth disobeys her mother and targets the creatures in a rampage of extermination during the late-night hours. When the insect problem gets out of control as a result, the girl's mother has the house fumigated. The only problem is that one centipede remains, and now mutated by the fumes, prowls around in the night with revenge on its mind.

4

THE CENTIPEDE

The Centipede

As the last few seconds of the final hour slipped away and a new day began, the enormous grandfather clock in the corner of the dark living room chimed twelve times. The sounds of the chiming and gentle swinging of the heavy pendulum seemed to flow together to create what most found to be an annoyingly noticeable noise and it was this very racket that awoke the sleeping girl who had fallen asleep just hours earlier in the same dark room and on the couch in front of a glowing television set. She lazily yawned and slowly opened her tired eyes. After taking just a moment to wipe the dried dirt from her eyes that her slumber had produced, she routinely looked around the dark room with the intention of immediately returning her gaze to the still glowing television screen. However, halfway through this habitual process, she quickly froze in terror as her gaze fell upon a long, spider-like insect that was scurrying across the carpeted floor just in front of the glowing television screen which gave off only enough light to illuminate the area in which the insect was scurrying. "OH MY GOD, WHAT THE HELL IS THAT THING?!" the frightened girl shrieked. It was a common house centipede.

As the centipede froze in its tracks to feign its death at the sound of the girl's loud shrieking, a light came on in the room. The girl's mother appeared at the bottom of the staircase steps with a concerned look on her face. "What's the matter, Elizabeth?" she asked. The still uneasy girl simply looked at her mother, back at the centipede, and back at her mother again, repeating the process several times. "THERE'S THIS HUGE, CREEPY, DISGUSTING BUG ON THE FLOOR! I DON'T KNOW WHAT IT IS AND I'M SCARED!" the girl panicked as her mother raised her left eyebrow and slowly approached the immediate area of the living room where the centipede was still sitting on the floor. "Oh, this bug? This one right here, Elizabeth? This is what you're so afraid of?" The girl nodded as she cautiously peered out of the blanket she was hiding under. "Well, its okay, it's just a little centipede. They're everywhere. It won't hurt you, so there's really nothing to be afraid of," the girl's mother tried to reassure her troubled, young daughter. "Okay, fine, but please just kill it! It's ever so creepy and scary and gross; I don't like it! Kill it!" the girl responded. The mother just smiled and gave out a slight giggle. "No, we're not going to kill it. Centipedes are very beneficial creatures to have around because they're harmless insects that eat all kinds of other bugs and insects that are harmful. They eat flies, termites, cockroaches, fleas, beetles, bedbugs, moths, and just all sorts of nasty things that we don't want in our home." "Really?" the daughter asked. "Why sure; when was the last time you saw a cockroach or a moth in here?" "Not for a while, I guess. But I still don't like that stupid, horrible bug! Kill it!" the girl yelled as she jumped up and tried to stomp on the centipede. "No!" her mother cried as she stopped the girl and touched the centipede to scare it off. Both women watched as the bug scurried under the television set. "You can't kill the centipedes, Elizabeth, okay? We use to have a really bad bug problem here and we couldn't afford to have an exterminator do anything about it in terms of bug control, so a friend recommended that we put centipedes around. It's our only means of bug control. So, don't be killing them!" The girl looked down in disappointment. "Okay," she said as she watched her mother leave the room.

Elizabeth watched as another centipede began scurrying across the floor. Being sure that her mother was gone and had left her again completely alone, the defiant young girl put her shoes on and smashed the centipede with her foot and began grinding it into the carpet. Finding it to be an easy kill, she turned off the living room light and the television set and spent the rest of the night roaming about the dark house, hunting and destroying the innocent, nocturnal creatures that she so feared.

Finding both her fears of the centipedes as well as the pleasure she derived from killing them growing, Elizabeth continued her nightly hunts every night for months. She killed hundreds each night and probably thousands in all and she had yet to notice any significant increase in the insect problem of her home. "Stupid mother," the girl thought, "she actually put these disgusting bugs in the house thinking they would help the insect problem! Ha! They are the insect problem!" And so, the spiteful, insect-fearing girl continued her hot pursuit of the centipedes, smashing, killing, and relentlessly destroying large numbers of the humble bugs like there was no tomorrow, each and every night for months.

Close to a year later, as Elizabeth's centipede genocide continued to rage on, the girl and her mother began to notice a growing insect problem in their home. Initially, it just was a subtle difference involving a small increase of the common housefly population, but the problem seemed to worsen with time until the day finally came when Elizabeth's mother noticed a few cockroaches scattering about on the kitchen floor. It was then that her curiosity got the best of her. "This is strange," she thought, "I haven't seen any centipedes around here lately. I wonder where they all went."

The curious woman then began to walk around the house and for the very first time in her life, she found herself actually looking for centipedes. She searched in dark closets, in the basement, underneath furniture, and in dark corners – all of these being places where centipedes hide during the day, but to her great amazement, there were none to be found. Instead, she found nothing but cockroaches, ants, and flies. "Damn it! Where in the hell are all the damn centipedes! Roaches are taking over the place and the centipedes aren't doing anything about it!" she thought to herself with frustration as she watched a cockroach crawl out of a small hole in the side of the couch. But then, suddenly, she heard something; it was her daughter talking and stomping her feet on the floor in the next room. "Take that, you damn centipede!" she heard Elizabeth scream. To the mother, the mystery had now been solved.

Rolling her eyes and sighing with disappointment, the woman walked into the room where her daughter was stomping her feet. When Elizabeth saw her mother standing in the doorway of the room with her arms folded across her chest and a frown on her face, Elizabeth became quiet and froze in her tracks as still as a statue. "Uh, yes, mother?" Elizabeth asked in a shaky voice. "Step aside, please," her mother asked. Hesitantly, the girl complied, revealing a dead centipede that had been smashed into the carpet by the sole of her shoe. Elizabeth's mother stared at the dead for what seemed like an eternity, as the nervous girl's heart raced with apprehension. Finally, the woman spoke, "Elizabeth, I thought I told you not to kill the centipedes. I remember specifically telling you that there are some bugs you kill and some that you don't. I told you that the centipedes are not to be killed. So, tell me, how long have you been doing this? It's obviously been awhile because I looked everywhere and there are none left." Elizabeth looked down at her feet with shame. "I know, Mother, but they're just so disgusting! I'm sorry, but I don't like the centipedes!" The mother nodded. "I see. I agree; they are disgusting. But let me show you their alternative. If you think centipedes are so horrible, then I have no idea how you think you'll be able to handle what I'm about to show you, but oh well. Follow me." Elizabeth followed her mother into the living room. "Okay, so what am I looking at?" the girl asked her mother. "Lift a cushion off of the couch," the mother replied. So, Elizabeth took a slow step forward and pulled up a cushion and there underneath where the cushion had been, she saw several hundreds of thousands of writhing cockroaches. The girl stared in horror as she watched them squirm and when she noticed a bunch of the disgusting insects climbing out of the cushion that she held in her hands, she threw it across the room and began screaming in extreme terror.

The very next day, Elizabeth's mother hired an exterminator to fumigate the insect-infested house. The exterminator agreed to do the job and was successful in his efforts to kill all of the unwanted insects. However, what nobody realized was the fact that the original centipede, the very one that set Elizabeth off on her anti-centipede activities and was the last centipede alive up to that point, had been hiding in the house during the fumigation and somehow survived. And, as the old saying goes, "what doesn't kill you only makes you stronger," the centipede was now immune to all of the fumes, pesticides, and insecticides that were used during the extermination efforts and worse yet; it was now severely pissed off and had only revenge on its mind.

For months, the centipede had been overeating due to the steadily increasing insect population and especially during the height of the problem when the cockroaches were at their worst. As a result of this overeating, the ambitious creature also found itself to be more active during the night hours. The combination of eating extra food and being more active only caused the growth of body mass and the strengthening of muscle tissue and surviving the fumigation directly resulted in a building up of the immune system and making the insect stronger and more durable overall. However, benefiting the immune system was not the only contribution of the fumigation; but also, the fumes had somehow managed to mutate many of the insect's muscle cells. And so, due to all of these uncommon developments, the centipede was now about the size of an overfed house cat that could simply be killed just by stepping on it.

The gigantic centipede hid in strategic locations during the day; places where nobody would find it and kill it in its sleep. Nobody knew of its existence, so it continued to live its life in extreme secrecy by staying well hidden during the day and discretely going about its nocturnal feeding activities at night. As time went by, the centipede became larger and wiser and realized that it could no longer scurry across the floor in silence or climb walls, furniture, or stick fast to ceilings. It was now a relatively slow moving creature that made an audible sound when it moved, much like a dog, and had no climbing or clinging abilities anymore whatsoever. What it did have, however, was a strong grudge and a growing hate for Elizabeth and it vowed to itself never to forgive her for destroying its simple, nocturnal empire.

When the day had finally arrived that the centipede realized it was the size of a large German shepherd dog that had run out of comfortable places to hide and that the house had a shortage of insects to eat, it decided to take its revenge on Elizabeth since she was the reason for it having to suffer such a fate. So, one night, while Elizabeth was fast asleep, the spiteful and vengeful centipede slowly and articulately climbed the creaking stairs towards her bedroom door. Upon reaching this destination, the clever bug slowly and quietly pushed open the partially closed door, producing the eerie squeaking sound of the gradually rusting hinges that the door hung on. Peering inside the dark bedroom, the centipede spied the blanket-covered girl sleeping peacefully upon her single bed located along the far wall in line with the middle of the room. Slowly and stealthily, the vengeful centipede crept across the smooth wood floor towards the bed. Then, ever so carefully, one leg at a time, the centipede slowly began to pull itself up onto the end of the bed with each of its one hundred legs applying the same amount of pressure to the mattress. This strategically thought-out plan took about half an hour to execute, but when the centipede was finally completely on the bed, it had no problem evenly distributing it body weight upon the bed without disturbing the sleeping girl that it was now hovering over.

As the centipede stealthily inched its way up the bed without touching Elizabeth, it quickly found more comfortable and stable footing along the sides of the mattress and when it looked down, much to its great delight, it found itself face to face with the sleeping girl. "Time to die, bitch," the centipede thought to itself as it quickly and forcefully slammed its fangs into the Elizabeth's neck, injecting abundant amounts of its foul and poisonous venom directly into the bloodstream leading to her brain. As the sharp fangs pierced her skin, she immediately awoke and opened her eyes, but only to see the one she had once tried to kill now slowly killing her. Elizabeth opened her mouth to let out a bloodcurdling scream but nothing came out and as she could feel her gradually tensing muscles forcefully closing her throat, her whole life just flashed before her eyes. She wanted to scream but could not and she repeatedly tried to talk, even if only in a whisper, but also had no luck. And, as she had also suspected, only a few seconds later, she found that she could not even breathe anymore. She struggled despite that and made every attempt possible to thrash her arms and legs about in an effort to knock her assailant off of her rapidly stiffening body, but quickly found that all of her efforts were futile and her hope in vain. Slowly, while still helplessly gasping for breath, her already blurry night-vision began to lighten until she saw nothing but a bland shade of white light that soon faded into black. Before long, Elizabeth was dead.

The satisfied centipede then pulled its fangs from the dead girl's corpse and was left with the sweet taste of blood as it dripped from the sharp fangs of the victorious insect. The taste of blood was so invigorating and energizing that the centipede wanted more. Slowly, it crept from the dark bedroom across the hallway and into the next room. There, the centipede spied Elizabeth's mother, fast asleep upon her bed but not covered with a blanket at all. Again, the spiteful insect worked its way up onto the bed and hovered over the sleeping woman. "Why did you bring me here in the first place? So that you're uneducated, stupid-assed, ingrate daughter could slaughter my entire family and destroy the empire that I have worked so hard to build all of these years? And for what? So you could have a few less houseflies buzzing around your kitchen? Why not just take out your damn trash once in awhile, instead of letting it sit there to rot so that it attracts cockroaches whose only aspiration in life is to compete with me for control over my kingdom? I'm afraid its time to die, bitch," the furious centipede thought to itself before slamming its fangs into the woman's neck, killing her in the exact same manner that it had killed Elizabeth just moments earlier in the next room.

With all other inhabitants of the house dead, the centipede could rule as it pleased, whenever it pleased, day or night without any limitations or the need to ever hide. It continued to eat select insects, but mostly procured its nourishment from the food that it found in the kitchen, the pantry, and the refrigerator. As a result of this, the cockroach population again began to grow in large numbers as they infested the house. The centipede did not mind this invasion, however, because it viewed their presence as its alternative food supply; its main source of nourishment that would only make it stronger.

Eventually, the cockroach population had grown so far out of control that the presence in the house was becoming noticeable to the neighbors and other residents of the town. The large black insects were crawling out of cracks in the walls, underneath doors, and windowsills, among other places. When city officials finally noticed the problem, they attempted to contact Elizabeth's mother, but without avail, so they concluded that the house had been abandoned and made the decision to condemn it.

On the scheduled day of the condemned house's demolition, the workers in charge of the project kicked open the locked door and entered the house. They were horrified at what they saw: cockroaches all over the place in such abundant amounts that it looked like the floor was moving. Cringing, the workers continued to push on through the house and made their way up the stairs to see exactly what the situation was on the second floor. It was while checking the second floor that the workers discovered the long dead, bloated, and rotting corpses of the two women. The odor was so horrendous that the workers gasped for air and then ran from the building, only to return with police officers and the town coroner.

As the men worked and the coroner was writing his report, the centipede was awakening for the day. When it opened its eyes and took a look around, it noticed the men working in the house and the coroner hovering over the corpses, writing his report and preparing to remove the bodies from the building. As the current owner of the property, the centipede felt that the men had wronged it by breaking and entering into its dark lair. As the puzzled and frustrated insect continued to watch what it considered to be a violation of its habitat, it became severely angered at what it saw. "NO WAY, PUNKS, THIS IS MY DOMAIN NOW!" the centipede thought to itself in a state of extreme rage and hostility as it leaped from the corner where it had been sleeping and jumped on the coroner's back, knocking him over besides Elizabeth's rotting corpse.

"AAAAHHH!!! WHAT THE HELL IS THAT THING?!" the coroner screamed at the top of his lungs as the centipede implanted its fangs into the back of the man's neck and began injecting him with its venom. Then, the centipede opened its mouth really wide, exposing long rows of sharp, jagged teeth, and started chomping down on the coroner's dying body with its powerful jaw. Saliva, venom, and blood dripped from the jaw as the centipede slammed its neck against the floor, snapping the coroner's crippled body in half. Moving its head from side to side with intense strength and speed, the pissed off insect began grinding the coroner into a fine paste as its flung blood all over the room, coating the floor, walls, and ceiling. When the man was nothing but a thin, pasty liquid, the centipede swallowed him and jumped with surprise as two police officers ran into the room and began shooting. The furious insect laughed to itself as the bullets pierced its thick hide as they flew from the direction of the trespassers. The bullets, however, only felt like slight bee stings and did nothing more than increase the state the anger that the centipede was already in. Slowly, it stepped towards the two men and exposed its crocodile-like teeth, still dripping with blood, now turned a bright shade of pink from its contact with the thick saliva of the hungry, salivating, and vengeful insect. The two men took a few steps back as they continued firing their weapons at the relentless insect. As the centipede continued to approach the two police officers, it noticed the faint smell of fear in the air and recognized the look of terror in their pupil-dilated eyes that seemed sunken into their hastily paling skin-covered, quivering skulls.

The panicking police officers continued firing bullet after bullet at the slowly approaching insect, but before long, what seemed like an endless sequence of "bang, bang, bang, bang," ended when it was interrupted by a "click" sound. The two men just looked at each other in horror and then immediately back at the approaching insect. "RUN!" one of the men screamed, but just after they had turned towards the doorway of the room and before they could actually take a single step in that direction, the centipede lurched at the two men with full speed and force, knocking them both over into the corner of the room and pinned them down to the floor. Then it bit both of them with its fangs and injected their bodies with its foul venom of death. A few minutes later, the two men were dead.

"Does anybody else want to fuck with me?" the centipede thought to itself as it left the room and descended the stairs. Finding nobody else in the house, therefore making it apparent that all of the workers had simply dropped what they were doing in fear and abandoned the building, the centipede was once again left in solitude. "That's what I thought," the proud and victorious insect pondered to itself. Then, with a smile and the strong feeling of triumph, the centipede made its way to the front door of the building, reached up to the door knob with its mouth, pulled the opened door closed with its teeth, and lived happily ever after.

Copyright 2008 by Anthony G. Roof

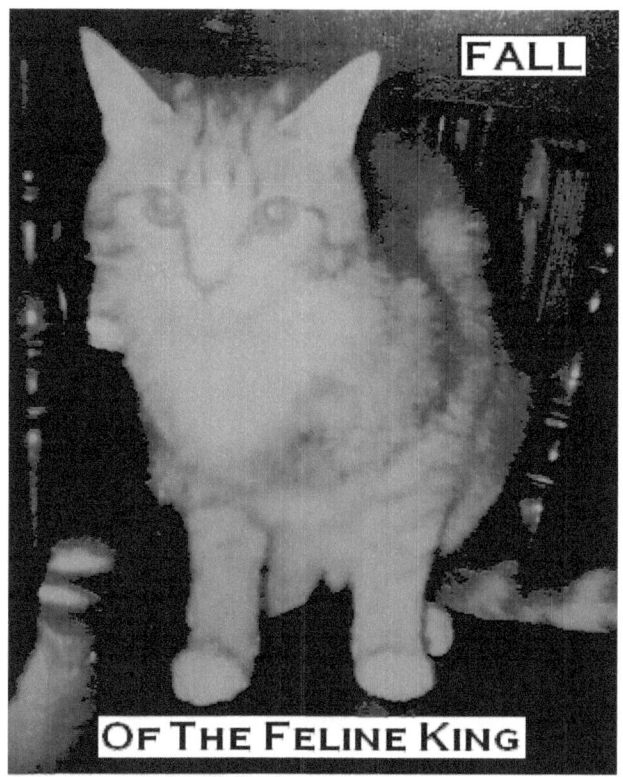

FALL

OF THE FELINE KING

Sean always takes care of his grandparents' pet cat when they leave town. He feeds it, waters it, plays with it, and does anything else he can do to protect and please it. But one day when the cat turns on Sean and attacks him for no apparent reason and the grandparents choose to side with the animal claiming that the young man must have done something to deserve the attack, Sean decides the cat must die.

5

FALL OF THE FELINE KING

Fall of the Feline King

"Sean, will you feed my cat while your grandfather and I go away on vacation next week?" Sean's grandmother asked. "Sure, I'll take care of him while you're gone," the young man responded. "Now remember, you have to feed him his dry food every night and when he's finished eating, you have to give him some of his treats. Then, in the mornings, you need to give him his milk. But remember, he doesn't like the regular skim milk that we buy, so he has to have special milk. You will remember all of this, right?" "Sure." Sean answered.

"Oh and also, you don't have to pen him up in the shed because he is an outside cat and can take care of himself." "Yeah, but do you remember the last cat that I penned up every time you went away so that I knew it was safe and then the one time when I didn't, he got hit by a car on the road?" "Now I told you a hundred times that these things happen and that it wasn't your fault! I'm not going to worry about this cat this time around, I'm just going to enjoy my trip and I'm not going to worry about him and you shouldn't either. He has everything he needs here and if he thinks he has to go off somewhere and get killed, that's his problem. But I don't want you worrying about this cat because he should know better by now not to go out on the road." "Yeah, but the last cat died because you weren't here and he wasn't used to my schedule, so naturally, he thought that you had abandoned him and was probably off to find a new home. And besides, this particular cat, the one that you have now, likes being in the shed." "I know, really, but you have your own problems to worry about. Just feed the cat and let him be responsible for himself this week. He's an adult cat, so there is absolutely no excuse for him to be stupid and get smashed on the road." "Okay, then, I'll just make sure he has food at night." "That's all that I ask."

A week later when his grandparents departed for their vacation, Sean went to their house to feed the cat as promised. Every night he did this and while he was there, he fed the cat well and spent time with it, playing with it, talking to it, and petting it. The cat seemed appreciative of being given this attention. "You're a good cat, aren't you, Mitch?" Sean would say to the skinny, orange tabby cat among other things to keep the purring animal content while his owners were away on their vacation.

127

At the end of the week when his grandparents returned to their home, Mitch, the cat was happy to see them again. He purred and rubbed up against Sean's grandmother's legs. "Thank you for taking care of my cat," she said to her grandson, "perhaps you should care for my cat every time we go away." Sean simply nodded and over the next four years, he took good care of the cat every time his grandparents went away.

"Oh my god, there's the cat! Let's pull its tail and rip out its fur!" screamed Sean's eight year old cousin, Heather. "Oh, I see the kitty! Let's harass the hell out of it and make it totally miserable!" screamed Lindsay, Heather's four year old sister. Then, the two little girls went charging at the cat, screaming his name and waving their arms in the air as they ran. Sean watched as the pupils in the cat's eyes dilated with fear and as his fur stood up and puffed out. The terrified cat then jumped into Sean's arms for protection.

"Why does the cat like you so much?" Lindsay asked Sean. "Well, maybe it's because I'm nice to him and I don't try to chase him away." "But we're just playing with him," the little girl replied. "Yeah, I know, but this is a cat, not a dog. Cats don't really like that kind of attention, so if you chase him, he'll just get scared and run away and then he'll hide every time he sees you." "You lie, Sean, you're a liar!" screamed Heather. "What do mean?" Sean asked. "The cat only likes you because you play the guitar! I saw on television that animals like music too and that some times they like to play in a band! I bet that cat plays the drums and you two have some kind of secret band that nobody knows about!" "Yeah!" screamed Lindsay. "Uh, yeah, well as cool as that would be, I'm afraid that animals don't really play in bands. I think what you saw was just a cartoon, which means it's not real." "Well then why does the cat like you?" Lindsay asked again. "It's like I told you, because I'm nice to him," Sean answered, but needless to say, the two little girls continued to scare the cat away every chance they got until it came to the point where the cat wouldn't even come around if it knew they were there.

Then one summer on the fourth of July, Sean and his girlfriend were taking a walk in the development behind his grandparents' house. They were both a little drunk as they walked, talked, and enjoyed the fireworks that filled the air. It was a really calm evening with clear skies, which made it perfect for the holiday tradition of setting off fireworks. The couple was thoroughly enjoying the evening's festivities when they arrived in one section of the development where the neighborhood children were also setting off fireworks of their own. The air was thick and heavy with smoke and the smell of burning gunpowder and the sky would light up with each and every loud explosion of the fireworks. And then, in-between the noises of the fireworks, Sean heard something familiar: the frightened crying of a cat coming from a bush just a few feet away. Sean and his girlfriend walked over to the bush to see what it was and sure enough, there was Mitch, the skinny orange cat that belonged to Sean's grandparents. He was so frightened that he couldn't find his way home, so Sean picked him up and carried him home.

About a year or so later, Sean walked over to his grandparents' house to visit. They were both sitting out on the back porch with their cat. When the cat saw Sean, it ran away. Sean thought nothing of this until he noticed a repetitive pattern: every time the cat saw him, it ran for its life. Pretty soon, Sean's grandparents and all of his relatives that knew of the cat were making jokes and laughing about how much the cat hated him. Sean couldn't figure out why the cat would hate him, so he ignored the jokes and continued to live his life like nothing had ever happened between him and the cat.

When another year had passed and Sean was walking to his grandparents' house one day, he stepped onto the back porch. There, curled up on a chair was the cat. While walking past the cat to get to the back door of the house, Sean instinctively lowered his hand to pet the cat, not thinking anything of it at all. Then, to his great surprise, the cat bit his hand, sinking its front teeth all the way into the young man's flesh and wouldn't let go. The cat then proceeded to sink its front claws into Sean's arm and start kicking his wrist with its back claws, completely breaking the skin and causing him to bleed.

While screaming in pain, Sean slammed the fist of his free hand into the cat's head and managed to pull his arm away from the vicious animal that had absolutely no reason for doing what it did. Sean entered the house and cleaned up his wounds. "What happened to you?" his grandmother asked. "Oh, the cat got me for no apparent reason. I just tried to pet him and he attacked me." "WHAT?!" the woman shouted. Sean smiled because he thought the cat was in trouble for what it had done, but to his surprise, the cat wasn't the one she was mad at. "What did you do to my kitty?! He didn't just hurt you like that! You must have done something to deserve this!" This angered the young man. "You mean to tell me that your cat massacres my arm and you're siding with him? I did nothing to that asshole! Nothing at all – I was just being nice to him. So now if I just randomly hurt somebody like this for no reason, would it be okay? Would you just assume that that person did something to deserve it? Do you always blame the victim? Or would I need actual proof that they did something to me? So if I ever do this to somebody, I would need to have a reason for it, but this cat can do whatever he wants for no reason at all with absolutely no recourse?!" "NO! NO! NO! NO! Even if you did have a reason for doing that to somebody, you still don't! It would still be wrong, reason or no reason!" "But that makes it even worse then! You're telling me that the cat can hurt people with absolutely no reason whatsoever, but I can't even do a fraction of this kind of harm to somebody even if I had all the reason in the world?! What, do you really think that an animal can do no wrong at all, that they are without fault, without sin, without flaw? Do you mean to tell me that your cat is innocent just because he is an animal as where if I did the same thing, it would be wrong? What the hell is different about it?!" "Well you know better. The cat doesn't know what he's doing; he doesn't know any better, so that makes it okay. Attacking people who make him mad is just a part of his instincts and culture, but you and I live in a society of rules, so is not okay for us to act like that. Therefore, even if the cat had no reason to do what he did, you are still at fault!" "Yeah," the young man's grandfather spoke up, "and I saw you hit the cat." "Well it's no wonder he hurt you then! You hit him! I would have bit you too!" the grandmother exclaimed. "But I only hit him because he bit me! It was the only way I could free my arm!" "That doesn't matter," the grandfather commented. "So not only did you hit him, but then you interrupted his revenge on you? You should march right back out there and put your hand back into that cat's mouth and let him finish your punishment!" the young man's grandmother said. By this point, Sean was extremely angry and went home without saying another word, because it was obvious to him that his grandparents were under the rule of the feline king; they seemed clearly blinded by the supposed cuteness of the spoiled cat that had tricked them into being its servants in the yard it had apparently perceived as its kingdom, therefore making the couple blind to reason and all arguments absolutely pointless.

The next time he went to visit his grandparents the cat was sitting on the same chair on the back porch. While keeping his distance from the spiteful, backstabbing creature, Sean rolled up his sleeve to reveal his scarred arm. "You see what you did?" he asked the cat. "Do you see that? You did that to me. After everything I've done for you. After I've fed you and took care of you, after I've protected you from the little kids and fireworks, this is how you repay me? Well, fuck you then, because one day, your empire will crumble and I won't be there to protect you." Suddenly the young man's grandparents emerged from the house and onto the porch. "Its nice out, so let's sit out here today," his grandmother said, so the young man complied and sat down on a chair far away from the cat.

The three people visited like always, by talking and sitting on the porch. But eventually, the cat got off his chair and walked over to Sean, jumped up onto his lap and clawed his chest right through his shirt. Then it ran away. As Sean's white t-shirt became stained with blood, his grandmother laughed her head off. "Wow! That cat really hates you! I can't wait to tell everybody about this!" That was when the young man decided that the cat needed to die.

That night, Sean walked to his grandparents' house and as slowly and as quietly as he could possibly be, he crept up onto the porch and approached the chair that the cat was sleeping on. Slowly, he positioned his leather-gloved hand directly in front of the animal's sleeping face and then with speed and accuracy, he grabbed the cat's head. The animal immediately woke up and began thrashing its feet in an attempt to claw the young man. "That bullshit won't work tonight, asshole," he whispered to the struggling beast.

"Tonight is the night you die," Sean told the animal as he violently and brutally began punching the cat in the stomach as hard as he could. "After all I've done for you over the years, you somehow think its okay to hurt me? After I've fed you and took care of you all of those many times, you want to bite the hand that feeds you? After all the times I've protected you from the little kids and from the fireworks, now all of a sudden, I'm not good enough for you?! You think you're so cool attacking me for no reason and then you have the nerve to hide from me?! What, were you afraid that I'd be nice to you or something?! Oh, how horrible I must be to think that it would be okay to be nice to you, you ungrateful, furry-ass son of a bitch!" Sean whispered as he punched the cat, but then it managed to free its head as it cried out in severe pain and then it tried to bite the young man, but only to get its teeth knocked out as it was brutally punched in the face. "I don't think so, asshole!" the young man said to the cat as he continued punching it like a punching bag at the gym. But then it managed to get away and speedily ran across the yard, away from its assailant.

"I DON'T THINK SO, PUNK, YOU'RE NOT DEAD YET!!!" Sean belted out as he produced a bow and an arrow and lit the tip of the arrow with a cigarette lighter. Then he quickly aimed it at the absconding animal and let the arrow fly through the air, striking the cat all the way across the yard. The flaming arrow stuck in the cat's side as the flames began to engulf the beast's entire body, scorching its stupid orange fur. The beast began to stagger around the yard, completely disoriented as fire consumed its body. "NOW YOU KNOW WHAT IT FEELS LIKE TO BE BETRAYED, YOU BACKSTABBING SON OF A BITCH!!!" Sean roared at the beast.

The cat continued to stagger about the yard disoriented as it cried out in pain. Finally, it approached the fish pond and fell into the water. Steam filled the air as the fire was extinguished. The now completely hairless animal simply treaded water as it thought it was safe. Then, a few minutes later when it thought it was ready it began to climb out of the pond. But suddenly, a large snake jumped out of the water and wrapped its entire body around the cat, slowly constricting the animal to death as it glared at its excited young spectator. "I am proud to inform you that your reign is over and you shall rule no more, for I have overthrown your sick monarchy, Sir Royal King Ass Face!" Sean said as he watched with the satisfying feeling of triumph as the snake unhinged its jaw and slowly began swallowing the dying cat whole. When the cat was completely devoured, the snake, now with a huge, cat-sized lump in its stomach, slithered back into the pond and disappeared deep into the murky water.

Sean returned to visit his grandparents about two weeks later and they informed him that they had not seen their cat for some time, nor could they seem to find him. "I wonder what happened to Mitch," the young man's grandmother said, "we haven't seen time for a long time and I kind of miss him. I thought it was so hilarious how he hated you so much and I always got a kick out of watching him run away when he saw you! Oh well, I just wonder what happened to him." Sean smiled grimly and responded, "I guess we'll never know.

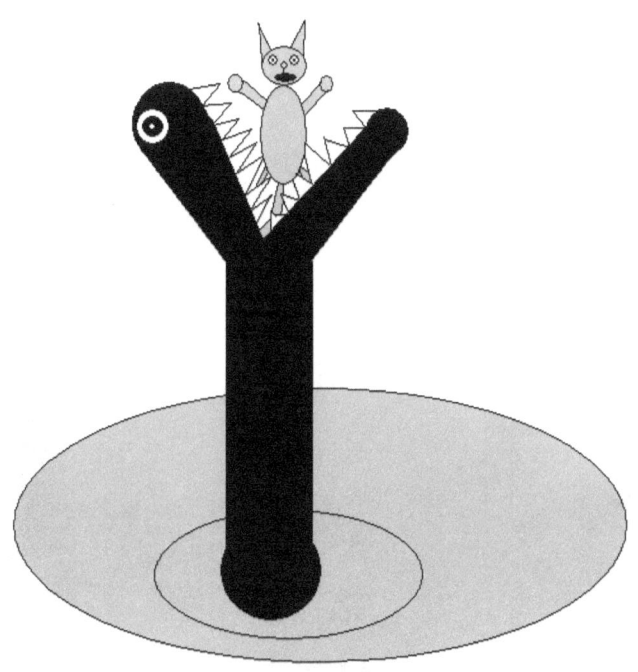

"I am proud to inform you that your reign is over and you shall rule no more, for I have overthrown your sick monarchy, Sir Royal King Ass Face!"

133

Copyright 2008 by Anthony G. Roof

The small rural town of Oak Springs, West Virginia is a quiet and peaceful place to live and work until the town experiences a crime wave. As the crime rate increases, the local police department enlists the help of the most feared man in town: Frank. Living in an abandoned mansion in the middle of a cemetery, Frank uses an old hearse as his patrol car. When he catches violent criminals, he secretly locks them in caskets and deports them to the town of Hell, Michigan. Eventually, when the corrupt mayor of the town begins to suspect foul play, Frank makes him disappear as well.

6

HELL UNFOLDS

Hell Unfolds

The inhabitants of Oak Springs, a small rural town located in the backwoods of West Virginia, were very friendly, yet stubborn people. Most of them were upper middle-aged to elderly folk and by nature, they tended to be very conservative and skeptical of new ideas and change of any kind. The town's population at the time was approximately 20,000 and steadily growing, which, by some, was considered to be significantly large for its location and the period in which it existed. Of that number, the senior residents of the town worked hard to promote good values and morality because the traditions, old customs, and principles that the town was built on were very important to many of the people living there. It was in this way that the townspeople found true happiness; by practicing many of the virtues that they all claimed to nurture, such as peace, love, and harmony. Such a concept could easily be described as having a simple relationship with their God, without all of the bells and whistles of modern-day organized religion. In fact, it was just a different time; a time when people kept things in perspective by practicing what they preached in their attempts to live up to their fullest potentials so that they could easily enjoy the gifts of their day that resulted from their highly productive rural farming lifestyles.

While the residents of Oak Springs were proud and simple people who believed in love and helping one another, they were also protective of their town and dedicated to preserving the values of their culture by remembering and celebrating their rich heritage. This meant that although the townspeople warmly welcomed strangers and were always willing to offer a helping hand to someone in need, they were not hesitant to resort to violence if they believed that it was necessary for the protection and preservation of their small and delicate society. Such dedication to the town often manifested itself through violent disputes with seemingly ill-minded strangers and brutal assaults upon perpetrating criminals who were caught engaged in their illegal activities. In fact, despite the intents of the protective actions carried out by the townspeople being almost completely contradictory to their religious teachings and beliefs, the actions actually carried out were done so to the most reasonable degree possible to avoid walking on the line of hypocrisy and unnecessary sinning, as well as to be fair to the people whom the town was being protected against. Though controversial, it was meant to be a simple, yet understandable concept of protecting what they had worked so hard to create, nourish, and preserve through police ideology and not an ordeal of senseless slaughtering in a morbid parade of brutality and gruesome bloodbath. Because of this common understanding among the townspeople, if a well-known resident was witnessed assaulting or manhandling a stranger, it was often overlooked and ignored; generally witnesses of such activity usually minded their own business and simply assumed that the resident was only taking responsibility for his or her own personal safety.

One man in particular was very interested in protecting himself and his hometown. His name was Frank and he had grown up in Oak Springs in a family with a rich history of farming and had lived in the town his entire life. Frank was a tired, middle-aged Caucasian man who worked very hard for everything that he had in life. Though going against the family's grain, he labored twelve hours everyday of the week as an independent contractor within the town and a hired construction worker in other towns and as a result, he was financially secure and doing relatively well in life. Although his career was demanding and tough, Frank greatly enjoyed his jobs and was grateful for each and everyday that he was alive. However, Frank realized that he was only going to live once, so he was not in anyway about to sit back and allow criminals to invade his property to steal away his hard-earned assets and belongings, nor destroy the harmony of his beloved town. These things had happened before and since the last incident that occurred on his property, Frank had become an intolerant, merciless, protective, and almost cold-hearted person to suspicious looking strangers whom he was highly skeptical of. In fact, Frank was very protective of himself and everything even slightly related to himself, like his property, his vehicles, his town, his friends, his family, his job, his heritage, and even his beliefs. Nobody could even begin to suggest the possibility of equating Frank to the concept of selfishness because the protection that resulted from his convictions covered and served the entire town much better than the local police department could ever hope of doing themselves. Because of this, Frank was a very valuable member of the community. He protected and served just like a police officer but better and on top of his own demanding daily obligations. Frank was a man with a mission; he was not a force to challenge, because he was an undefeated and undisputed hero of the small town. In fact, to many, he was both a feared and respected mercenary whose best friend was a handgun.

Frank owned a large, seventeenth century gothic stone mansion that sat in the middle of an enormous cemetery spanning for acres. The house had a very interesting history that fascinated Frank to no end. As a child, he and his school friends would dare each other to sneak inside but none of them were ever brave enough to actually follow through with the dares. They were all deathly afraid of the old, abandoned structure and the many ghost stories and rumors featuring the house that circulated among the school children did nothing to help Frank and his friends overcome their intense fear of the building. But despite of all of his fears and nightmares, the mysterious old mansion remained a great legend that fascinated Frank well into his adulthood. Eventually, Frank overcame his fears and purchased the house, making it his home. As the years went by, the history of the old house slowly revealed itself to its curious new owner.

Frank had learned that the house at one time belonged to the cemetery owners and served as the caretaker's homestead. Back in those days, modern mortuary work was in its infancy and a very gruesome job that nobody ever wanted to do, so anybody who did agree to take the job was highly compensated and treated with great respect. This was mainly due to the fact that finding all of the necessary personnel with which to staff a cemetery was so difficult, that often there would be only one employee who performed all of the chores and that was the caretaker. But not only was it the mansion's purpose to provide shelter for the caretaker; it also had to serve as a funeral parlor located on site for the convenience of grieving families that chose to bury their loved ones in that particular cemetery. As time went by and mortuary and burial practices became simpler with technology, more and more people were employed to work for the cemetery. This advance in cemetery management eliminated the job of the traditional caretaker and spurred business. As a result, the cemetery eventually filled up and was turned over to the township. The land and the mansion quickly fell into disrepair and when it was realized that nobody visited the premises anymore, the township made the decision to demolish the mansion, remove all of the grave markers, and build an interstate highway over the valuable land. Surprisingly, nobody spoke out against this proposed desecration, even people who had family members buried there, because the cemetery had become so gloomy and frightening that nobody even wanted to see it anymore. All of this was happening right around the time when Frank, completely oblivious to the news, made his decision to purchase the property. It was his good timing that saved the old building and cemetery from demolition, but much to the dismay of the townspeople who feared the property intensely.

Frank remembered the day that he had purchased the mansion in quite vivid detail. It was also the day that the mansion was scheduled to be demolished and Frank just happened to be driving by and noticed all of the heavy equipment parked within the confines of the cemetery and an orange spray painted sign nailed to the mansion door that read "CONDEMNED – KEEP OUT." As a skilled construction worker, Frank knew that there was nothing structurally wrong with what he considered to be a beautiful, historic building, and as a historian he felt that it would be a crime to destroy a building dating back to the late 1600's. And even though he was not thrilled by cemeteries, Frank could not help but to feel that demolishing such a large field of graves was disrespectful beyond all belief. "Those idiotic morons," Frank thought as he drove slower and slower in an effort to get a better look, "How could they be so ignorant? I don't know why people are so afraid of that awesome house. I would pay a lot of money to be able to live in it. Well, maybe I can just drive up and get a better look. I'm sure they won't mind."

Frank slowly turned onto the long, gravel road leading into the old, run-down cemetery, passing the big, rusted, metal gate as he drove up the hill towards the mansion. When he reached his destination, Frank turned off his pickup truck's engine and stepped out onto the weed choked lawn just in front of the mansion. He looked around at the property and was disgusted with how badly it had been neglected over the years. Grass, weeds, and random trees were growing all over the place and many of the tombstones were broken and faded, some dating back to the early 1700's. Many of the newer, larger, marble stones were covered in dirt and thick vegetation and some were even covered in spray-painted graffiti. Frank could not believe some of the things that had been spray-painted onto several of the stones within his sight. Phrases like, "Siegfried is a faggot," "Michael sucks," and "See you in Hell, motherfucker," desecrated the markers of the final resting places of their owners. "Oh well, whatever. I just came to see the house," Frank thought as he walked up a slight hill and into the cool and serene shadow of the enormous structure standing before him.

The house was very old and run-down. Most of the archaic, gothic style arched windows were broken and the heavy grayish-blue limestone of its exterior that was not covered by the dense growth of

140

ivy vines was badly weathered and faded. All of the visible wood surfaces on the outside of the house, like windowsills and doors, were severely bleached by the sun and rapidly decaying. The lawn surrounding the house was littered with thousands of pieces of broken slate from the roof and from what was visible of it, Frank noticed thick patches of heavy, green moss growing on the structure. The intrigued man stood in silence as he studied the decaying building, depressed by its pending fate of demolition. "This is sad," he thought as he rested his hands on his hips and gazed up at the roof once again, totally losing himself in thought as he studied the tall, stone towers that graced each end of the building. "CAN I HELP YOU, SIR? YOU BETTER HAVE A DAMN GOOD REASON FOR TRESSPASSING! WHAT IS YOUR BUSINESS HERE?!" a loud voice suddenly demanded, startling the unsuspecting Frank as he nearly jumped out of his skin and spun around to face his visitor with a sickened and startled sense of rage.

Frank took a deep breath and could feel his heart having palpitations from the sudden scare. When he was finally able to think again and had fully turned to the source of the voice, he realized that he was standing face to face with the mayor of the town. The mayor was a very serious man who was once noble, caring and protective of citizens much like Frank, but only before he was driven insane and corrupted by his encounters with cold-blooded criminals who constantly threatened the town's prosperity. But these days, he trusted nobody but himself and was now a notorious, bitter old man who hated everybody and lived his selfish life only to pursue his own greedy interests. His name was Donald Furnington and everybody in town feared the hateful man. The only reason he had been able to serve as the mayor of the town for so long was because the leaders of other towns feared him as well and so the townspeople of Donald's territory usually got the better end of the stick when it came to negotiations with neighboring communities. But other than that, the townspeople avoided Donald and very rarely attempted to speak with him out of the fear of negative consequences. As Frank stood there, paralyzed in fear at the sight of Donald, his arch nemesis who constantly tried to imprison him for his intolerant, take-no-crap attitude and town-protecting qualities, Frank could see that Donald was becoming impatient. "Well? I asked you a serious question! You will answer me right now or I'll have the police take care of you!" the old man snarled as his dark pupils narrowed and became almost snake-like in appearance above his curled upper lip. Frank realized that he needed an excuse, so he said the first thing that came to his mind without giving any thought to what he was saying, "Uh, yes, Mr. Furnington! Please excuse my nervousness; you simply caught me off guard. Listen, I'm really sorry that I trespassed on this property; I didn't know the area was restricted. You see, I'm a construction worker and a historian and I've always admired this building. I heard that it was condemned and I came here looking for somebody that I could ask about the possibility of purchasing the property. But now that I found somebody, or rather have been found, would you like to talk about it or should I just leave? I'll gladly leave if you want me to; I'm really sorry that I intruded..." "NONSENSE!" Donald barked, "I wasn't born yesterday! I know you don't intend on buying this run-down, shit-hole property! What kind of sick morbid bastard would want to live in that old shack in the middle of a graveyard? What, do you also plan on hanging upside down from the rafters or sleeping in a coffin or something like a vampire? Or perhaps you plan on digging up rotting corpses to fuck? No, I'm not convinced. I know why you came here," the bitter old man snapped as he directed his glance at the graffiti on a large tombstone and then back at Frank. "Do you know what the penalty for vandalism is?" Donald inquired, even though his agenda was to perpetrate a greater form of desecration.

By this point, Frank was beginning to worry. "Uh, Mr. Furnington, I'm a construction worker, not a destruction worker. I didn't vandalize anything and even if I did, what does it matter to you? You're planning on bulldozing all of these graves anyway, which is very sick, I may add. Honestly, I was just curious about buying the property. I don't see how it is any of your business what my intentions are with it, but you have an opportunity to make some money and get this eyesore off of your hands. What do you say to that?" Frank mustered the nerve to say to the old man, but only after he had said it, he wondered if it was really a good idea. Nobody spoke to Donald Furnington like that; nobody. Donald was not pleased with Frank's attitude and it was apparent by the disgusted look on his bright red face as his stare burned deeply into Frank's soul. After a few minutes of awkward silence the old man replied, "Normally, I would serve you with a citation for being insubordinate to my authority, but you mention money. Now, I don't believe you for a second; I think this wanting to buy the land bit is all just an elaborate excuse to cover your ass for trespassing. But I'll tell you what. If you buy the property as it is right now at my price, I will let you off the hook. However, if you don't agree to buy the house, I will charge you for trespassing among other things and go out of my way to make your life a living hell. So what is it; yes or no?" Frank was completely caught off guard with this kind of answer. Of course, buying the land was just an excuse, but he didn't want to get into trouble and let Donald be right. He hated the old man's condescending, know-it-all attitude and strongly felt the need to prove him wrong. Frank decided to give in and buy the property. After all, he had always loved that old mansion. "How much?" Frank asked. "No, no, young man. You don't answer a question with a question. I asked you a question first. What is your answer; yes or no?" "I need to know your price before I can commit to it." "Look, you made the mistake of coming here so now you forfeit the convenience of organization in this deal. Yes or no?" Frank took a deep breath while looking down at his feet. "Yes," he answered.

There was a short pause and Frank glanced up to see Donald looking at him with a menacing smile on his crooked and greedy face. It was believed that nobody had ever seen the old man smile before, but there it was, right in front of Frank. The only problem was that it was not a pleasant or reassuring smile, but one that sent chills down Frank's spine. "Okay, very good," the old man began, "my price is two million dollars." Frank felt his jaw drop as cold sweat began to bead up on his brow. "W-W-W-WHAT?! ARE YOU INSANE?! THIS BUILDING IS SO OLD – THE ELECTRICAL WIRING IN IT IS SO ANCIENT THAT NO BANK WILL GIVE ME A LOAN OR A MORTGAGE TO BUY IT! WHO HAS TWO MILLION DOLLARS JUST SITTING AROUND LIKE THAT?!" Frank yelled at the old man. "Yes, sir, that's my price. You didn't think that I was going to sell this valuable land to you for less than I could potentially make from bringing in more business once this interstate highway was in place, did you?" Donald taunted with pleasure, as Frank felt the gradual losing of his temper. Frank paced around in disbelief. "Furnington, really, if that story was true, you would make far more than two million dollars, you know you would. Just admit it; you really have no intention on selling me this property. You just want to give me false hope so that I can scramble for cash on a wild goose chase before you and your henchmen come after me to cart my ass off to your sleazy jailhouse. I don't have time for that; I have a job and work to do," Frank tried to reason with the mayor, who was laughing with a sense of evil pleasure as he placed his fingertips together to form a pyramid of evil contemplation. "You sure are smarter than you look, son. Of course I don't want to sell the property to you, but if you were able to somehow pull off some miracle and come up with two million dollars, I would let you go free. You see, the reason I am so confident is because I know you'll never pull it off! Now, you have twenty four hours to pay me or you'll be promptly locked up." By this time, Frank was finding it difficult to cope with his anger. Slowly, while keeping his eyes trained on Donald's fat, red, laughing face, Frank reached into his jacket and tightly grasped his gun. Slowly, he began to pull it out, but before he could reveal the weapon, Donald took notice to what was going on and immediately stopped laughing. "I wouldn't do that if I were you. I don't believe I have to explain why not, now do I, young lad?" Frank knew that Donald was right and pushed the gun back into his jacket. "Meet me here this time tomorrow with my money or with your hands out to be cuffed," Donald bravely declared as Frank turned his back and walked towards his truck, boarded it, started the engine, and drove away.

As Frank drove away, he thought about the situation and whether or not it would be in his best interests to buy the property. Being a successful and wealthy working-class man, Frank had well over two million dollars invested in various savings and checking and different business accounts, but the problem was that most of his funds were invested in IRAs, retirement funds and cash deposits that tied his money up until a certain date. The money that he did have access to that he could actually spend was just a little over two million dollars, but he had plans for it to invest in more heavy construction site equipment. Although the money was there, it was not like Frank could just frivolously spend it on whatever he wanted. This was because all of his funds were there to serve practical purposes and so the budget that he could reasonably use for his own personal luxury and recreation was not at all large enough for buying expensive houses. In fact, at the time, Frank actually lived in a trailer park to keep his costs low, which was a testament to just how much of his money was actually tied up in the banks and his business interests. And so, as Frank drove, he weighed his options and realized that going to prison for a day and paying a few hundred dollars in fines was the much more economic choice, but he hated Donald so much that he could not resist the opportunity to prove him wrong and cause him to lose billions of dollars worth of income by preventing the construction of the new proposed highway. So, although a difficult decision to make, Frank decided to purchase the property when he discovered that he could free up some cash by putting off buying the new construction equipment for a few more months. And it was upon that decision that he wrote a check for two million dollars to the township and met the miserable old man in the cemetery the next day to pay him. Donald was devastated upon receiving the check, but there was nothing he could do about it due to the fact that the demolition crew was present and witnessed the whole meeting between Frank and Donald. "Get off my property or I'll call the police on you for trespassing!" Frank told Donald with a smile of triumph as the angry old mayor slowly walked away with his disappointed eyes to the ground.

Frank remembered that chapter in his life very well and in the most vivid detail, but that time was now just a distant memory in the past. He was now the sole owner of the property and did everything that he could to clean it up. As the years went by, he completely repaired and renovated the old mansion, accurately restoring it to its original appearance to the best of his abilities. He built a new wall around the cemetery and replaced the old rusted metal gate at the entrance of the property, repaired and replaced many of the damaged tombstones and kept the grass freshly mowed and the lawn healthy. However, although he had made the property look nice and presentable, most of the townspeople were still fearful of it. A few people overcame their fears and were grateful to Frank for saving the cemetery; this was evident by their frequent visits to the graves of their deceased friends and family members, but this number was quite small. Most people continued to avoid the property out of their fears and unease for the gloomy and eerie atmosphere that seemed to fill and surround the entire area, but Frank did not mind because he liked his privacy.

As time passed and Frank became an older, wealthier, and more respected figure in the town, he became active in the politics of the local government. Mayor Furnington continued to disrespect, mistreat, hate, and look down upon Frank, especially since their transaction involving the mansion. In fact, Donald would constantly go out of his way to oppose everything that Frank did, claiming that if a gun-toting street-prowling scoundrel supported something, it had to be a bad deal with corrupt intent. However, Frank ignored Donald's stupid remarks and worked hard to serve his town, because he had a greater agenda than fighting with the mayor, which was to keep the town safe from criminals as the population increased. Frank continued

145

to roam the streets at night in search of criminals, fighting with them, deterring them, turning them into the local police and even killing them when necessary, but he now also served in the local government of the town because he believed that he could better influence the system from within. As Frank continued to protect his town, many of the townspeople, despite their great respect for him, continued to fear him. These days, Frank's vehicle of choice was an old, black 1950 Cadillac hearse that he had found in the mansion's accompanying carriage house and restored to its original driving condition. He would often drive up and down all of the streets in the town, dressed in his usual attire of all black clothing, listening to his favorite heavy metal music and smoking a cigar as he patrolled the streets in search of criminals. It was no wonder that the townspeople feared him, but Frank just hoped that criminals would as well.

The nights were long and boring for Frank as he patrolled the town because the event of actually locating, identifying, and picking up a criminal was a rather rare occurrence. However, for Frank, it was all worth it due to the local police department's strong appreciation of his services and his highly held belief that there was no better feeling than being appreciated for protecting and serving his community. Just about every night, Frank would go out on patrol, usually to finish empty handed. But then, one night, as Frank was slowly cruising down the main street of the town, out of the window to his left, he was both excited and angered at what he saw in the shadows: a tall, thin man clad in bright, baggy clothing with an abundance of gold jewelry about his face and neck mugging an elderly woman at knife point.

Frank eagerly slammed on the brakes of the hearse and skidded to a stop diagonally in the middle of the street, completely blocking both lanes of traffic. Without even turning off the ignition, Frank hastily flung open the driver's side door of the car, jumped out, drew his gun and ran as fast as he could towards the scene of the crime. As he approached the startled criminal, Frank started screaming in a loud, deep voice, almost a loud, belting growl, the words "DROP WHAT YOU'RE DOING, ASSHOLE! STOP IN THE NAME OF THE LAW!" To this, the criminal dropped his knife and quickly ran down a dark alley. Frank ran after him, firing several shot as he ran, but to his great dismay, the criminal safely fled the scene. Feeling a sense of horrible disappointment and irritating grief at losing the perpetrator, the one and only criminal to ever escape him, Frank slowly walked back to the improperly parked hearse with its engine still running and driver's side door still wide open as loud heavy metal music flooded the streets from the speakers of the car's radio. As he approached the vehicle, the elderly woman walked up to him and asked if the criminal had gotten away. "Why yes, I'm afraid so, Mrs. Hearthside, I'm terribly sorry. I've never had that happen to me before," Frank responded. "Yes, yes, I know, Frank, you are a diligent young man and your heart is in the right place, but I do wish you would be a little more careful. You take awfully dangerous chances, you do." "I know, Mrs. Hearthside, but I have to for the protection and safety of Oak Springs. I try to be careful, but what about you? Are you okay? Are you hurt in anyway? Do you need a ride anywhere?" The elderly woman looked at her feet and then back up at Frank before speaking again. "Well, Frank, I think I'm okay; I don't seem to have any bruises or cuts. Only problem is that I have no money now because of that selfish rascal. Can you drop me off at the police station so I can report the crime and describe the man who robbed me?" "Sure," Frank answered. He was happy to help but he could not stop apologizing for his failure in catching the criminal as the two people walked to the hearse and Frank opened the passenger side door for the old woman before boarding the vehicle himself and turning off the radio.

"My, this sure is a dreadfully frightening patrol car, you've got here, young man," the old woman observed. "An old hearse; a rather odd choice of a vehicle, scary in its own ways," she continued, "Frank, I know you do the community quite a fine service and for free too, I may add, but why such an eerie car?" Frank sat in silence for a few seconds before answering, still disappointed with his failure in detaining the criminal. "Oh, the car, well, you know I own the cemetery and this was in the garage there. You're absolutely right, it is pretty scary; morbid actually would be a better way to describe it. But you see, Mrs. Hearthside, the whole point here is to scare criminals into submission. I choose to patrol in this car as a way of deterring crime, you see." "I suppose," the woman started as Frank pulled the hearse up to the police station, "oh, there it is! The station! And there is Officer Jacobs! I sure can't wait to tell him about this nasty selfish young man who robbed me! Thanks for everything Frank and you try to enjoy the rest of the night, you hear, and be safe!" As soon as Frank brought the car to a complete stop, the elderly woman opened the door and climbed out to greet Officer Jacobs who was standing on the sidewalk looking in the direction of the hearse. "HEY THERE, FRANK!" the officer shouted while waving as Mrs. Hearthside approached him. Frank did not respond; he was too in shock at his failure as he sat in the idling vehicle watching the officer wave to him. In fact, Frank watched as the police officer and the elderly woman walked up the large cement steps and entered the police station before he dared to drive away.

As Frank continued to patrol the streets that night in search of crime, he carried with him the great weight of disappointment. He had always believed in the strong moral values and the special ways of life of Oak Springs and it was upsetting enough to him to think that anybody could ever want to disrupt the harmony of such a great and humble community. That was why it was perfectly acceptable for the townspeople to act on their own accord when it came down to protecting the town or to taking responsibility for their own safety, taking into consideration that the police could not be everywhere at once. It was also why Frank patrolled the streets and worked close to the police when there was a serious job to be done; it was why Frank was even allowed to do the things that he did and to act in such a manner. But perhaps what bothered the troubled man the most was the very concept that within a small town heavily watched and patrolled by police, protected by Frank's violence and protected by the individual town residents themselves, that crime could even exist at all, especially considering how many of the neighboring towns that were larger in size and only had basic police coverage had a much lower crime rate. This meant to Frank that the crime rate in Oak Springs was way too high and out of proportion with its number of inhabitants, indicating only that criminals were invading the town in droves to escape the law enforcement of the neighboring communities. This thought made it difficult for Frank to clearly understand whether he was failing at his mission or whether Oak Springs was just simply playing criminal ping-pong with its neighboring towns. So far, since Frank had been patrolling the streets, his ideas have changed almost constantly as have the policies of the police department and now it seemed almost to the point where Oak Springs needed one set way of handling crime; one unchanging way that was final in its design and not open for debate – Oak Springs needed a final solution and Frank was thinking about the illegal deportation of captured criminals.

That night, as Frank sprawled and stretched his tired body upon his bed and stared at his dark bedroom ceiling, trying to fall asleep, his mind wondered intensely. "My final solution," he thought out loud to himself, "Final solution, hmm, it sounds a bit too Hitler-like. I am not a neo-Nazi; I'm just a man who is trying to keep his town safe and orderly. How can I fight fire with fire and win without becoming a corrupt hypocrite like Donald? After all, I wouldn't be in this house right now if that crook hadn't cheated me. The real question is how can I fight crime without becoming a criminal myself? If I deport the criminals that I catch in the hearse, nobody would know or even question what I am doing and sure, it would be illegal, but it would also cut down drastically on the crime rate in town. It would be a beneficial crime to the townspeople because it would keep them safe and happy. Hell, the government does it sometimes and they call it justice. When I do something illegal, it's a crime, but when the government does it, its justice? What a joke. Well, I have to think about it like this: what would the lesser of two evils be? Allowing criminals to run free after a short stint of locking them up, feeding them, housing them, and clothing them at the taxpayers' expense or just simply deporting them somewhere else, far, far away from here?" After having these thoughts, the tired, disappointed man yawned, felt his eyes getting heavy and rolled over onto his side. "Deportation it is," he said out loud and then, he fell asleep.

A few nights later, Frank was out on patrol and having a slow night when he decided to take a break and parked his hearse along the main street of the town. He put his cigar out and emerged from the vehicle with the intentions of walking to the bar just half a block down the street. After stretching his back, he stepped up onto the sidewalk and began walking in a slow and steady pace in the direction of the bar, when suddenly a black leather-gloved hand grabbed Frank by the face, covering his mouth, followed quickly by a sharp knife poking him roughly in the back. "Make one move and I kill you, mudda-fugga, I shank you up and spill yo blood all over the place, fool!"

Just then a million thoughts began to surge through Frank's mind as he awaited his yet unknown fate with his sick-minded fear of death and bitter feelings of defeat and disappointed as his assailant's knife was slowly pushed harder and harder into Frank's back. Frank wondered why such a crime was happening to him, since most people tended to avoid him, but just then the criminal spoke in such a way that it answered Frank's question. "You thought you were so cool da other night, like you were da hero of the day of somethin'. You had to be Mista Tough Guy, didn't you, by puttin' yo nose where it didn't belong. Mah homies and I, we gots enough problems just by dealing with the po-po, but you aint no cop, you should be mindin' yo own business! I don't know what yo job is, but whatever it is, I don't tell you how to do yo job, so you shouldn't be out on da streets tellin' me how to do or not to do mine, sucka!" And then it clicked; to Frank, it all suddenly made sense. This was the criminal who had gotten away from him the other night. Frank had forgotten that a criminal always returns to the scene of the crime, but here he was again and this time in contact with Frank! "What a wonderful opportunity," Frank thought to himself, "to have another chance to catch this sleaze bag and also to test my new deportation strategy! This is so great! A second chance!" A jubilant and grateful Frank began to fill with excitement at his discovery, when just then the criminal shoved the knife even deeper into Frank's back, giving him the ultimate reality check. "Oh, yeah," the now disappointed man thought, "he's the one who caught me, it wasn't me catching him. Look's like I'm screwed because he'll probably kill me now since I pose a threat to him and his slime-ball criminal friends...." Frank's thoughts trailed off as he was interrupted by the criminal shoving him into the alley as a police car drove by. Once in the dark alley, the criminal shoved Frank against an exterior building wall and put the knife to his throat so that the blade was actually breaking the skin and shedding a small amount of Frank's blood. "What, you daydreamin' or somethin'? You not appreciate the seriousness of da situation? Why you not signal to me or nothin' when you saw that pig mobile comin'? Yeah, fool, you'd love dat, wouldn't you, cops all at me again! I don't think so, punk!!!" the criminal screamed into Frank's face, sending large amounts of spit as well. Just then, it again dawned on Frank just what was going on. He realized a second time that he had not finally caught the criminal who had gotten away before, nor had he been caught be a random criminal who wanted to kill him, but rather, he was caught by the same criminal from before who now wanted to kill him! The criminal who had Frank so filled with disappointed, sorrow, grief, and rage for the last few days; the same loser who had caused Frank to lose sleep the night before and now he wanted to kill Frank! Frank could hardly cope with his sickened sense of disbelief as his heart started pounding in his chest simultaneously with his anger filling him with hatred, both causing his muscle tissues to become tense as they filled with the blood that surged from his excited, racing and pissed-off heart.

"Okay bitch," the criminal began lecturing Frank, "dis is what's going down. You gonna give me yo money and I gonna take off down da alley. You try anything cute, I shank you. You do anything after I roll, me and mah homies hunt you down and end you! You got dat, lemon-squeeza?!" Of course, this remark only angered Frank even more and resulted in him having a total burst of adrenaline that went rushing through his body at an intense and painfully rigorous speed. Just then, Frank roared out an extremely loud and deep guttural growl as he slammed his boot into the criminal's crotch and pushed him over with both hands onto the paved floor of the alley way, completely catching him off guard. The criminal then quickly attempted to stab Frank in the leg with the knife, but Frank was too quick for him and stomped his boot down onto the criminal's hand with all of his strength, completely crushing it, complete with the sound of breaking bones as the criminal screamed in agony at the very top of his lungs. "Hey man!" the criminal pleaded, "what you doin,' man, we can work dis out! Let's rap, brotha!" "SHUT YOUR FACE, ASSHOLE!!! THE TIME HAS PASSED FOR NEGOTIATING!!! YOU SHOULD NOT HAVE FUCKED WITH ME!!! NOW YOU'RE GOING TO HELL!!!" Frank roared at an ear-shattering volume as he kicked the knife out of the criminal's reach.

Frank then produced his gun and a pair of handcuffs and ordered the criminal to get to his feet, which he did but with a bit of nervous hesitation. "Hey man, you no cop! You can't touch me! You breakin' da law, man!" the terrified criminal said with a shaky voice. "YOU'RE RIGHT, SCUM-BAG! I'M NOT A COP! I ONLY HAVE MORE AUTHORITY THAN THE POLICE, BECAUSE I AM A HIRED AGENT BY THE CHIEF TO DO WHAT I DO! SO I CAN DO WHATEVER I WANT TO YOU AND THERE'S NOT A DAMN THING YOU CAN DO ABOUT IT! AND FURTHER MORE, IT'S TOO LATE FOR YOU TO START WORRYING ABOUT WHAT THE LAW SAYS! IF YOU CARED ANYTHING ABOUT THE LAW WHATSOEVER, YOU WOULDN'T BE IN THIS MESS RIGHT NOW, SO SHUT YOUR FACE!!!" Frank screamed as he handcuffed the criminal and shoved the cold, metal barrel of his gun into his prisoner's back. "You wouldn't shoot me! You too scared of what mah homies gonna do to you when dey find out bout dis!" Frank yawned and then aimed his gun at the criminal's lower leg and pulled the trigger, sending a 45 caliber hollow-tip round into the flesh with a loud bang that echoed in the alley. "Oh, wouldn't I?" Frank asked as his prisoner screamed in intense pain and agony and hobbled on one leg. Frank stood firmly in place with no facial expressions whatsoever until the screaming had died down and eventually stopped before he proceeded. "Now," Frank warned, "this time, shut your mouth, keep it shut and do what I say or I'll do it again. Do you understand?" The criminal nodded quietly as Frank repositioned the barrel of his gun against the criminal's back and slowly directed him towards the parked hearse.

Once at the hearse, Frank opened the door the on the back of the vehicle and pulled the empty casket out half way on the rollers, just out far enough to open the first section of the lid, exposing half of the inside of the white-linen lined box. Then he looked over at the criminal who seemed to be paralyzed with fear at the sight of the casket. The pupils of his eyes were dilated along with the complexion of his skin being slightly paler and on top of it all, the leg that had been shot was now standing in a puddle of blood but the man himself was speechless. Frank laughed as he wondered what thoughts, if any, were going through his prisoner's mind just then. "Okay. Get in," Frank said to the criminal who just looked at him and back at the casket and then back at him again, all with a look of shock and disbelief on his face. Then the criminal started to speak the words, "hey man, is dis really necessary…" but stopped talking when Frank held up his gun to the criminal's head and cocked it. Slowly, the criminal climbed up into the hearse the best that he could with his injured leg and then carefully crawled into the casket, feet first, so that only the upper part of his body was exposed. Frank then spit a huge wad of flam thick from cigar tar into the criminal's face while smirking grimly with menacing laughter as his eyes gleamed with morbid delight, clearly proud of his triumph over the criminal who had defeated the town's crime control systems just a few nights earlier. But while Frank was enjoying the maiden execution of his newfound crime-handling methods, his prisoner's body was quickly becoming more and more tense from the worst feeling of terror that it had ever experienced in its entire life; a feeling so intense and beyond even the most evil of imaginations that the very thought of it seemed to shock every cell within the body into a hopeless state of instant helplessness. A short moment later as the laughter roared on, Frank slammed the casket shut, locked both sections of the lid, shoved the entire box back into the hearse on the rollers, and then completed the restraining of his captured prey by slamming shut the back door of the hearse. Then, while still inflicted by a state of nonstop laughter, the proud man reclaimed his seat behind the steering wheel of the vehicle, lit a fresh new cigar, started the engine, and drove off into the night.

As Frank drove home that night, he made it a point to play a compact disc of assorted black metal music featuring some of the most satanic bands in history from Norway and a few of the surrounding European nations at full, ear-splitting volume as an effort to instill an even more intense state of terror into the already fear-stricken criminal. As the disc played, the inside of the hearse was filled with the extremely loud and eerie sounds of classical music and down-tuned heavy metal, both played in minor keys and topped with the shrieking and growling vocals of pissed-off devil worshippers, all screaming at the very tops of their lungs about how much their lives sucked. However, during the quiet parts of some of the songs and while in between songs, the violent kicking and muffled screaming of the criminal became audible, filling Frank with a great sense of pride and amusement as he drove down the dark city streets.

When the cemetery became visible from the street, Frank turned the vehicle onto the narrow gravel road leading up to the mansion and drove up the hill into the dark night with the only light sources being the hearse's dim headlights and the light of the full moon that seemed to loom over the intimidating and spooky looking mansion that sat surrounded by old tombstones and large twisted trees on the top of the hill. But as the hearse reached the top of the steep hill, the violent kicking and screaming of the frightened criminal became louder and louder as the music blared on. Evidently the prisoner, used to the relatively flat city streets, noticed the steepness of the hill as the hearse traversed it and realized that he was being transported to some unfamiliar territory that was most likely not populated enough to sport a witness to what was occurring. Frank smiled as he thought of this and brought the hearse to a stop in the middle of the section of cemetery hidden in its location behind the enormous mansion. This location seemed to be the most fitting, because not only was it not visible from the street, but it was the only section of cemetery that had enough space in between burial plots for Frank to be able to dig a new grave without disturbing any of the surrounding graves. And so Frank turned off the engine of the hearse, though leaving the radio on repeat mode to play Black Sabbath's "Electric Funeral" just loud enough for his prisoner to hear over and over again, and climbed out to leave his prisoner inside to wait in fear as Frank prepared to dig a new grave.

One old and rusted spade of soil at a time, the new and shallow grave was dug under the dim and eerie light of the full moon as Frank's evil laughter filled the cool and calm air of the otherwise silent night. It was the silent, but perfectly fitting night; for the air was almost chilly to the feel with no wind or noise, the full, yellowish-white colored moon sat up in the dark skies with its subtle dried-blood colored craters occasionally interrupted by a slowly passing cloud and black and speedy bats filled the air as the cemetery echoed with menacing laughter. It was also about this time the kicking and screaming of the casket-caged criminal became more frantic, louder and rowdy, rocking the hearse back and forth on its parked and idle tires as the vehicle's suspension system slowly and quietly squeaked with every rocking movement.

Once the project had been fully completed to his satisfaction, Frank rushed into the mansion to produce a small bottle of chloroform; the colorless, volatile, heavy, and toxic liquid with an ether odor that he had planned to use on the criminal to initially produce a slowly confusing feeling of insensibility followed quickly by a numbing and defeating anesthesia effect. However, realizing the readily and widely recognizable smell of the substance, Frank decided to fill the half empty bottle with urine to produce a new but remarkably similar chemical that he called urinform; the same makeup of $CHCl_3$ but now combined with nitrogen, bacteria and the other common properties of piss. After quickly recapping the bottle and mischievously smirking with enthusiasm, Frank pulled on an old, black, hooded undertaker's robe, picked up an old, rusted sickle and exited the mansion with anticipation as he walked swiftly back to the parked hearse. Once where he needed to be, the innovative man gently shook the bottle for a few seconds to thoroughly mix the chemicals and then placed it in a robe pocket. He then produced his gun and unloaded it of all live rounds, promptly replacing them with blanks. After this, he re-concealed the weapon, put down the sickle and quickly got to work lugging out a casket-lowering mechanism from the carriage house and carefully arranged it over the open grave. Then, he opened the back door of the hearse and began slowly and carefully pulling out the casket and inching it towards the lowering mechanism. It proved to be a rather difficult task for one person to do alone but once his efforts proved successful, Frank purposely positioned the casket so that the lids would open away from the large pile of soil that he had removed from the earth when he dug the grave. "Let's get this interment started," Frank spoke out loud, answered only by the sudden kicking and screaming of the casket-bound criminal who had been quiet and still just a few minutes earlier.

With his heart now racing with excitement, Frank unlocked and opened the section of the lid that covered the upper part of the criminal's body, exposing his intensely frightened and worried face and violently heaving chest to the dim moonlight. When the fear-tortured prisoner saw Frank's shadow hovering above the casket, he panicked and asked Frank in a shaky and nervous voice what was going to happen but much to Frank's dismay. "SILENCE!" Frank roared as he slapped the criminal across the face with all of his strength, literally leaving a handprint on the left cheek. When the criminal cried out in pain, Frank hit him again and covered his mouth with a long piece of silver industrial-strength duct tape. Now not being able to speak, the jittery criminal began nervously peering outside of the casket, his eyes darting around at everything from the large pile of soil, to the several old and creepy tombstones, to the parked hearse and even up to the full moon. Then he looked back down to the casket that he was restrained in and his eyes began to fill up with an abundance of wet and steaming tears, much to his catcher's great feeling of victory and triumph. Frank smiled grimly with glee as he watched each and every one of the salty tears roll down the side of his prisoner's face; the few that did not manage to hastily crystallize upon his cheeks quickly soaking the white, fluffy pillow beneath his head. But just then, a dark cloud slowly began to pass the moon, slightly blocking out some its dim, yellowish light. Frank glanced up at the sky, his smile sluggishly fading and then looked back down at the criminal with a very serious look on his face. "The time has come," Frank began speaking as the local church's bells began tolling in the distance, "the time has come for your ultimate moment of truth." When the criminal heard this, he began squirming and Frank paused to produce both his gun and the bottle of urinform, just as a violent thunderstorm began to move in, filling the night sky with enormous streaks of bluish-white lightning followed by loud crashes of thunder.

　　Smiling, Frank held up the bottle for the criminal to see. "See this?" Frank spoke in a deep, almost evil growling voice, "this is piss; some from each of your victims, including Mrs. Hearthside and even myself. Why piss, you may ask? Because its symbolic of your crimes, your pitiful and piss-poor, ungrateful lifestyle during your time on this earth, your greedy and selfish piss-ant personality and more importantly, the most common and intensely felt emotion that you have caused all of your victims to feel; anger, or as more frequently phrased, being pissed-off. You see, by committing your crimes, you, in your own way, have pissed on each and every one of your victims as you violated them. And now, before you die and enter the kingdom of Hell, before I in a sense damn you, it is time to return the favor by allowing each of them to piss on you, literally, which tonight, they shall do through me." Frank told the uneasy and paling criminal just before pushing a button on a remote control, causing the song "Black Sabbath" to blare through the cemetery at full, ear-spitting volume as several tall pyrotechnic towers of fire randomly placed throughout the immediate area burned so hot that the criminal could feel the heat on his face although lying beneath the robed and sickle-baring figure of what appeared to be the Grim Reaper.

As the blaring song progressed and the lyrics, "what is this that stands before me; figure in black which points at me," filled the night air, Frank put down the sickle and extended his arm to point at the still casket-bound criminal without hesitation and then with both hands, the proud man uncapped the bottle and slowly poured it upon the criminal's face while laughing menacingly. As the chloroform began to take its effect and Frank noticed the criminal slowly beginning to pass out, he quickly grabbed his gun and aimed it at the criminal's head so closely that the muzzle of the barrel was practically touching the nose. "SEE YOU IN HELL!!!" Frank roared at the very top of his lungs before firing several blanks into the criminal's face, coinciding perfectly with the very last few seconds of consciousness. Without a trace of doubt, the criminal now thought he was dead, though unfortunately for him, he was not.

When Frank was absolutely sure that his prisoner was completely unconscious, he turned off the music and the pyrotechnics, took off the robe, put away all of the weapons and cemetery equipment that he had used in his prank and then finally, he gave the criminal an injection of another anesthetic that would keep him asleep for about another six hours. Frank then closed and locked the casket and carefully loaded it back into the hearse and closed the back door of the vehicle. When everything had been perfectly cleaned up and returned to its original state, Frank boarded the hearse and slowly made his way out of the town as heavy rain pounded down on the hearse and began to flood the city streets. Frank simply smiled as he set out on the long and tedious, seven and a half hour drive to the mosquito-infested swamps of Hell, Michigan, only stopping about halfway through the drive to inject the still knocked out criminal with yet another shot to prolong the state of unconsciousness and also to fill up the hearse's fuel tank with gasoline.

Upon their arrival in Hell, Frank drove around the town streets in search of the ugliest, most miserable section of swampland that he could find near a public road and stopped when he found it conveniently next to a large billboard featuring the phrase "Welcome to Hell" in huge, black, bold, capital letters with the word "Hell" painted to appear to be on fire. The side of the street that this billboard was on sat down in a swampy, mosquito-infested ditch that was also filled with rotting, maggot-covered road kill and an abundant amount of littered trash. When Frank spotted this, he climbed out of the hearse and opened the back door of the vehicle to pull the casket halfway out on the rollers. Immediately after completing this task, Frank opened the first section of the lid, grabbed the unconscious criminal underneath the armpits and pulled him out onto the street. Frank was then careful to position the criminal perfectly on the pile of road kill and trash along the side of the road in such a way that when he came to, the very first thing that he would see was the large billboard looming in front of him that welcomed him to Hell. Frank then made it a point to remove the handcuffs and opened and poured an entire bottle of whiskey all over the criminal, including his face and mouth and placed the empty bottle by the unconscious man's side. Promptly after completing those deeds, the clever, yet devious Frank then carefully opened the criminal's mouth, stabbed the tongue with a sharp knife to create a speech impediment, attached a festive-looking sombrero to the criminal's head with super-glue and removed his wallet, replacing it with a fake Mexican identification card. While staging all of these things, Frank was careful not to disturb the huge bags of cocaine, marijuana and heroin that the criminal already had in his possession prior to being captured, for these items would only add to the overall effect of the final solution for the criminal. Then, using a nearby pay phone, Frank called the local police to report the criminal for public drunkenness, quickly re-boarded the idling hearse, and began speeding all the way back to West Virginia.

When the criminal finally came to and realized that he had been sleeping, he could not help but to believe that what had happened the night before was just a horrible, horrible nightmare. But once he had wiped the sleep from his eyes and took a look around, the very first things that he noticed were the enormous "Welcome to Hell" billboard, the mosquito-infested swamps and the fact that he was lying on a pile of rotting, maggot-covered road kill reeking with the unbearable stench of death. Then he noticed the millions of mammoth-sized mosquitoes that were feasting upon his already swollen skin as the tanning sun began to bake him into the pile of decomposing animal carcasses. Screaming, the terrified criminal jumped to his feet and attempted to run away, but only fell flat on his face as pain surged through the bullet-shattered bones and torn muscle tissue in the calf part of his leg. To the panicking criminal, this only confirmed to him his death and admittance into Hell. "OH MAN! DIS CAN'T BE HAPPENIN' TO ME, MAN! I CAN'T BELIEVE I ACTUALLY IN HELL! DIS SUCKS, MAN! DER BE JUST NO WAY DIS CAN GIT ANY WORSE, MAN, JUST NO WAY!" The upset and frightened criminal struggled to sputter out despite his knife-inflicted speech impediment.

Just then, a police car approached the area where the criminal was sprawled out face down on the ground. Normally, the criminal would have attempted to run away at the very sensing of a police officer, but this time he decided there was no need to abscond due to the fact that he thought he was dead and in Hell and also because he did not want to strain his leg anymore than it already was; so, in a careless heap with disbelief, the criminal remained on the ground. "Sir, get to your feet now. You have been reported for public drunkenness. I'm going to have to ask you a few questions and do a few tests to confirm whether or not this is true, so get up slowly and do as I say," said the voice of an approaching police officer. "HEY MAN! I DON'T HAVE TO LISTEN TO YO! I BE DEAD NOW SO PISS OFF!" the criminal responded but to the police officer, such an answer was not very amusing. "Sir, you are not dead. Just get up and cooperate with us or you'll find yourself in even worse trouble than you are already in," the unusually patient officer tried again but devoid of luck. "MAN, I TOLD YO ASS, MAN! I DEAD! I DON'T HAVE TO DO NOTHIN' FOR YO! THIS IS HELL; I ALREADY BE A PRISONER SO YO CAN'T LOCK ME UP! DAT'S RIGHT – DER AINT NOTHIN' YO CAN DO TO MAKE DIS WORSE!!!" "Sir, you're not dead but you've obviously been drinking. If you really think you died and went to Hell then you are not fit to be out in public. Its okay to drink and get intoxicated now and then but you cannot legally do it in public like this. If it should happen to you at a bar or restaurant, that's fine, but you must remain there until you are sober again or unless you have a designated driver. But you can't be walking around like this in public;

158

its just plain illegal. Now get up and I'll go easy on you. I can tell you're obviously not from around here. Okay, so up with you, now." "MAN, YO THROUGH WIT YO JIBBA-JABBIN' CAUSE YOU CRAMPIN' MAH STYLE, MAN! I TELL YO AGIN, BIOTCH, DIS BE HELL, AINT NOTHIN' ILLEGAL HERE! NOW PISS OFF!" "Sir, just get up, I'm not going to tell you again, just get up, slow and easy – NOW!" "PISS OFF SLOW AN' EASY – NOW!!!" By this time, the officer had lost his patience with the insubordinate criminal.

The frustrated police officer took a deep breath as his face slowly became an even brighter shade of red. "GET TO YOUR DAMN FEET, ASSHOLE! I AM IN CHARGE HERE, NOT YOU, NOT THE DEVIL AND NOT ANY OF YOUR IMAGINARY, FAT, DRUNKEN SUPER-HEROS EITHER! I'VE BEEN PATIENT WITH YOU BUT NOW WE DO THINGS MY WAY!!!" the enraged officer shouted as he began violently kicking the criminal in the ribs. "HEY MAN, WUT DIS ABOUT?!" the criminal screamed back as another officer arrived on the scene. "Larry, what are you doing?" the new officer calmly asked. "This jerk is giving me a hard time and won't cooperate with my orders. He just keeps making these really smart-assed remarks when I tell him to get up off the ground." The new officer gently scratched his chin and spoke again, "Is this the call for the public drunkenness situation?" Larry nodded. "Well, Larry, it seems to me that he can barely speak English, I mean, listen to how he tries to pronounce such simple words and fails. And didn't you notice yet that he's wearing a sombrero? How do you miss a thing like that?" "Tim, okay, this is Hell. You run into all kinds here, besides, he's drunk." "HEY MAN! I TOLDS YO DIS WAS HELL!!!" the criminal interrupted but only to be ignored. "Well, I'll tell you what, Larry, I think this is much more than just a public drunkenness issue. We're going to have to take him in." "Okay, lets do it," Larry responded and with that, Tim and Larry handcuffed the criminal and lifted his entire body up and carried it to the back of a parked police car.

As the criminal was being transported to the Hell, Michigan Police Department, Officer Larry made several attempts to recite the criminal his rights under the due process procedure. However, the criminal kept interrupting with loud screaming of obscenities and violent kicking and thrashing around in the back seat of the patrol car. So Larry gave up and simply drove to the police department as the criminal went totally berserk in the back seat. When they had arrived at the department, Tim came to help Larry transport the kicking and screaming criminal into the building but found that it was not very easy to control the violently panicking man, so Larry cracked the criminal in the head with a baton and Tim sprayed a whole can of pepper spay into the criminal's face. These actions, however, did not improve the criminal's behavior but only made it worse. "I think we're going to need to tranquilize him," Larry volunteered and Tim agreed as he administered an injection into the criminal's arm. Within the minute, the criminal lost consciousness and began to slide to the floor. Tim and Larry once again lifted his entire body and carried it into a cell so that they could lock him up while they processed his information and another officer conducted a strip search.

A few hours later, Tim, Larry, the Chief of Police, and all other officers involved with the criminal had a meeting in the police department's conference room. "So, what did you guys find?" asked the chief. "Well, Chief," one officer began, "we've concluded that he is an illegal immigrant from Mexico because upon doing the strip search, we found a Mexican identification card, which makes perfect sense considering the sombrero and his lack of ability to speak English." The chief simply nodded and took a look at the identification card that the officer handed him. "Anything else?" the chief asked. "Well, he had a lot of drugs on him. Three huge Ziploc freezer bags of marijuana, cocaine and heroin, so we figure he was here on business," Tim replied. "Okay, drug trafficking. What else?" "That's really about it, on top of being drunk and disorderly," Larry answered. "So what are the total charges?" the chief asked, to which another officer answered, "illegal immigration, public drunkenness, disorderly conduct, resisting arrest, and illegal drug trafficking. So what do we do about this, Chief?" "I believe we're going to have to…" "Lock him up forever!" Tim interrupted. "Lock him up until he can pay his fines?" Larry offered. The chief just frowned and shook his head. "No. We can't lock him up forever, that wouldn't be fair to the hard-working tax payers of our humble town. Besides, how can he make the money to pay his fines if he's locked up in here? I'm afraid we're going to have to deport him. That being said, which two of you are up for the long drive to Mexico?" Larry and Tim looked at each other and smiled. Tim was slowly drifting off into a daydream about Mexican food and tequila and Larry enjoyed long drives. Finally, Larry volunteered, "Tim and I will do it, Chief, since we found this guy and brought him in, if that's okay with everybody here." The chief briefly looked around the room and upon returning his gaze to the two volunteering officers, he nodded approvingly. "Alright then, men, you better hit the road. It's actually a very long drive to Mexico; about twenty-five hours one way if I am not mistaken, so be sure to take plenty of tranquilizers with you to keep Santos or whatever the hell his name is, under control.

Upon being granted the chief's approval to make the trip to Mexico, Larry and Tim packed up a patrol car with everything that they would need for the long drive. When everything was in order, they carried the still-unconscious criminal out to the car, tightened his handcuffs, gave him another tranquilizer injection and locked him into the back of the vehicle. The two excited officers then boarded the vehicle themselves and began their trip down south. During their drive, they listened to the radio, talked, told jokes, ate donuts and even took turns driving and sleeping, stopping only occasionally for gasoline. Every so often, one of the officers would give the criminal another injection to keep him asleep for the entire drive; a ride they actually found enjoyable with the criminal kept quiet, since it was not often that they were paid to take long trips, which pleasantly broke up the monotony of their day to day jobs. In fact, they did not really mind the drive, due to the fact that being police officers provided the convenience of being able to drive as fast as they wanted to, which made the overall trip take considerable less time than it should have.

Upon crossing the border and arriving in Mexico, the two officers pulled over to the side of the street, got out of the car and pulled the sleeping criminal from the back seat. As Larry held the criminal still to keep it from falling, Tim removed the handcuffs and together the two officers brutally heaved the still unconscious, sombrero-clad criminal into a ditch along the side of the road. They then took the opportunity to urinate, which they made a point of doing on the criminal, before reclaiming their seats in the idling patrol car to depart from the scene. The two police officers then drove far away to enjoy the rest of their day in Mexico before leaving to return to Michigan the very next day.

As the criminal was beginning to wake up, all he could feel was the intense pain of his sunburned skin and swollen leg. He was still wet with piss but now also soaked with his own sweat as the temperature easily exceeded one hundred degrees Fahrenheit. Slowly, the criminal climbed to his feet and carefully worked his way out of the ditch. He limped around the hot, desert streets but could not find another living person for miles around. He was very thirsty so when he found a small, stagnant pound, he took a drink to quench his unbelievable thirst, however, drinking that water made him urinate blood for almost three straight days. When the criminal eventually made his way into a large, Mexican village, he found it impossible to communicate with anybody there because nobody spoke English. Instead, the Mexicans, all of them wearing modern clothing, believed that the sombrero-clad criminal was making fun of their culture and national heritage. As the criminal tried to speak with his knife-inflicted speech impediment, the Mexicans thought that he was mocking their native tongue. These things irritated and angered the Mexican people so much that they took turns brutalizing the criminal and upon finishing they had him locked up in a Mexico City jail cell for the rest of his miserable life, which to him was a true example of Hell unfolding upon the dismal earth to swallow him up forever.

Meanwhile, Frank had long since returned to West Virginia and upon his arrival in Oak Springs, he was confronted by the local Chief of Police, whom came knocking on the mansion's front door. "Frank, I don't know what you did, how you did it, or where you've been for the last few days, but I have to tell you, something has happened around here lately. There's virtually no crime at all; it's like something bad has happened to the gang leader of the criminal underground and now all the criminals are too afraid to do anything illegal. From what I hear, the word on the street is that somebody has captured or kidnapped one of the toughest, most notorious criminals in the tri-county area and has somehow made him disappear. I mean, it's really weird around here; you know, like the calm before a storm – the kind that you think are going to be really bad but then never actually come. We literally have no crime rate at all anymore because of a rumor that's going around that somebody has made an example of this one guy," the chief excitedly but with evident confusion, informed Frank. "Well, Chief, that is certainly good news. I wonder what happened. Oh well, I guess we'll never really know for sure," Frank answered with a devious smile on his face. The chief started laughing. "Frank, I know you had something to do with this. But don't worry, I'm not going to harass you or try to bust you or anything like that. I just came to thank you, which I want to do on behalf of all of the citizens of Oak Springs, whom now can all go about their lives feeling safer than they had previously. So, thank you, Frank, it really means a lot to us all," the chief said as he shook Frank's hand. Still keeping a straight face, Frank replied, "Well, you're very welcomed, Chief, but I really don't know what you're talking about. I'm glad to hear the good news, though." "Well, whatever, Frank, nevertheless, whether you did anything or not, I still just wanted to fill you in on this wonderful news." "Thanks, Chief," Frank answered as he closed the mansion door. Slowly turning around and leaning against the door, Frank menacingly smiled and before long, the entire mansion was filled with the sound of his morbid laughter; for Frank knew that it was only a matter of time before Donald Furnington suffered the same fate as the criminal and in his absence, Frank would rise as the new mayor of Oak Springs, forever "damning" anybody who dared to cross his path.

INTO THE NIGHT

COPYRIGHT © 2008 BY ANTHONY G. ROOF

Bill hates his life. Everybody takes advantage of him, lies to him, cheats him, and blames him for things that he did not do. Bill gets treated like crap at home, picked on at school, and taken for granted at work by bosses and fellow coworkers who do not appreciate his service. Eventually, Bill gets sick and tired of constantly being screwed over and as he takes an inward journey to his soul in a pathetic attempt to understand his place in the world, he goes insane and starts killing people.

7

INTO THE NIGHT

Into the Night

The summer air was cooling down one August evening as Bill sat silently in a lawn chair and watched the dark orange-colored sun slowly set, leaving the area in a gradual state of increasing darkness. Bill loved the summer season, but that particular night proved to be nothing more than yet another depressing disappointment to him because as he watched the sun disappear beneath the horizon, he somehow felt it strangely symbolic of his own life. The setting sun seemed to represent the death of something good, something that made him happy and yet was just never enough. Bill was saddened by the recurring realization that all good things must end and not a day went by that something or everything didn't remind him of that dismal fact. Even the passing of a day itself seemed to take a massive toll on the young man's troubled mind as he counted the stars that now filled the night sky and contemplated their death and even that of the sun he had just watched set.

The stars were infinite in their numbers but each and everyone of them had its own lifespan and this very concept only reminded Bill that even though days were very plentiful and numerous to come, the days of his life would not be, nor was any specific number to ever be guaranteed. Bill sat back in his chair and studied the night sky, but only to be distracted by a shooting star. He found it odd how people would excitedly celebrate the death of stars by making wishes upon their final travels through the solar system, but yet never take the time to think, or to care for that matter, about what would happen to the earth if that shooting star had been the sun. And just as the setting sun at the end of a day seemed to symbolize nothing more than just that to most of its observers, Bill could not help but to wonder what would happen when that very star shot wildly across the sky and ended what would be the final day the planet would ever see.

Each and every single star seemed so small to him when he looked at them, but he was well aware of their great distance and realized that if he could even see them at all from such a distance, than they had to be monstrous in their actual sizes. But there were so many of them and to each one, even to the earth itself, Bill was nothing more than a speck of dust; he was insignificant entirely. But why, then, did his life have to hurt him profoundly as he found himself completely devoid of monetary resources on a perpetual basis? Now rising to his feet and bringing his gaze back to his immediate surroundings, he pondered such troubling questions that there seemed to be no answer for; the answerless problems that hung over him like black rain clouds.

Bill watched now as a bug crawled by his feet, a black water-beetle to be exact, and realized that he in comparison to the bug in its eyes was like the stars were to him. So in perfect logic, the stars to the beetle would have to be so devastating that they could not exist due to the frightening distractions and mind-troubling thoughts. But yet, these humble insects did exist and did not seem at all concerned with anything around them; while simply accepting the ways things were, they moved upon the turf in nothing less than a carefree manner. Now Bill was realizing that everything in the universe was relative to something else and that there could never be any true answers because perception did not matter and it was perception alone that determined one's standard of comparison with which to judge the world around them. However, perception would only change depending on who you asked and therefore, there could not be any truly universal standard for comparing anything, because everything was relative to something else. There could be no good without evil, no happiness without misery, no love without hate, and so on; one could never know true happiness unless they had something horrible with which to make the comparison. Maybe things could make more sense if everybody simply agreed to a set standard, but naturally, differences in perception had to fuck that up. The only real question that needed to be answered before anybody could answer any other question was: who do you ask? And so, all of these ideas could only mean that Bill was both significant and insignificant at the same time, which made no sense whatsoever and ultimately meant that Bill could not actually exist in reality. But somehow, he did exist and all he knew was that everybody wanted money from him.

Both in his own mind and to others, Bill only existed when it benefited everybody else around him but never himself. When something would benefit him or make him happy, Bill did not exist at all; he was not even allowed to exist. Murphy's Law always got the best of Bill because everybody around him was selfish and only cared for their own self-interests; majority rule thus facilitating the unfair concept that Bill could do nothing about due to being outnumbered. And so Bill was there when he needed to cater to the selfish whims of others, but he was not real otherwise. None of this made sense to Bill or anybody around him; however he was the only one who ever made the effort to understand what was happening. Nobody else cared because to them, the truth was too inconvenient to think about. All they cared about was the almighty dollar; the blood that these hungry parasitic ticks would suck until it was all gone – and then suck some more.

Bill was twenty eight years old. He had no money, hardly any friends, no luck, and absolutely no time whatsoever for anything in life that he truly wanted to do. He had lived a sheltered childhood with one older sibling, a sister six years older than him, and with very few privileges. At home, he was constantly finding himself in trouble, even for things that he was not responsible for and told that his mouth got him into more trouble than anything else ever could. Bill was not allowed to watch television, be with school friends, or go anywhere. Whenever he asked for anything or to be allowed to do anything, the answer was always "NO," because of his supposedly bad attitude. Ironically, Bill did not have a bad attitude or any attitude at all as far as that went, because he had learned to keep his mouth shut and to do absolutely nothing that other kids his age were doing. In fact, Bill was practically idle in every possible manner; he did not talk back, he never, ever, ever, even dared to defend himself or in any way at all attempt to stand up for himself, and he was overly submissive to any parental-imposed legislature that affected him even in the very least. Before long, Bill had been conditioned to believe that he was always wrong in every way possible and that there was never even a snow ball's chance in Hell that he could be right about anything. Bill was always wrong, even when he was right; in the extremely rare circumstances that he was actually correct about something, it was either dismissed as luck or coincidence or was just conveniently "forgotten." But if Bill was wrong, there were other penalties to pay, for there were a set of rules designed only for him to obey in addition to the rules that everybody else was required to follow. And so, Bill quickly realized that only the most spineless, most emotionlessly stoic, quietest, and most passive of demeanors got him through a day with minimal bitching; he could actually eat dinner and only be yelled at, criticized, and blamed for things he didn't do nine tenths of the time rather than all of it, which was the closest thing to paradise that he could ever even begin to imagine. And at those earliest of times in his life, he found that if he could go through the dinner hour and not get yelled at the whole time; if he could go through a single day and only get beat two or three times for things he didn't do; if he could make it through a day and only lose about maybe five or six privileges – then he was living the high life, even if to most "normal" kids, this seemed like a nightmarish hell that threatened to consume their very souls.

But what worked at home did not necessarily work at school. Being spineless and passive and refusing at all costs to stand his ground only got Bill made fun of and taken advantage of by the other kids. It was at school, however, that Bill was exposed to what modern "normality" supposedly was; the very thing that kids judged each other by and determined the ease in making friends and so he experienced a relatively loose environment where he thought he could get away with being a child more so than he could at home. However, this was not the case. Bill's parents picked his clothing and dressed him so at school, the kids just made fun of him and made it impossible for him to fit in. The only real friends that he had made at school would occasionally ask him to do things outside of the classroom with them and of course when Bill would ask his parents' permission, the answer was always "NO." Eventually when asked by his few friends to spend time with them outside of school, Bill wouldn't even ask his parents, but instead lie and say that he did and the answer was "NO." So, needless to say, it was not very long before Bill lost all of his friends and found himself completely alone with absolutely no self-esteem or confidence whatsoever. He had exerted such a strong and dedicated effort to keep the two worlds of his home life and his social life at school from colliding, but to no avail. When the other kids discovered the passive role he played at home to keep out of trouble, they naturally took advantage of it by accusing him of everything bad that happened. With Bill around, he served as the scapegoat and proved to be the other kids' ticket to ride; Bill was their license to do anything wrong that they so pleased because afterwards, they would just blame the incredible master of sin, Little Billy. In time, this concept established Bill as a "bad kid" and many phone calls were made to his parents. Now, with both of his nightmares combined, Bill's life truly was pure hell.

But now with his childhood well over and most of the bad things from it gone, things still were not right. The crippling depression that he had back then lived on stronger than ever and therefore made him submissive to the influences of the few people he actually trusted. When he had graduated high school, he was excited to get a real job and in time find a home of his own where he could be free of all of the things that had troubled him in his past; things that "normal" people often took for granted as being good, like the celebration of holidays and family gatherings. But those he trusted pressured him into attending college, even though Bill had absolutely no faith in continued education programs. With the relentless nagging not ceasing, Bill gave in and enrolled at a small-town college and took the required courses supposedly necessary to his "development." Many of the classes had nothing to do with what he was there for and the prices were outrageous, but his parents only waited until he was too far involved in his second last term to whine and cry about how stupid he was for going to school because college was nothing more than a scam that would never, ever pay off under any circumstances whatsoever in the real world. They told him and rubbed in his face the fact that he had wasted precious money that he would never live to see again. When Bill asked why they didn't just tell him that in the very beginning before he enrolled, rather than pressuring him to enroll, the answer he received was that they wanted him to learn a "valuable" lesson the hard way, in how life screws you over and stops at nothing.

And now, with all of the nonsense of his past finally over, Bill stood outside in the night, gazing at the stars and reflecting on his life. He had nothing but debt and an unfulfilling job at a hardware store that worked him like a dog and paid him minimum wage. He had been there for over six years and new hires walking in off the street were making more than him just to start. Then, after ninety days, they were all given raises when Bill was not. And on the rare occasions that Bill was given a raise, so was everybody else so that it would be "fair to everybody else." It frustrated the young man to no end how he was easily the hardest working employee in the place and busted his guts out while everybody else fucked around and did very little in comparison and they all made more than him; on one occasion when Bill did ask for a raise, he was told that he was not worth it. This remark left a lasting impression on the young man as he now wallowed in the agony of his empty life without a dime to his name as he felt nothing but a strong, burning, and intense anger that drained him of what little energy he had left at the end of every single day.

But perhaps what pissed off Bill the most was the fact that all throughout his entire life, all of the kids made fun of him for being neglected and poor and for not being a stupid, spoiled brat like themselves who had everything possibly imaginable under the sun simply handed to them on a silver platter. They were all sheltered from the misery of the world and showered with wealth and all kinds of other good things; anything that they wanted they were given immediately with no questions asked. Bill's life was exactly the opposite. He was sheltered from the goods things and purposely exposed to the bad things. So, the only comfort that Bill had was convincing himself that all of the other kids who were given everything they ever wanted would become total failures later on in life because they were never taught the value of a dollar or about the concept of work or about how the world really works. The only thing that got Bill through the day was believing that all of these spoiled brats would fail miserably in life while he was extremely successful and wealthy, all due to their drastic differences in parenting. Bill believed that life was like a battery; one half was positive and one half was negative and it was absolutely necessary for it to be that way so that the individual could establish the reasonable standards of comparison needed to extract the great value out of life. He believed that if a childhood was good, the adulthood would be horrible and vice versa. The charge of life could not possibly exist without both sides of the equation. So, by this time in his existence, Bill found himself completely depressed beyond recovery when he discovered that nothing in anybody's life had changed; those spoiled kids with the golden childhoods that he believed would never amount to anything were out succeeding, becoming successful business people and executives of top-notch companies, and needless to say, disgustingly wealthy, while on the other hand, Bill, who had been miserable as a child and believed he would be doing well as an adult, found himself with nothing but loneliness, grief, and a crippling debt that he could never repay. It was only at this time in his life that Bill seriously wondered if it was ultimately the parents who determined whether or not their children were destined to be losers simply by the manner in which they had been raised. If this were idea was to prove so, it would do nothing short of challenging every belief that he had ever held in his entire life, but finding no other logic or reason, Bill concluded that the answer to that question was "yes."

So into the night the young man walked knowing that he would be in debt for the rest of his life. Nothing made sense to him anymore and probably never would. He took only one step at a time in his efforts to contend with his gradually pending fate of intense misery. There would never be a single penny that he could ever call his own, there would never be a single meal that the world felt he deserved, there would never be a good paying job within his reach, and there would never be a home that he felt he belonged in. The world was a wicked place full of pain, suffering, misery, corruption, and deceit. The night was his only true friend now; as he drew his inspiration from the stars, it was under the cover darkness that he hunted for his food in the trash cans of the city park and slept in the park bushes in a total state of crippling solitude.

He had no friends, he had no family, he had no home, he had no money, he had no food, no water, no car, no bike, no shoes, no future, no more clothes than what was on his body, and the one semi-good thing he did have, a job, did nothing to help him advance in life. So at that very moment in time as he walked, he made the decision within his own mind to quit that unfunny joke of oppression that he called a job. And now, he realized, he was left even without that and certainly no destination or plan for what was to come next. Nope – now the only thing that he did have was a college degree which was nothing more than a worthless piece of paper for which the only practical purpose would be to wipe his ass later when he ran out of fresh tree leaves in the park.

As Bill walked, he remembered why he never told anybody about his bizarre life story; they would just stare at him with a puzzling combination of horror and disbelief in their eyes and even if he were to dumb it down and simplify it, there in the eyes of his listeners would still be the ever-present state of disbelief. In fact, Bill wasn't even sure whether or not he believed his own story. It was a grim tale that he didn't often want to think about, so telling it would only force him to and of course, he would feel like his listeners who were only hearing it for the first time ever. And so, left without even the credibility of his words to his name, Bill continued walking late into the night.

The next night, once darkness had fallen, Bill continued walking without any destination as he traveled further and further from his hometown. Now without a job, there was just no reason to stay there, so the young man simply roamed the land aimlessly in search of nothing. He used his time to gaze at the night sky and to think as he walked. What came to mind, however, was the question: "what did I do wrong?" Bill pondered for several minutes as he recalled countless images of spoiled kids being given the world on a silver platter; kids who frolicked and played during their childhoods and refused to have anything whatsoever to do with work. Then when they decided that they wanted to go to college and had no money, they were rewarded for their irresponsibility by getting to attend college for free, either because their parents paid for it or because the government did. As he recollected these things, he remembered his endless days of working and saving money as a child instead of having a childhood and being able to play with the other kids. When all of the money that he had saved up fell short of paying for college in full, nobody helped him; he was punished for having done the mature, responsible thing by working in that he received absolutely no government support like every other snot-nosed, worthless brat under the sun. As Bill walked the streets late into the night, his thoughts shifted to his working experiences. He recalled how hard he worked for nothing but then watched as minorities were hired and paid triple what he was to do far, far less. It just seemed that in the workplace, the more a person was paid, the less they were actually expected to do. Why then, Bill wanted to know, did he always get in trouble for slacking off when all he wanted to do was test his theories and build a life for himself? It just didn't make any sense.

Then Bill looked at the stars and saw the constellation "Orion." He remembered reading about the constellation and how the ancient Egyptians had built three massive pyramids directly beneath the three stars in Orion's Belt. Modern scientists had long since learned through the use of highly-advanced computer technology that the pyramids matched up perfectly with the three stars and that this was most likely not done by coincidence. But how did the ancient Egyptians know to do this without any kind of technology whatsoever? Bill was confused by this concept because he realized that most people today are completely stupid even though they live in a time of outstanding technology. Perhaps, Bill often wondered, maybe technology does little more than dehumanizes people and weakens their minds as they experience a decreased need to think and figure things out on their own. It just didn't make sense. Nothing made any sense.

After several long nights of walking, thinking about the world, pondering philosophy, and reflecting on his life, Bill had come to a conclusion: he simply did not exist. No, everything that he had remembered or thought about the world was a sugar-coated bullshit lie. Everything that he had believed or fantasized about was a dream and nothing more. Everything that he thought he had lived through and thought he had clear recollections of and every place he thought he had been to – they were all nothing more than elaborate illusions. Nothing was real, nothing was true, nothing existed, nothing was happening, nothing ever did happen, nothing could ever happen, and certainly, nothing made any sense. But that was okay, because nothing mattered.

Once several months had passed of Bill thinking in this manner, he had managed to fully convince himself that he did not exist. He thought nothing of walking leisurely across busy interstate highways and freeways, he thought nothing of not eating or sleeping for days on end, he thought nothing of committing any kinds of crimes; he thought nothing of anything, because in his own mind, he simply did not exist. He wasn't worried or in the least concerned about getting hurt or killed, because he thoroughly believed that pain was just an illusion and that death was just a myth; true death didn't exist, so Bill's logic was: "how can somebody who doesn't exist die when death itself doesn't exist either?" So the young man continued to roam the land with his mindset that nothing was real, nothing mattered, and that there were no consequences for his actions, playing life like a video game. Nothing could stop him, not even fear, because fear was only an illusion; fear did not really exist – fear was just another lie.

Before long, Bill became a criminal in the real world, but an action hero in the video game he thought he was playing in his mind. Anything he wanted, he simply took. Anybody who got in his way, even police officers, he shot. By this point, the way that Bill saw the world was like how he had always saw it, only now there was a point total up in the air, a health meter to his right and an ammunition count to his left. He saw the world the same way that one saw a video game on a television screen, but what everybody else saw of Bill was an out-of-control maniac prowling the streets with a loaded, pump-action, twelve gauge shotgun, killing everybody that he meant and then screaming: "Yeah! I got ten more points!"

As Bill's mental video game raged on, so did his relentless killing spree. Not long after he had begun living out what he believed to be a role playing game, his number of confirmed kills quickly reached fifteen hundred. Bill was on a roll as he prowled the streets late at night, lurking in the shadows and attacked people in dark alleys. With each and every shot of his gun, the recoiling motion would kick back into his shoulder, bruising it and rubbing the skin tender, but Bill ignored the pain he believed to be an illusion as he gleefully continued to open fire on the masses of innocent people.

Certainly no college degree mattered anymore; he had long since wiped his ass with it and mailed it back to the school. In fact, nothing mattered anymore because nothing was real. Anything that had ever had any value to the young man suffered the same fate as his college degree; his high school diploma, various certificates of achievement, autographed pictures, important letters, family photographs, and even dollar bills – all were used as toilet paper because none of that stuff mattered anymore or ever should have mattered in the first place. The only thing that mattered now was staying alive throughout the game long enough to get a high score. That didn't seem to be much of a problem for him so far, due to the abundant supply of readily accessible materials to aid him in his quest. For instance, when he was running low on ammunition, all he had to do was rob a gun shop. This was something that occurred so frequently that at one point he simply stole a large backpack and loaded it with unboxed shotgun shells. There just didn't seem to be any shortage of this valuable resource as he plundered on into dark streets, moving from town to town, scoring mega-high points everywhere that he struck.

Eventually, without realizing it, Bill had made his way back to his hometown where a lot of people were waiting for his return. They were all armed with various weapons, some with weapons far superior to his, and the local and state police were scattered around everywhere he looked. As Bill unknowingly walked into the middle of the town hoping to score some more points on humanity, out from the shadows his armed opponents emerged. There were hundreds of guns all pointed at Bill and there seemed to be a high degree of certainty in the air of his capture. However, Bill was not in the least afraid, but rather relieved that what was becoming an almost boring game had just gotten a lot more challenging. "Alright, I guess this means I made it to the next level!!!" Bill excitedly shouted out to the armed and waiting crowd.

"No, I'm afraid not," one armed man said to Bill as he was carefully aiming his gun at the young man's head, "I'm afraid this means 'game over,' scumbag!" the man exclaimed as he pulled the trigger of his gun, sending a shot flying through the air at Bill. But unfortunately for the shooter, at that same moment Bill had move and the bullet flew into the crowd behind where he was standing and hit another one of Bill's armed opponents in the head, killing him instantly. "Why did you move, you asshole, now Joseph is dead! You killed Joseph!" the man who shot Joseph cried. "GET HIM!" the crowd roared as it moved in and gunshots filled the air.

Bill quickly rolled about in the street and pushed his way through the crowd, ducked, jumped, and moved around as much as he possibly could. The angry mob continued firing shots, but they were all missing Bill and killing each other instead. Bill continued to hide among the masses until enough people had died that hiding was no longer feasible. Then, instead of trying to hide or trying to run, Bill went into a shooting frenzy and commenced pumping shot after shot after shot in all directions around him until the sounds of mob's screaming and shooting silenced. Bill, however, continued firing, hastily reloading, and firing again until he had completely run out of ammunition. The thick puddles of blood began running down the street towards a storm drain as the heavy odors of death filled the air and attracted flies by the thousands to hover about and lay their eggs upon the dead and the rapidly dying bodies. Eventually, everybody except Bill was dead. Slowly and carefully, the young man stepped backwards out of the bloody mess of freshly massacred corpses. Then he counted them finding that there were sixty two. He did not know exactly how many he had killed himself, but he figured that since they had all died one way or another because of his presence it would be okay to take the credit for their deaths. "Okay, let's see here, sixty two times ten – alright! I just earned six hundred, twenty points! I guess this means its time to advance to the next level!" Bill excitedly exclaimed as he stepped up onto the sidewalk and walked away from the crime scene, tracking bloody footprints as he walked.

As Bill walked down the street, he heard the sirens of police cars in the distance. The sound was becoming louder and louder with every passing second and before long, Bill was surrounded by police cars with armed police officers emerging from the vehicles. "FREEZE, PUNK!" one officer yelled as he drew and aimed a forty caliber pistol at the young man. "Aw, man, not right now, okay, I'm out of ammo so I'm just going to pause the game and take a short break, is that okay?" Bill responded. "SHUT YOUR STUPID FACE, ASSHOLE!!! YOU ARE UNDER ARREST!!! YOU HAVE THE RIGHT TO REMAIN SILENT!!! ANYTHING YOU SAY CAN AND WILL BE USED AGAINST YOU IN A COURT OF LAW!!!" the cop roared. Bill just laughed. "I have the right to remain silent, do I? Well, I think I'm going to waive that right, because man, you guys are taking this game way too seriously! You need to just relax and take it easy, besides, it's more fun that way! Oh, and for the record, I am not under arrest because you haven't actually touched me yet. Those are the rules; it's kind of like playing tag. But really, I could just turn around and walk away right now. And another thing, how can anything I say be used against me? What if I say something like 'I enjoy cold popsicles on a hot, summer day' or something like that? How are you going to use that information to incriminate me?" "SILENCE!!! JUST SHUT YOUR HOLE, RIGHT NOW OR WE WILL USE FORCE!!!" the serious cop responded without amusement. "No seriously," Bill began again, "I'm interested in this now. How are you going to use that information against me?" "I SAID SILENCE!!! THIS IS NO JOKE!!! THIS IS SERIOUS BUSINESS!!! YOU KILLED ALL THOSE PEOPLE BACK THERE!!! NOW WHAT HAPPENS?! HUH?! DOES THIS MEAN 'GAME OVER' FOR THEM?!" Bill just looked at the cop with confusion, like he had just been asked the dumbest question in the world. "Dude, just tell them all to press the restart button on their controllers. It's not that big of a deal."

"Alright," another officer said, "this moron obviously isn't going to listen to us, so on the count of three we all fire." Bill watched as many of the officers cocked their weapons and the counting began. "One, two…" "WAIT!" he screamed. "I forgot to mention something! You see I just realized that even though I'm out of ammo, I'm not totally defenseless, because I still have this grenade! And I'll pull the pin out of it right now and kill us all if you don't all put your guns down! Oh, and you know what else, shooting me wouldn't do any good anyway, because I have special wizard-armor on!" Bill said as he produced a large grenade with his left hand and took a hold of the pin with his right hand. "HE'S GOT AN EXPLOSIVE DEVICE!!! PUT YOUR WEAPONS DOWN!!!" the officer in charge shouted. Bill watched with amusement as each of the police officers put their guns down on the street. "HA HA!!! SUCKERS!!!" the young man screamed as he pulled the pin, threw the grenade into the crowd of cops and ran off into the forest.

"BOOM!!!!!!" the grenade sounded as it violently exploded and blew up the entire area where Bill had thrown it. Looking over his shoulder he could see overturned police cars in flames and burning corpses scattered all about in the street and on the sidewalk. Once again, nobody but Bill survived the grenade-induced disaster. So, seeing no other living people left in the street, the young man walked back to the crime scene and produced a can of neon-green spray paint from his backpack. Then, in large green letters, Bill sprayed his name and his high score in the middle of the street next to a mangled corpse. It read: Bill = 78,360.

After doing that, Bill walked up the street towards an already harvested wheat field. When he had reached this destination, he was just about to take a step into the field when he heard the voice of an upset woman. Slowly, he turned to face her. "What do you want?" he asked the troubled woman. "You killed my father, my brother, my uncle, my husband and my son earlier today! I saw you going on your little killing spree! How could you?! How could you kill so many innocent people like that?! You're a monster; a cold-blooded snake! Why did you do it?! Have you not even a shred of remorse?!" the panicking woman shrieked at him. "Uh, lady, calm down, okay, it's just a game," Bill patiently replied. "A game?! This is a game to you?! People lost their lives today and to you it's just a game?! Well, I'll tell you what, you Hell-bound monster, this is real life! This is really happening; it's no game! This is serious business! This is reality!" the woman tried again, but by now, Bill was tired and decided that he had had enough for one day. "Look, lady, I don't know what you think this is, but so far I have the highest score, so I'll be the judge of what reality is. Do you understand? Reality is whatever I say it is and I'm telling you that none of this is real. When you acquire the winning score, then you can decide what's going on here, okay, but right now, we're playing by my rules." "THIS IS NOT A DAMN GAME! WAKE UP! THIS IS REAL!" "I told you lady, none of this is real. None of this is really happening right now. I do not even exist, nor do you. Everything you see, hear, feel, think or in any other way sense – it is all just an illusion. You see, none of this makes any sense whatsoever," Bill said as he turned away from the weeping woman while wondering why she even cared about anything, because in his mind everything that he had told her was the truth. He did not exist, she did not exist, the people he killed did not exist, the very concept of killing did not exist, the concepts of caring and of weeping did not exist, the black shroud of night did not really exist, nor did the very concept of existence itself even exist.

Slowly, Bill shifted his head to gaze at the night sky and all of the stars that filled it. Then he looked over at the moon and studied its lunar characteristics. Then he looked back down and studied his own two hands. Then he peered off into the dark of night before returning his gaze to the still weeping woman. "It's all just an illusion. Nothing is real," he calmly said to her. And then the young man resumed walking, only to disappear into the night.

THE END

About the Author

ANTHONY G. ROOF was born in 1985 in Lebanon, Pennsylvania, where he still resides. In 2007, he received a bachelor's of science degree in business administration from Central Pennsylvania College where he had completed the writing of his very first short story, "The Cardinal Sin." This is his first book.

Copyright 2008 by Anthony G. Roof

ANTHONY G. ROOF

www.ingramcontent.com/pod-product-compliance
Lightning Source LLC
Chambersburg PA
CBHW020441180626
46812CB00003B/1345